DEATH GRIP

A Dr. Annabel Tilson Novel

DEATH GRIP

by Barbara Ebel, M.D.

A Dr. Annabel Tilson Novel

Paperback ISBN-13: 978-0-9977225-7-4
eBook ISBN-13: 978-0-9977225-8-1

This book is a work of fiction. Names, characters, places and events are the product of the author's imagination or are used fictitiously. Any resemblance to actual events, persons, or locations is coincidental.

CHAPTER 1

Medical student Annabel Tilson's night-on-call with the internal medicine service began with an unexpected chore. It was her own fault. She had practically volunteered herself.

She closed the door of her Nissan with a sideward shove and trotted towards the submarine sandwich shop. Breaking away from the grind of beeping monitors, the rush to fetch lab results, and the confinement of their cramped office in the hospital wasn't so bad after all.

Tonight, she was her medical team's gopher.

Her designated purpose was to bring back tastier food for dinner rather than the bland, lumpy food from the hospital cafeteria. The chief resident, the two female residents, and three other students waited for her.

She stepped up on the curb and extended her arm to pull open the door. Almost as close to the entrance, a toned, earthy-looking man attempted to grab the handle before her, but failed. She kept the door ajar as he made a weak attempt to smile and then followed her in.

The square tables were dotted with customers and, as she passed the counter displaying sample barbecue sauces and other condiments, a greeter rattled off a welcome. The man prepared take-out orders behind the glass case and a menu of hot and cold subs and salads graced a long board behind him.

Annabel stopped under the "place orders" sign.

"What will you have?" a man wearing a "Manager" tag asked.

"I have an easy and hefty order of seven subs - all beef and cheddar briskets on wheat rolls - four large and three medium. It's to-go and I don't need drinks."

"Will that be all?"

"That's plenty."

The man who came in with her stood close. She stole a harder look at him. His jacket was unzipped, his cheeks appeared flushed, and he wiped his forehead. He had full lips and hairy, thick eyebrows; she figured him to be in his mid-thirties.

"That'll be $71.19," the manager said.

1

Each member of her team had given her a flat ten-dollar bill, so she pulled out their money, added to it, and passed the correct amount over the counter.

"You placed a lofty order for a slender lady," the man next to her said. Even though he spoke softly, his New York accent was distinct. "Are you feeding a basketball team?"

Annabel snickered. Since she stood five-foot-eight inches, she understood why he mentioned a sport known for tall players.

"The food is for a group of folks I'm working with tonight."

The man jostled a few inches forward to rest his hand and the weight of his upper body on the counter. His posture sagged as well as his eyelids as he gave her a slight nod. She stepped to the nearest table to wait for her order.

"What can I get you?" the manager asked the man.

"I'll be back. I'm not feeling well."

Annabel watched the male customer tread on hiking boots over to the men's room. As she waited, she pulled a few napkins out of the dispenser and noticed the wall picture of a firehouse. Meanwhile, folks were busing red trays to a garbage container, dumping their trash, and placing their trays up top. A mother nearby nodded at her and a couple came in and discussed what to order.

She glanced over to the bathrooms. The men's room door gingerly opened and the man who entered the sub shop with her finally made an appearance. Instead of walking back to order at the counter, he slowly made his way to the table next to her. He almost stumbled as he pulled out a chair, eased into it, and rested his head into his hands. His eyes closed.

Annabel moved her chair sideways and leaned forward. "Sir, are you all right?"

"I ... I don't think so." He squeezed his eyes tighter and pressed the palms of his hands on his forehead. "I was sick in there. There's no way I can order any food."

"Don't worry about it. You can't help that."

"I never suffer from headaches, but my head's about to explode."

"Is there anything I can do for you?"

"I don't know. I better leave." His attempt to stand was fraught with weakness, so he placed his hands, which were usually strong and robust, on the table.

"Why don't you wait here for a moment," she said, "while I snatch my order and bring it to my car. Then I can walk you out."

He nodded, caving in to her suggestion, and sat back down.

Annabel walked to the area for "pick-ups" and, one at a time, a woman handed her two brown bags. "The first one has the bigger subs," she said.

"Thanks." The contents warmed her hands right through the bag as she headed for her vehicle. The mild winter had only snow-dusted southern Ohio several times so far and, besides a few unfathomably warmer days, now the weather hinted at spring. The early evening was a balmy fifty-six degrees. She opened a back door, placed the meals on the seat, and ran back to the poor man waiting for her inside the sandwich shop.

"What is your name?" Annabel asked as she stood over him.

"Jae. Jae Nixon."

Annabel nudged an arm close to him. With hesitation, he wrapped his hand around her with a slight grip and they began walking out.

The manager planted his eyes on them as they passed.

"I'm walking him out to his vehicle," Annabel said as an explanation. "His stomach is apparently upset, so he won't be ordering."

"Okay. Come back soon."

Annabel and Jae made it out the door. By the looks of him, she figured he felt embarrassed about his present circumstance. He seemed to be a fit male - maybe a hiker or some sort of outdoorsman - and relying on anyone, especially a woman, to walk him somewhere was probably an embarrassment.

"Where's your car?" she asked.

"Pickup truck." He nodded at the dark Chevy Silverado in the next row of parking spaces and then stopped and stooped over.

"Are you going to be sick?"

He dry-heaved and shook his head. "There's nothing left in my belly to come up."

"Are you sure you're going to be able to drive home?"

"No to both."

Annabel wondered what to do with him; she needed to peel away and depart for the hospital. The students had taken their internal medicine mid-term test that morning and she was now technically in the second half of the rotation. She couldn't afford to botch up her night-on-call by being late because she had volunteered to be the team's lackey and procure their dinner. Plus, they were salivating for their hot subs; she was sure of it.

"I think I need to go see a doctor," Jae said.

"There are no doctor office hours now. How about the ER?"

"That would be better."

"Then you're coming with me."

Jae nodded with approval at her suggestion. "Now it's my turn. What's your name?"

"Annabel. Annabel Tilson. I'm a third-year medical student and I'm bringing you in."

CHAPTER 2

The smell of beef brisket wafted through Annabel's red SUV during the short drive to the hospital. It made her stomach churn with hunger, but it made Jae want to pinch his nostrils and put his head between his knees to quell his nausea.

"I forgot to ask you," Annabel said. "We're going to the V.A. Hospital. Will that work for you?"

"I served in Afghanistan." He exerted more pressure against his forehead. "I carry my military card with me."

"That's like your passport to care. I'm taking care of a female patient right now about your age. She was there too. Before rotating at this hospital, I had no idea how many of you served and are living here in Cincinnati. You must be told all the time ... thank you for your service."

"Yeah ... right. I came back and saw people and society differently. Eccentric, overindulgent, wasteful, and ungrateful."

"I'm sorry. I also shouldn't be talking so much. You aren't up for a conversation and you don't look like you could drink a cold one or do the cowboy cha cha."

"The cowboy cha cha?"

"I'm from Nashville."

"That explains it."

Annabel turned into the hospital parking lot but veered directly to the ER front door. She turned off the ignition. "Wait here." She jumped out, grabbed a wheelchair from behind the automatic doors, and came back.

Jae eyed the medical prop. "Is that necessary?" He grasped the door frame, rose with difficulty, and plopped into the chair.

"You are weaker than you think."

Annabel wheeled him into the lobby and parked him in front of the admitting window. "I have to run. My team is waiting on me and I have work to do. If I have time later, I'll check on you."

"I can't thank you enough. I don't understand why I'm ill."

"That's what you're here to find out." She patted him on the shoulder. "Hope you start feeling better."

Annabel moved her car to the staff parking area. With the two bags of sandwiches, she hurried into the hospital cafeteria. The area for serving hot food was closed for the night and the dining room was mostly empty. She sat at a table near the window and began texting each member of her medical team. Their office on the medicine ward was cramped for them to spread out and eat, so they had agreed to meet there. She hoped none of them was involved with a patient admission in the ER.

She texted the three other students, two residents, and her chief resident, Dr. Donn Schott.

Food's here!

It didn't surprise her when her laid-back chief showed up first.

"You're a sight for sore eyes," Dr. Schott said. "What took you so long?"

In his forties, Donn maintained a chubby appearance along with his early gray hair, beard, and mustache. She kept from chuckling; the sandwich meant more to him than the rest of them.

"In my defense, I was half-working. A customer fell ill at the submarine sandwich shop."

Donn wagged his finger at her. "Dr. Tilson, you're a magnet for all sorts of events and behavior."

She shook her head in disagreement.

"Besides doctoring," he said, "you have a history of … shall I tell you?"

"Being privy to murder cases," she said. "Crime, bad drugs, a robbery …"

"A robbery? I didn't know about that one."

Not wanting to explain, she ignored his remark. She opened the heavier bag and slid out the four large subs.

"Dr. Schott, help yourself."

Donn spread open the paper wrapping and his eyes bulged. He had his first bite chewed and swallowed by the time she turned around and headed for an iced tea. When she came back, her other team colleagues were gathered around, diving their hands into the bags.

As Annabel situated herself in the middle of the table, her best buddy on rotation, Bob Palmer, sat across from her.

"Thanks for bringing these back," Bob said, his blue eyes coming alive as he cast a glance at her.

"They aren't the only things I brought back. I drove a man who needed medical attention to the ER."

"That sounds crazy," said Jordan, one of the other students. "Why didn't you call EMS?"

"My clinical judgment told me he didn't need that kind of immediate treatment … like CPR or an IV or nitroglycerin. He was young, not even as old as Dr. Schott."

Donn peeked up from his sandwich, cheddar cheese sauce clinging to his fingers. "I'm not sure if you complimented me or not."

"So why did he latch on for a ride with you?" Bob asked.

"I detect jealousy in that statement," Jordan butted in. "Like the other night when Annabel left us at her neighborhood cafe and her sister told us she went to meet some guy. You didn't seem that happy about it."

"What?!" Annabel exclaimed. "I told her not to say anything about that because, otherwise, you all would give me grief about it." She frowned at the discovery. The students had met for dinner a few days ago at Annabel's neighborhood coffee and sandwich café. Her sister, Nancy, was visiting for the weekend and promised she wouldn't tell her fellow students that she was meeting someone later. That someone was a failed date she'd arranged from a social dating app.

"All right, already," Dr. Schott inserted. "Annabel, get back to the medical part of the story."

"Thank you. Gladly. I didn't think the man was capable of driving himself. He exhibited lack of coordination and weakness. He probably has the flu."

"Then you earned a humanitarian award tonight, but you better start eating like the rest of these vultures or you'll be sitting here by yourself soon."

Annabel and Bob both stared at Dr. Schott's empty sandwich wrapper and then smiled at each other. The rest of them weren't as voracious as their big chief.

"The first medical patient is already in the ER," Donn said, "and, Dr. Palmer, you're the student up for the first admission."

"I'm ready," Bob said.

"Dr. Burg," Donn said to the resident sitting next to him, "let's go ahead while Bob is taking his time eating the only sustenance he'll enjoy until tomorrow."

Melody Burg was an internal medicine resident with deep southern roots. She sprang up with enthusiasm to follow Donn, especially since she wasn't wobbling on high heels like she did on normal days in the hospital. When on-call, she eventually ditched heels for flat clogs – the signature comfort shoes when the in-training residents and students were on overnight call.

"I'll be there in a few minutes," Bob said, and then savored a few more bites as Donn and Melody disappeared from the cafeteria.

Annabel and Bob weaved through the hallways to the back section of the ground floor. They passed a patient in a squeaky wheelchair pushed by a hospital employee, a visitor looking for the cafeteria, and a couple sitting on a bench glued to their iPhones.

"Are you sure you want to follow me?" Bob asked.

"Yes," she said, "but not for long. I hope your admission is interesting."

The ER automatic doors slid open, revealing a night which was fairly busy as Bob split off to find Dr. Schott. The health care workers reading charts or writing orders didn't make a peep. The noisy, active areas of the room were from physicians and nurses interviewing sick vets, patients in pain, and the cacophony of monitors.

Annabel headed straight to the wall board with the names of patients, their ER room numbers, and the providers taking care of them. She gazed up, spotted Jae Nixon's name listed in Room 6, and pondered how to check on him because of patient privacy laws. The best way was the direct way, she thought, and eliminated the idea of prying information out of the ER doctor.

"Mr. Nixon," she said, poking her head into his room. "It's Annabel Tilson, the medical student you met. Are you doing any better? May I come in?"

Semi-elevated on a stretcher, Jae tilted his head to see her. A sheet partially covered him and he wore a generic hospital gown.

"Sure," he mumbled. "If not you, then who? My knight in shining armor. I mean, my fairy princess."

Jae centered his head back straight as Annabel approached. His right bicep displayed a magnificent tattoo – an American Indian with a bald eagle to his upper right and an American flag draped behind them.

It took her a second to peel her gaze away and notice the IV in his hand

8

with fluids dripping in from the bag hung on the pole above. His whole arm was tan, like he wore summer sunshine all year long, and he wore a scissor-sharp haircut. Sure, she thought, he still carries habits from serving time for his country.

"Then anyone can be a princess," she said, "if giving someone a ride to the hospital is all it takes. You don't have to tell me anything because it's none of my business, but I came to check on you."

"No problem. The consensus is that I have the flu. I'm a bit ... dehydrated, they said. I'm running a low-grade fever, which explains a lot."

The word "flu" registered in Annabel's brain. It was a lucky guess on her part; she was happy to hear she was on the right track for his diagnosis.

"That makes sense. The flu didn't hit a staggering number of patients this winter, but the season was a bit more extended into this month. You caught the tail end of it."

"Just my luck," he said, shutting his eyelids. "In medical terms, they said they're going to treat my symptoms here and I should be able to go home in a few hours. 'Supportive care,' they explained. The pain medicine they gave me for my headache should kick in soon as well."

"I hope so, but now I feel responsible. Your car is in the parking lot of the submarine shop. What are you going to do?"

"I could call someone to give me a lift there, but there's no need. I have my cell phone and plan on calling Uber when they let me go."

Annabel nodded and glanced at the monitors - heart rate a little elevated, but not a big deal due to his slight fever - and his IV fluid bag was half-drained. He had also regained some color back to his face since she dropped him off.

"I better go," she said. "Looks like you and the ER doctor have your situation under control."

"Thank you again. I'm sorry I'm not more hospitable. Before I go, I'm going to doze some more."

Annabel sighed. Even though Jae would not be one of their admissions, she was glad he was successfully being treated and would soon be sleeping in his own bed.

As she twirled the long waves in her medium-blonde hair, she realized she'd be lucky to even open the door of a call room later and glance at a bed ... because outside Jae's room ... medical patients were stacking up.

9

CHAPTER 3

Annabel felt a tug at her sleeve when she left Jae Nixon's room, which forced her to stop. Dr. Schott was beside her and yanked on her short white lab jacket again.

"You have a real admission," Donn said, "not someone you drove in here for an ER visit."

"Are you annoyed at me for bringing that man in?"

"On the contrary, but don't worry. This patient is more interesting than one having the flu. Her suspected diagnosis is a stepping stone to studying normal and abnormal heart conditions."

Dr. Schott pointed towards Chineka, who was writing at the desk. "You're working with her on this one. She's writing up the patient's H&P."

Annabel knew the familiar jargon – "H&P" stood for history and physical. She also liked both the team's female residents, so it didn't matter which one she worked with. Chineka Watt and Melody Burg were sound teachers to the students and vastly unalike in their backgrounds and personalities. Based on what Chineka had told her, her upbringing as an African-American had been probably more difficult than Melody's. She also lacked Melody's fashion flare, but she was more focused and attentive to her patients.

Donn's hand brushed over his beard. "Your patient's name is Meagan Helm. She's complaining of heart palpitations and, like me, she's in her forties. A tech is doing an EKG on her right now. Go ahead, skedaddle."

Annabel gave him a questioning look.

"Scram. Get in there."

She did an about-face and surveyed the board again, this time for Meagan Helm. She didn't want to disturb Chineka by taking the chart away from her so, in essence, she felt like an airhead marching into Room 8 unprepared.

Mrs. Helm's door was wide open, so she went straight in and found a group of people swarmed around her. The EKG technician, finished using her machine, was coiling up the wires which had extended to the electrodes on Meagan's chest.

"Now who might you be?" Meagan Helm asked and then took in a deep breath.

"Dr. Tilson, a medical student. I work with Dr. Watt and Dr. Schott. May I ask you some questions?"

"Like all my kids here, you're probably learning your future career, so I don't mind."

Annabel nodded at the man and two young women.

"That's Walter," Mrs. Helm said. "And the twins are Sally and Susan."

The three of them, close in age to her, nodded hello.

"You have more family around you than I normally see from patients in here," Annabel said.

"I'm a lucky lady. They all live in the general Cincinnati area." As if Meagan was having trouble with her heart, she patted her chest.

"I have a close family too, but no one lives nearby."

Sally sat on the stretcher, smiled at Annabel, and then went back to watching her mother.

"This will be on the chart," the technician said, waving the EKG as she approached the door.

"Aren't you going to look at that?" Mrs. Helm asked Annabel.

"I am only in my first year of clinical rotations, which is my third year of medical school. I must confess - I am not yet a wizard at reading them. I'll scrutinize it with my upper level residents giving me guidance."

"I understand, and feel free to ask me questions with my children here."

Walter hovered on the other side of the stretcher with his sisters; their devotion to Meagan apparent. His deep set eyes stayed focused between the door and his mother.

"What made you come to the ER tonight?"

"Ah-ha, in other words, what's my chief complaint?"

Annabel raised her eyes with surprise.

"I work part-time in a doctor's office, on the business end of things. Although I don't know enough about medical illnesses, I do hear the buzz words."

"It's always helpful when patients understand the lingo. In my limited experience, they tend to answer questions more succinctly."

"So true. Patients can diverge into long-winded stories instead of getting to the point of the health-care worker's questions. I hear that complaint all the time." She took a quick breath and patted her chest.

Annabel nodded and waited.

Sally spoke up. "My mom's heart is beating funny. It's been speeding up today."

Meagan's hand slid up and glided along her long brown braid sitting on the front of her print blouse; she gulped for another mouthful of air. "I didn't work today," she said. "Otherwise, I would have said something in the office. I've been short of breath, my heart's palpitating, and I hear a 'ba-boom' echoing in my ears."

"Plus," Sally said, "she told me on the phone she was feeling dizzy."

"Ever experience this before?" Annabel asked.

"I don't remember too much about it, but a long time ago when I was pregnant with the girls, my heart rate went crazy. My mother told me I had rheumatic fever when I was a kid and that could possibly cause problems later on."

Rheumatic fever, Annabel thought, puts a spin on the problem. More assured that she had a clear understanding of her patient's chief complaint, she asked Meagan more questions. Mrs. Helm denied taking medications, using tobacco, alcohol, or illicit drugs. Her other past medical and surgical history was insignificant.

Annabel slid her dangling stethoscope off her neck and placed it on Meagan's chest to listen to her lungs and heart. Listening to her heart sounds, she thought she heard a murmur like a diastolic rumble, which would signify turbulent blood flow across one of the heart valves.

"I'm finished," Annabel said and smiled at the twins. "It looks like that pregnancy a long time ago turned out really well."

Meagan agreed with a nod of her head. "Both pregnancies and all three kids."

Meagan Helm's H&P should be easy enough, Annabel thought as she walked over to Dr. Watt. Except, of course, for the last part of it - the "diagnosis" and "plan." That was where the students had to rely on their two residents and chief resident for their expert clinical judgment. One more person was involved in the equation as well - their attending doctor, Dr. Sebastian Mejia, a sixty-year-old cardiologist who Dr. Schott reported to and who occasionally showed up for rounds.

"What do you think about Mrs. Helm?" Chineka asked, glancing up.

"I'm out of my league; like a plumber trying to do electrical work."

"We're soon going to fix your deficit because the heart's electrical activity is exactly what you're going to learn."

Annabel swung around the corner of the desk, eager to examine the EKG with her.

Dr. Watt held the electrocardiogram in front of them. "You have heard some of this already, so in addition to new information, you're going to hear a recap of what you think you know. There are four chambers to the heart – two upper atria and two lower ventricles – as any fifth grader knows."

Chineka began pointing to the spikes and dips, or waves, in the line tracings. "The P wave is a record of the heart's electrical activity through the atria and the QRS complex signifies the electrical impulses moving through the ventricles. What you heard with your stethoscope and what we see here is an abnormal heart rhythm with chaotic generation of electrical signals in the atria. Or …?"

"Atrial fibrillation," Annabel guessed.

"Spot on. I bet you wish you were earning a cardiologist's salary."

"I'd even settle for the electrician's."

"When you listened to her lungs, did they sound clear?"

"I believe so."

Chineka motioned Annabel into the side room, holding a long brown envelope, and took out Mrs. Helm's chest x-ray. She slid it up on the viewing box. "Yes, her pulmonary status seems fine … right now. However, when atrial fibrillation develops with the erratic firing of the atria, the ventricle responds rapidly and causes shortened diastolic filling. The result is usually pulmonary congestion."

"So why hasn't she developed that?"

"She made it to the ER quick enough. A big consideration is what caused her atrial fibrillation."

"Her heart rhythm was not only irregular, but there was a murmur and I learned she has a history of rheumatic fever."

"And a late sequela of rheumatic fever is rheumatic heart disease with the mitral valve between the left atria and left ventricle most frequently involved." Chineka pulled down the X-ray and sat back at the desk. "See how far we've come? The cause of her atrial fibrillation is most likely mitral stenosis. However, I had the benefit of Dr. Schott's input."

"So what do we do for Mrs. Helm?" Annabel asked with a worried tone.

"There is an urgent treatment plan if a patient is hemodynamically unstable, they're having angina, or they're experiencing pulmonary edema. In which case, she would need a direct current electrical shock to her heart ... to convert her to a normal sinus rhythm. However, we recognize that she's pretty stable and lacking lung congestion. What we're going to do is control her ventricular rate - her fast irregular heart beat - with intravenous drugs to slow the conduction through the atrioventricular, or AV, node. Beta-blockers, calcium channel blockers, or digoxin are the drugs of choice."

"Lucky for her no one is going to loom above her with electrical paddles. That would be a frightening scenario for any patient."

"If that were the case, we'd ask an anesthesiologist for assistance to make her comfortable."

Annabel nodded. "They sure come in handy."

"You better start writing your H&P. I'm going to show Dr. Schott the EKG, find out which drug we should order, and use it on her as soon as possible."

Annabel found a cubicle off to the side to write Meagan Helm's H&P. The main desk didn't need to be cluttered up by a medical student where ER physicians and other doctors and nurses had more important work to do there than she did. She first read every morsel of information written by everyone else who had written a note and then penned her own. When she finished, she regarded the board again. Jae Nixon's name was still up there.

Annabel slipped Mrs. Helm's chart in a slot and noticed the nurse next to her was the one taking care of Mr. Nixon.

"Is Jae Nixon still going to be discharged from the ER?" Annabel asked.

"Sure is. He won't be needing your team. The secretary is getting his paperwork together. Besides the needed medical care, he seems to like the rest. Keeps closing his eyes and nodding off like he's catching up with his dreaming."

Annabel smiled. "Maybe you made him feel comfortable."

14

"I wish most guys who show up in here were as polite and down-to-earth as him," she said, unwrapping a stick of gum.

The night wore on and Annabel realized the students had scattered, so she headed upstairs to the office. However, once Mrs. Helm was transferred to a room, she would check in on her and also gather any pending lab work. One thing making her case easier was the absence of a pile of old charts from previous admissions and medical problems. Some of the vets had stacks of them from chronic admissions for their heart and lungs.

"There you are," Annabel said when she found Bob on the couch. "What was your admission?"

"An elderly man with COPD having an acute exacerbation. I still need to take a quick survey of his records and figure out what usually works best for him."

"You're not going to practice cookie-cutter, one-size-fits-all medicine, are you?"

Bob chuckled. "Hey, admit it. There's some truth to that."

"Although my dad always tells me: just when you think you've seen it all, something new pops up."

Annabel's father was a famous Nashville neurosurgeon whom Bob had met. "How is your dad, anyway, and the rest of the family?"

"He's still mourning the loss of our family dog, but other than that, they are all good. And get this … my sister, Nancy, who came up from Nashville and went out with us all recently, has taken up texting with Jordan."

"I was wondering about them. They seemed a bit chummy that night. Jordan is not the most stellar medical student for her to become involved with." He frowned, but Annabel laughed.

"He thinks he is. I suppose that to many people our age, dating a medical student may be a great catch. At the end of their training, their pockets may plunge deeper."

Annabel wondered if she should mention to Bob that she saw Jordan cheating that morning while taking his midterm test. It had surprised her and sickened her that one of them would do such a thing. At least for now, she decided to keep the information to herself.

"Distance is a problem if your sister and Jordan are going to date," Bob said. "Nashville is not exactly down the road from Cincinnati."

"She says she's going to drive up again when she can. Like my apartment is her apartment, or something like that."

Bob rolled his eyes. "An intermittent roommate? Have fun trying to study."

"Right. Tomorrow after call, how about we check our grades from our test today?"

"It's a deal, but our results may either spoil the rest of our day or give us cause to celebrate."

"My celebration, if I am rested enough, will be to run down the steps in the neighborhood and then along the Ohio, or maybe go jogging at Eden Park."

"Can I join you?"

"Sure. I never knew you enjoyed running as a sport."

"There's a lot you don't know about me. I rarely do, but a trip to the park for a run with you sounds like the perfect excursion away from the wards and books."

CHAPTER 4

Jae Nixon was as patriotic as they came for his age. He had served his country for a short time when many his age never contemplated doing such a thing. He figured a guardian angel protected him after that because he succeeded in paving his destiny to work in his dream job.

During high school and college, Jae burned through biology books like a chain smoker. He absorbed the biological classification of living things - from families to genera to species - like a sponge.

Taxonomy was only one aspect of what he loved about the field. In those days, he suspected that learning biology would give him the background necessary and foster the ability to later work in the great outdoors. He was born to comingle with nature and vowed to stay away from a desk job, or in an inside, full-time biology job confined to the four walls of a scientific lab.

He knew exactly what he wanted to do after procuring his bachelor's degree in the natural sciences - become a U.S. park ranger.

Jae prepared a smooth, easy way to attain his goal by gaining experience in seasonal park ranger jobs and doing volunteer work. By doing that, he also fully realized the scope of going into that career. The men and women wearing ranger uniforms and telling tourists about the sites they were visiting were not just "park rangers."

They were, in essence, police officers - police officers of state parks or "law enforcement park rangers." Jae was proud to have completed special law enforcement training to do his job.

There were no regrets. He had found his own heaven with his guardian angel in tow. He enjoyed being outside, he helped protect the animals and plants in the parks, and he passed on his enthusiasm to visitors from around the world.

Jae also liked one of the aspects of the job that some rangers despised. They did not stay posted to one park; they were subject to transfers. Although they needed to "get up and move," they broadened their experience and horizons by being stationed at a variety of national parks. It could be an American president's historic site such as the Hermitage in Tennessee, Acadia National Park in Maine, or the vast Yosemite National

Park out west.

A ranger could even be assigned to the National Parks Service in Washington, D.C., the service in charge of the capital's major monuments. He enjoyed and welcomed each new assignment.

Jae was now in his second year of working at the William Howard Taft National Historic Site in Cincinnati. It didn't have the grandeur of the Great Smoky Mountains National Park or the Grand Canyon, but it embraced the history of the 27th president of the United States. Since he had a strong patriotic side to him, he enjoyed the spot as much as the other two places he'd worked.

Plus, he beamed when he told clueless vistors the history of William Taft – the only American president to have served as both president and as the chief justice of the Supreme Court.

Since Jae intermittently napped in his ER room, he wished someone would snuff out the brightness of the overhead flourescent light. It bothered his headache as well as his sleep. But, he thought, ERs weren't for a patient's comfort. His visit to the hospital was meant to get him back on his feet and normal again. He had no plans to miss work the next day. There was enough to do every day for him and the other ranger, Patty Caye.

Jae and Patty each lived in separate small wooden one-story houses on the park premises. Rangers lived at their work site but, of course, being one mile north of Cincinnati wasn't exactly living in one of the mountainous park spots. There was, however, a feeling around their cabins like being out in the country and enough greenery and woods to make him happy.

Too busy lately with school field trips to the visitors' center and hikes for the kids on the adjoining trails, he was overdue to take care of a chore at work.

Tomorrow, he wanted to address the upsurge in the mouse population on the property.

Even though the mice were sneaky about not being seen, they were running around between their cabins, in the storage shacks, and in the vicinity in and around the woods. His own cabin showed signs of increased mouse droppings as well.

Because of the mild and shorter winter, the damn white-footed mice were rampant and proliferating like stray dogs in heat. The successful rodent, native to Eastern North America, was expanding northward and responding to climate warming by pushing its tolerance and adaptability to its limits. It was a fact that its population and expanse was increasing as far as southern Quebec at an unparalleled rate.

Even though mice also have an important part in nature's ecosystem, such as to provide food for "good" black snakes, he knew their numbers needed to be culled. He must go outside earlier than usual, he thought, and selectively put down poisonous bait feeders to kill them and also traps to catch them. He should have done it a month ago.

He opened his eyes for a moment and checked the status of the fluid bag hanging from the pole. There didn't seem to be a drop left to drip into him and he did feel more revived. Knowing that the ER was in the middle of a shift change, now he waited impatiently for his discharge.

Finally, an RN showed up, introduced himself, and explained the paperwork and medical instructions.

"You're good to go," he said, taking out his IV. "See your primary care doctor if you deteriorate after tonight and obviously come back to the ER if you need emergent care."

"Thanks. I plan on staying away."

Jae tapped his phone app for Uber transportation outside the hospital and, in a short while, after his ride appeared and drove him to the fast-food sandwich place, he drove his own pickup truck and pulled up to his home at the park.

Although he never ate dinner, he had no desire to eat and was soon out cold in a deep sleep.

At six o'clock the next morning, Jae stepped outside on the squeaky boards of his porch with a cup of coffee in his hands. The cool, crisp air was not cold enough for him to don a jacket. The quietness broke when Curley and Twist came bounding toward him and shook their torsos. He had selected the names for the two dogs based on their furry coats. They were not exactly strays any more since he and Patty put food out for them, let them in and out of their cabins whenever they needed shelter, or when the two dogs gave them a pitiful look like they wanted human companionship.

Jae patted Curley's back as the mutt pushed against his leg. He tried to be cognizant of both the dogs' health needs and caved in to take them to the vet six months ago for annual vaccines. But then again, between the two rangers, they were not that careful about keeping up-to-date with their monthly parasite prevention medications.

"Good morning," Patty said loudly as she pranced across the grass between their cabins. "I was concerned about you last night because your place stayed dark up until I went to sleep. I'm not spying on you; it just crossed my mind that you never mentioned any plans for being out late. I never saw the truck lights come in or any lights go on over here."

Jae smiled at the five-foot, three-inch ranger. She was not as old as him, looked younger than her age, and could be mistaken for a boy when she wore her ranger's hat. Although she was little, she was tougher than she appeared – mentally and physically. Alongside him, she had helped rescue stranded and sick visitors, and always pulled her weight when it came to clearing tree limbs and brush from the trails after storms.

"Thanks for your concern," he said. "I left in the evening to pick up a sandwich and, instead, ended up in the ER because I felt lousy. Turns out I'm walking around with the flu."

"Jae! Why didn't you call me?"

"Why? They put me back on my feet, as you can see."

"Still … I don't know about you. We should ask each other for help when we need it." She shook her head as Twist jumped off Jae's porch and sat next to her.

"I don't disagree. Had they kept me overnight, I surely would have called you."

"Under that circumstance, you would have been forced to. Are you okay to work this morning, or can I help you out with some of your duties?"

"I'll be fine. I'm going to go to war after the damn mouse population around here before I open up the visitors' center."

"I'll leave my cabin door unlocked so you can get in over there too. I'll open up the visitors' center, so don't worry about hurrying over there." She clicked her tongue a few times at the dogs. "Come on, you filthy beasts. Leave Jae alone. I'll grab you some food. You both could use baths, too, but it'll be hell or high water before I do that."

Jae took another sip of coffee as he watched them leave. Inside his cabin, he put down his mug. He hated to admit it to himself, but the coffee tasted lousy, his GI tract felt like it was stuffed with saturated sponges, and his headache was ramping back up to a dull roar.

He gathered more mental optimism about the rest of the day. It was probably crappy coffee that started him off on the wrong foot. He stepped in the laundry room at the back of the house where he owned a freezer chest and opened the lid. He grinned at the bags of venison, took one out, and couldn't wait to savor the rich, gamey taste, which reminded him of the diet the deer ate during it's own life: acorns, herbs, and sage.

Maybe he was run down to have caught the flu, so there was no better "meat" for him to eat than venison - abundant with vitamins and minerals and low in fat content.

For now, Jae put the bag in the kitchen refrigerator, gulped down a sample of orange juice, and reeled back with surprise due to its sweetness. It tasted terrible, so he dumped the rest down the sink. He reverted to getting out an ibuprofen for his growing headache and swallowed it with water.

Jae then gathered the supplies needed for his mouse-trapping chore. He realized something which had not occurred to him before. What stupidity. He and Patty should take in a cat or two; let them go in and out between the cabins and the woods like Curley and Twist. What better way to curtail the mouse population than with natural predators?

A big yellow school bus was parked in the lot of the visitors' center when Jae ambled over and entered the front door. The gift shop to the right, staffed with an elderly volunteer at the cash register, was cluttered with school kids.

"Did you accomplish your mission?" Patty asked as she approached him.

He nodded and brushed his hand along the crease of his forest green uniform trousers after all the crouching down he'd done. "I'm finished for the time being and came to relieve you. I can do half the paperwork in my cabin later."

"Appreciate it. I just gave these kids a tour of Taft's restored Victorian house. There's a volunteer over there starting another tour. I'll swing by later."

Jae opened the door for her since he stood closest to it. After Patty left, a woman leaning against the exit area of the shop pushed away from the wall and walked over. She wore a furry pink cap and stared at him with large brown eyes.

"Hi," she said. "My students are buying out the gift shop."

"We don't mind that," he said. "As long as their parents gave them a limited amount of money so they don't go home in trouble for spending too much. What grade are they in?"

"We're fifth grade. I've been teaching that grade for years, but to tell you the truth, I really envy your job. I would have loved to be a park ranger. It would be like being on vacation every day without a care in the world except for wondering what kind of wildlife you would see on a particular day."

Jae's energy was draining, even for a conversation, but he never gave up an opportunity to highlight the unseen and unknown perils of being a park ranger. Yes, it was glamourous. Dangerous too.

"It can be more involved than that," he said. "Who do you think has the greatest likelihood of being assaulted on the job: someone in the Secret Service; the Bueau of Alcohol, Tobacco, Firearms and Explosives; the DEA, FBI, or any other federal office?"

She scrunched up her eyes. "I would say the officers working with intoxicated people and those with weapons. So, the Bureau of Alcohol, Tobacco, Firearms and Explosives."

"No," he said. "It's a national park ranger."

"I'll be," she stuttered. "Why's that?"

"We rescue people out of dangerous situations but face the same perils ourselves; we fight wildfires; come face-to-face with wild animals, and deal with unhappy visitors with short tempers, to name a few."

"Hmm. I never thought about that." As if she lost her enchantment with park rangers, she went back to waiting for the students at the exit of the gift shop.

Jae left the lobby, went down the next hallway, and into a small office. The visitors' center had it's own stash of clerical work, which needed the ranger's daily attention. He sat and leaned over into his hands. It was lunch time, but he didn't feel like eating a thing. Hopefully, his venison would appeal to him that evening.

CHAPTER 5

After walking away from the call rooms, Annabel dropped her overnight bag in the corner of the office while Bob followed behind her.

"Did you get any sleep?" he asked.

"Enough," she replied. "How about you?"

"More than you. I stirred when I heard you come in next door."

"Sorry. I probably made more noise than I should have. I stayed up and monitored Mrs. Helm's atrial fibrillation treatment. That was pretty cool watching her heart's chaotic electrical impulses convert to a normal sinus rhythm." She sorted the index cards in her hands, each one representing a different patient. "We better go see our patients before official rounds, and before Dr. Schott shows up and starts reading his *USA Today* to us."

"Since we're post-call, he probably won't do that. He'll have yesterday's paper and he already read those highlights to us."

"You have him figured out."

"What's not to figure? He's super nice to us, a good teacher, likes his food, and, besides medicine, he keeps his finger on the pulse."

Annabel slid the white cards back in her lab jacket and smiled. "We should do something for him."

"Let's think about that. In the meantime, let's find coffee to gulp down and then see our patients."

"A lot of coffee. Dr.Mejia is joining us for rounds this morning, so we better be on our toes."

Annabel's current favorite patient was May Oliver, a thirty-two-year old-woman who came in with coughing up blood, or hemoptysis, as the medical team called it. She was diagnosed with lung cancer; the adenocarcinoma had already sneakily metastasized to her bones and brain. It was bad enough the young woman suffered respiratory symptoms, but having a cluster of the cancer in her brain had caused seizures, and the foci in her tibia, or shinbone, had made her more and more unsteady on her feet.

Annabel tightened the strings on her scrub pants as the entire team stopped in the hallway outside May's room. The students and residents needed to highlight the recent activities of their patients and thoroughly "present" any new patients that had come in during their call.

Their attending put his hand up to his hair as if checking the placement of his neatly organized comb over and then looked straight at Annabel.

"Mrs. Oliver had another radiation treatment yesterday," she said. "She kept down hot cereal this morning, her vital signs are stable, and the oncologist plans no more treatments for the time being."

"He wants to see her in a month," the resident on the case, Dr. Burg, added.

Dr. Mejia nodded his approval. "Sounds like she tolerated the third treatment the best."

"Third time's a charm," Dr. Schott said. "Whenever that happens with a patient getting chemo or radiation, I think of it like tolerance to a narcotic. The effect becomes less, but in this case, the nasty side-effects."

"For our patients' sakes, I wish that was a universal occurrence."

Dr. Mejia straightened his tie; the only team member wearing street clothes. He always dressed refined and wore what society expected of a distinguished cardiologist. "I suppose it's time, then. To send Mrs. Oliver home."

He frowned, making Annabel worry about May's fate. Her patient was too young for the cards she had been dealt and the two of them had bonded because of similarities in their lives.

Dr. Schott gestured and the group clamored into May's room. The woman slurped through a straw while holding a liquid nutrition drink. Only a stubble of hair clung to her scalp and she wore a green sweater, too loose for her slight frame.

May took her lips off the straw. "I expected you all to come traipsing in here after Dr. Tilson visited me before. These are your 'morning after' call rounds with Dr. Mejia, who is fresh as a cucumber giving you all his words of wisdom about diseases and patient plans and outcomes, and the students are dragging and dreaming of going home. I'm a frequent flyer in here, so I know these things." She said it in one long breath and again put her lips to the straw by her mouth.

Dr. Mejia laughed. "Dr. Tilson pegged you correctly ... you tolerated the last radiation treatment well. We will be sorry to see you go, but the excellent news is that Dr. Burg will be writing your discharge orders after rounds. Dr. Schott and this motley crew will expect you in clinic soon and you need to also be evaluated by the oncologist in a short time."

May shifted position and stole a glance at Annabel. "I can't thank you all enough. You broke bad news to me and then tried your best to cure me. Curing me was not meant to be; we have only stalled the inevitable. I'll try my best, however, and practice Dr. Tilson's advice to be optimistic."

Annabel gulped. She felt so bad for May, but there was nothing more the team could do. In her limited clinical training, she had yet to witness a braver patient.

Dr. Schott peeled his eyes away from May. "Yes, carry optimism with you at all times. Enjoy the rest of that strawberry drink."

The team cluttered back up the hallway and Bob patted Annabel's shoulder. "You made her hospitalization more tolerable," he said softly.

"Thanks. I'm going to do what my dad started doing a few years ago when he let religion back into his life. I'm going to say a prayer for her."

As if he was privy to Annabel's thoughts, Dr. Schott said, "Patients don't always get better from our health care. Sometimes healing comes from spiritualism or an unknown force which infuses someone with the ability to overcome their own medical obstacle."

"I tend to be more pragmatic," Dr. Mejia said. "Maybe that's why I went into cardiology and deal with the straightforward physical and electrical elements of the heart."

"I'm going into cardiology too," Jordan reminded him. "My thinking precisely."

Annabel wanted to say, "No one asked you," but she bit her tongue. She noticed Dr. Schott shake his head probably because Jordan had overstepped his rank in front of the attending doctor.

"Religious discussion aside, who's our next patient?" Dr. Mejia asked.

"We should do Mrs. Helm next," Donn said. "She's next door and is Annabel's new patient from last night."

All eyes focused on Annabel again as she slipped out her patient's index card and checked the patient's age.

"Meagan Helm is a forty-seven-year-old Caucasian mother of three who came in with an onset yesterday of rapid heart palpitations, shortness of breath, and dizziness. Her heart gave her similar problems when she was pregnant with twins and she has a history of rheumatic heart disease. Other than that, her past medical and surgical history is negative, and she never had a follow up for her heart."

Annabel slipped the cards back in her pocket and continued. "On her admission physical exam, her heartbeat and pulse were fast and erratic and her EKG indicated atrial fibrillation."

Jordan took a baby step forward, his enthusiasm for the heart condition as apparent as Dr. Mejia's.

Annabel continued. "Her diagnosis is atrial fibrillation and the plan was to convert her pharmacologically and not by cardioversion. Dr. Watts ordered an IV calcium channel blocker and Mrs. Helm's heart responded perfectly; her rhythm is now normal and regular."

Dr. Mejia rubbed his hands back and forth. "Ahh. A clean, classic case. Dr. Schott must have told you atrial fib is the most common cardiac dysrhythmia and mostly occurs in the elderly. However, cases are increasing in younger people without structural heart disease." He turned his attention to Jordan Maldonado. "They are a challenge and, by the time you are out of residency, you'll be seeing more and more of them in the ER where the first diagnosis and treatment occur.

"Now I'll ask the resident ... Dr. Wattts, now that Mrs. Helm's reason for admission is taken care of, are we sending her home?"

"We need to find out the cause of her atrial fib."

"Correct." Dr. Mejia turned to Jordan. "What causes a heart to be jumpy like that?"

All eyes rested on Jordan as his eyes grew smaller and no words came out of his mouth.

Chineka Watts waited like the rest of them, but then decided to salvage Jordan's pride and spoke up. "Structural heart disease, such as mitral valve disease, or from hypertension. Also hyperthyroidism, pulmonary disease, ischemic heart disease, and pericarditis, to name a few others."

Dr. Mejia nodded and then checked on his hair again with his hand. "What are you going to order first?"

"An echocardiogram, sir."

"Students, besides rattling off tests that we order on our patients, you must always know how they work. Echocardiography uses ultrasound waves which produce images of the valves, the chambers, and the pericardium, or lining, around the heart. What we're dealing with here, most likely, is mitral stenosis. If that is the case, what will we see on the echo?"

"Left atrial enlargement," Chineka said.

Dr. Mejia broke out in a smile. "Don't you just love it?" he asked, mostly to himself. "Let's go." He bobbed his head toward the door and went in. By the time they left, Mrs. Helm understood their reasoning to order her an echocardiogram.

"Who's going to the Medicine Department?" Annabel asked as the team piled into the office after rounds, minus Dr. Mejia. Their attending already parted ways to go roto-rooter a patient's coronary arteries.

Jordan's head was planted six inches from his cell phone as he texted. "I'm coming after I fire off this message to your sister."

"Tell her I said hello," Annabel said and frowned.

"Let's go," the fourth medical student said. "Jordan, we'll let you know if you passed." Stuart Schneider held his head down low, like usual, and was thin as a dime. The fact that he was in the top of their class overshadowed his quiet personality. Unless pressed, he never let on that he knew so much, but he did.

"I'm coming," Jordan barked at Stuart. Jordan tugged at Annabel. "Your sister said she and I should meet halfway between Cincinnati and Nashville one of these weekends."

"Better for your first date than one of you driving the whole way," Bob said.

Jordan stooped over and grabbed his bag and jacket. "And who are you dating these days?"

"Nobody."

"That older med student is out of the picture?"

"Totally."

"How about you, Annabel?" Jordan asked. "You snuck out for a date the other night after we were all together."

"Don't mention that one. However, the policeman involved with our medical case during the first half of the rotation has asked me out again. I actually met him while on my psychiatry rotation."

Surprised, Bob's pace slowed and he glanced at her. Maybe it won't go anywhere, he thought. Then again, he didn't know why the two of them had not continued dating before.

Stuart bulldozed ahead of them and, outside in the parking lot, they each climbed into their own car. Downtown on the main campus, the hallway of the medicine department came alive with their footsteps. Bob opened the door to the office and they lined up like school children waiting on the bathroom. The secretary sorted through the alphabetically arranged test results.

"Should I say the test scores aloud or do you each want privacy?" she said with utmost importance.

All four of them shrugged.

"We don't care," Stuart spoke up.

"Easy for you to say," Bob said. He smiled at the woman with a stacked figure and a tight permanent. "Yeah, it's okay. He speaks for all of us."

"You all passed, but Dr. Schneider wins the trophy with a perfect hundred."

"Congratulations," Annabel acknowledged in awe to her classmate.

Stuart hung his head. "To all of us," he said.

Annabel drove home with relief that her call night was over, she wasn't dead tired, and that she passed the mid-term test. She'd scored a ninety-one … not too shabby.

She was glad for Bob too, who surpassed her this time with a ninety-two. They knew Stuart's result, but Jordan did not divulge his. The way he acted, however, she almost thought that he was the one with the one hundred and not Stuart, especially since he had cheated.

She pulled off of I-75 and soon drove in her eclectic neighborhood of small houses, which were mostly three-story apartment rentals. The area was hilly and charming and had a small garden park close to the end of her street where the view encompassed the dark channel of the churning Ohio River making its way towards the great Mississippi.

Annabel weaved her SUV up and down the streets flanking where she lived and sighed with despair over the parking situation. Renting someone's garage for parking was a luxury commodity and garages rarely became available, so she did what most of the other younger people did who worked - be at the right place at the right time and snag a space when someone happened to pull out of a spot.

The sun was shining and she was in a good mood, so she cranked the top country playlist a little louder and kept circling.

It seemed like she heard Keith Urban a second time by the time a brown-suited young woman in heels beeped open her car door and scrambled in. Annabel gave her enough space to pull out and then she parallel parked like an expert. Luckily, the proximity of the fire hydrant was not an issue and she was at least on the upper end of her own street.

No matter how small her third floor two-room apartment was, it was always heartwarming to open the door to her own place. She dumped her things on the kitchen counter and went into the bedroom, which also housed her desk and only comfortable chair.

After peeling off her scrubs, she took a hot shower and dressed in polyester running pants and a long-sleeved T-shirt. All the while, she contemplated the parking situation. Jae Nixon, the sick man she drove to the hospital, had solved his transportation problem back to his parked vehicle without any fuss at all.

She had a parking problem, not so much a transportation problem, but why hadn't she thought of it before?

She grabbed her cell phone. Both her parents would be working, but they would either take her call or let it forward to voicemail if they were tied up. She called her dad, who might be doing surgery on a cranial case or seeing patients in the office.

"Hi, honey," he said right away.

"Hey, Dad. Can you talk?"

"I'm in the doctors' lounge between cases, trying to saw my way through a bagel with a plastic knife."

"You can get into someone's head easier than that."

"So true. Surgical equipment companies are more skillful making their products than the humans churning out plastic cutlery, that's all." He laughed and added, "Is everything all right?"

"I passed my internal medicine mid-term."

"Congratulations. Was there a doubt in your mind?"

"I suppose not. My friend, Bob, did well too."

"Treat yourself and Bob to your favorite restaurant. It goes on my credit card anyway."

"We're going to run together today, which we've never done before. We're post call and we weren't slammed too bad."

"I often have worse nights than you and I'm the one finished with training."

"Although you say you're always learning, Dad."

"That is the truth and the way it will be for you too."

"I miss Dakota," she said. "But I'm sure you grieve for him more."

"That dog is in my heart every day. Nevertheless, yes, I miss my faithful companion. I better go. Anesthesia is ready to put my next patient to sleep."

"Dad, another thing. Can I start putting something else on the credit card bill?"

"I'm listening."

"The parking around here has only gotten worse and I shudder every time I pull out of a space. When I come back home, finding a parking spot is as evasive as finding Bigfoot. I'd like to leave my Nissan where it is on hospital days and instead call Uber. The service is not that expensive."

Danny considered her request. His daughter never made outrageous requests when it came to money. "However, your safety comes first."

"The substitute taxi cab service is safe. In the major cities, people are using it like crazy."

"Okay. Give it a try. Let me know how it works out."

"Thanks, Dad. Say hello to everyone at home and good luck with your next case."

"I'll tell them."

Annabel closed the call and punched in another one. This time to Bob.

"A real phone call and not a text," Bob said when he answered. "Are you all right?"

"I'm fine. Can we change our plans from driving over to Eden Park and meeting there to run and, instead, run a loop from my place? Down my usual route?"

"It's alright with me. How come?"

"I spent freaking fifteen minutes searching for a parking space when I arrived home and I don't want to do that again today."

"Hmm. So what you're saying is that you want me to go there instead and enjoy the same hassle, eliminating it for you."

Annabel's hand flew to her mouth. "I'm sorry. I didn't think of it that way."

Bob grinned. "I know you didn't. I'm yanking your chain. I'll be over at 1 o'clock, but who knows when I'll be rapping at your door."

Annabel grimaced when she hung up. He tolerated her bright ideas a lot more than she deserved.

CHAPTER 6

Jae Nixon finished one hour of paper pushing in the visitors' center and ambled back over to the cabins.

First, he went inside to his kitchen and pulled out a drink mix. He mixed the orange powder with water and hoped the fluid and electrolyte combination would prevent him from wilting any more. Like a leaf blowing to the ground, his energy was draining by the hour.

Still wearing his outdoor walking boots, he gathered the bucket with mouse deterrants he'd used earlier in the morning when he had mouse-proofed inside the cabins, storage shed, and make-shift garage. Those spots were ideal for the white-footed mice in the cooler months, but now he needed to survey outside; it was time for them to begin their breeding season. Finding burrows and nests were on his agenda.

When he drove in from the hospital the night before, his headlights had spotted one of the nocturnal critters, a full six inches including its tail, scurrying ahead towards stumps and rock piles behind his place. The furry fellow's underside was white but the upper body coloration was dark. The bicolored fast rodents could zoom away from headlights like lightning compared to the stunned deer that froze when he rounded a corner and caught them by surprise.

When he poked at the ground where he saw one disappear the previous night, he knew the site made a fine protective cover for them to burrow. He found a soil crack with evidence of mouse droppings and not only did he drop down poison, but he took a shovel from the nearby shed and filled it in.

As he took a break, his eyes scanned the edge of the woods while he drank down the refreshing drink in stops and starts.

Two old rotting logs were several feet away. The second one proved to harbor a mouse nest underneath, so he dismantled it with the shovel.

An hour later, he struck gold several feet above ground with an abandoned squirrel's nest. Because of his thorough biology background, he could spot the usefulness of this newly inhabited mouse home for breeding purposes. Two startled white-footed mice practically flew off the tree above him while he was working.

Although he wore no jacket or hat and had done no strenuous work, moisture began to accumulate under Jae's armpits and the base of his neck. He finished the twenty-four-ounce bottled drink he had mixed, put the shovel away, and went back to his place.

Inside, he swallowed an over-the-counter pill for his headache first, took off his boots, and sat on the plaid cloth couch. He could barely fend off the tiredness, so he fluffed the pillow by the armrest and lay sideways.

Just a short catnap, he thought ...

Sitting at her desk, Annabel heard a thump and put down her pen. She scurried across the kitchen floor and opened the stiff door. Bob stood there in a short-sleeved T-shirt and navy blue running pants like herself. His hair was fixed just right and he wore a smile.

"Fancy sneakers," she commented.

"They're brand new and need breaking in."

She stepped aside, letting him walk in. "What's the deal with those shoelaces?"

He glanced at her shoes and grinned. "You're the runner, but you use traditional laces?"

"You answered my question with a question," she said, frustrated. "Besides our mid-term test, I guess you outsmart me in running gear too. I don't know anything about traditional or non-traditional shoelaces."

"Then it's my pleasure to show you something new. They are elastic no-tie shoelaces. These lock laces did not come with the sneakers; I bought them separately."

"So they are for people too lazy to tie their laces?" She kept a straight face and then tapped him and laughed.

"No. Why bother with regular flat nylon laces that drape over your shoes? You have to double knot them to prevent tripping over them. Or why bother making knots with them at all, causing you to waste precious time?"

Annabel shook her head. "Bob Palmer, now I understand. You're studying more than me because you're salvaging more study time by not tying shoelaces."

They both laughed "Are you ready to hit the pavement?" he asked.

"Follow me on this grueling route. We're going to do stairs as well.

They go down to the major thoroughfare along the Ohio. And by the way, my dad congratulated us on passing our test. He said a dinner for the two of us is on him."

"Can we take him up on it?"

"How about going up the block to Pete's for a late lunch when we're finished? That would be more our style."

"Your call."

Annabel grabbed her keys, locked the door behind them, and they scrambled down the two flights of stairs. She pointed down the narrow block but focused on the pavement as they began their jaunt. The blocks of cement were old and uneven and she hated the hazard.

"Falling is not permissible," she yelled over her shoulder. "We're finishing internal medicine without an incident."

"No problem." They joined alongside each other when they crossed the street at the end and followed a safer pavement through the little park ripe with greenery from non-deciduous bushes.

"Come on this way." They paused at the top of the staircase. "The hard part's coming back up." She grinned and took off ahead of him.

Bob followed, and at the halfway mark, they took an overpass across the road to the other side. They both walked a bit on the sidewalk and watched two barges going in opposite directions.

"Hold up," Bob said. He leaned over but changed his mind and sat down on the pavement instead. The tall grass flanking the sidewalk along the embankment qualified as overgrown weeds that had not seen a lawn mower for a year. He flexed his knee toward him, leaning back into the brush.

"What are you doing?" Annabel asked.

"Fixing my shoelaces."

"After telling me they're trouble free?"

"I'm breaking them in like my shoes. I need to pull the elastic tighter and cinch it into the lock device."

"Sounds like surgery, but the OR is sterile and free of living things compared to where you're sitting."

He rolled his eyes, fiddled some more, and then went to the other shoe.

"I beat you fair and square," Annabel said as they entered Pete's Café.

"Neither of us mentioned our run being a race."

"We're competitive; otherwise, we wouldn't be in med school."

"But at this stage, we don't need to be. The only person who qualifies as competitive is Jordan, and that's because he's a dick head."

"Bob!"

"Well, isn't he?"

"I'll refrain from saying." She waved at Pete as they approached the counter.

"Haven't seen you in a few days," Pete said. "I'm serving super scrumptious quinoa salad today."

"You sold me. I'll take it with a mocha cappuccino."

"Me too," Bob said. "But a regular dark roast coffee."

Pete rang up the total.

Annabel dug into her pocket and took out her credit card. "This is my dad's treat today."

"Thank him for me," Bob said.

They picked a table in front with a full view down Annabel's street. "You've never really mentioned how you're paying for medical school," she said. "Are your parents helping you out?"

"As you know, my mom's a nurse and my dad's an electrician. They paid my way through college and now they're paying tuition for my two sisters who are undergrads. They are being generous, but they surely can't swing my medical school bills. These four years are totally my expense; I'm strapped with big loans." He frowned. "The minor jobs I worked the last two summers barely covered my book bills."

"I'm sorry. At least you'll have a salary as a resident."

"True. At least then I'll be able to pay my rent without borrowing money."

"I'm fortunate and I never take my parents for granted. It's my dad's money from what he does, but my mom has worked all these years too … as a teacher. When we were real little, however, she stayed at home and I'm glad she did. I have nothing but happy memories. She went back to teaching when she could." Her eyes moistened. "I even had fantastic grandparents in my life. I couldn't have asked for more than that."

Bob shook his head. "We've both had hard-working parents. I want to instill that most important principal into my kids someday too. A solid work ethic."

One of Pete's regular waitresses walked over and placed down their lunch. "Look's good," Annabel said. "Thanks."

"Enjoy," she said.

Annabel opened up a napkin, drizzled dressing on her salad, and picked up a fork. "You plan on having kids?"

"Sure. Don't you?"

"I don't think about it." She glanced out the window; a car crept along looking for a parking spot. "Maybe. The other parent is the problem. Most marriages end in divorce."

"Your parents are divorced ... yet they're together."

"They're an exception."

Bob stirred a sugar packet into his coffee, put the spoon down, and wiggled in his shirt. He reached behind his neck and scratched. "Besides purchasing modern shoelaces, the next T-shirts I buy are going to be tagless."

"I'm ahead of you on that one. There's not one label in my top itching me like crazy or advising me how to wash the fabric."

The coffee had cooled enough and Bob raised it to his lips. Their conversation drifted to the hospital and the medical subjects they needed to concentrate on for the following few weeks.

At home, Annabel downloaded the Uber app onto her phone and registered for the service. She familiarized herself with the site, studied a few hours, and went to bed early.

The next morning, she woke fully rested. She factored in an extra ten minutes into her schedule since it was her first day to try the modern taxi service. In essence, it was a trial run. It had to be dependable or she would have to ditch the idea.

Lately, Annabel had definitely seen a few young people in the mornings come out of their apartments like her and get into the substitute taxi cars, so she figured it couldn't be all that bad. Plus, the ranger had used it and since he was law enforcement, the service must be trustworthy.

After punching in her destination and requesting a solo ride rather than a "pool" ride, she headed downstairs and stood next to the tree in front of her place. She often looked out her front window at its high branches, enjoying the leaves as they revised themselves through the seasons, and was often charmed by the bushy-tailed black squirrel who had thrown together a nest at the junction of a branch and the main trunk.

She monitored her app and saw her ride making a turn from around the block and then it was there in person. The driver's window rolled down.

"Annabel?" asked a young man.

She nodded and entered the spotless, spacious back seat with her backpack.

"How are you doing today?" she asked, like she was a regular. A GPS map streamed on the driver's phone mounted on the dashboard and a medal hung from the rearview mirror.

"I'm ready for the day."

She couldn't place his accent. "Will you drive all day?"

"I will."

"I'm new at this," she admitted. "Do most drivers make this a full-time job?"

"Some do. Some don't. I'm only a year in this country and this suits me fine. I can work as much or as little as I like, at any or all hours."

"Where are you from?"

"Nigeria."

Music streamed from his phone and now she understood his taste for the pleasant Afrobeat. "You must miss your family."

"I'm okay. I plan a visit next year. I'm becoming more acclimated by the day."

"Good for you," she said pleasantly. Her text message alert sounded. It was from Dustin Lowe, the police officer:

Medical students work early! I bet I'll catch your attention now rather than later. Interested in the rain check I promised you?

She smiled. They had an interesting roller-coaster ride since meeting and yet he knew more about her personal life than she'd like. To his credit, he still wanted to date her.

Hi, Dustin. Yes! Nothing like breakfast at night with a prior date, a friend, and someone who came to my aid.

Super. What night works for you?

Friday?

We're on. At the same diner? I think starting where we left off would be fun.

Sure. I'd enjoy that. Can I meet you there around 7?

See you then. Heal the sick today!

Annabel sighed with contentment. He was an attractive, likeable guy with the most glorious dimple in his chin. And after all, she had nothing going on at present through her dating app, and substantial dates with her former surgical chief resident, Robby Burk, had failed to materialize. She wished they would because she had the hots for Dr. Burk no matter what he did.

When she glanced up, the driver turned and slowed the car in front of the hospital entrance. Amazed she was there already, she grabbed her backpack and opened the door.

"Thanks so much," she said, getting out.

"Lekker dag," he responded. "Have a nice day."

She strutted into the hospital with plenty of time to see her patients before rounds and went straight to the cafeteria to buy coffee. She had skipped making it at home. With a medium-sized cup in her hand, she headed to the elevator, and hummed the driver's music in her head. Her life right now seemed fuller than usual and no bad things were happening. She planned to keep it that way.

CHAPTER 7

Jae woke up with a start and realized he had dozed for a half hour. Thirty minutes too much. He sat upright and rose slowly. Luckily, he had popped enough ibuprofen before falling asleep and his headache was behaving itself.

Patty must be at the visitors' reception desk waiting for him to relieve her, he guessed. She had other park tasks to do which needed her attention. He strutted to the main building and approached the desk.

"Where have ya been?" his partner asked with a hint of annoyance.

"I'm sorry. I dozed off by mistake." His thick eyebrows lowered as well as his head.

She frowned. "That's not like you, but I didn't mean to make you feel guilty."

"I'll make it up to you. I'll share my venison tonight."

"That's all right. I'll stick with my tabouli, quinoa, or tofu." She rested her hands on her belt and wondered about him. "If you're contemplating eating deer meat, you're holding up with the flu pretty darn well, even if you're suffering from a mild case."

"My dinner plan may be wishful thinking. However, I overheard a conversation in the ER; usually the young and the old suffer the worst with the flu."

She nodded as a couple walked their way. The man planted his cane carefully while his gray-haired companion stayed a step ahead of him.

"They're all yours," Patty said and stepped out from behind the wooden desk.

Jae thumped his finger on the counter. "Welcome to the park."

"Thanks," the old man said. "May we take a tour?"

"Sure. You can wait here or enjoy the premises outside. The volunteer starts another talk in forty-five minutes."

"We've got nothing better to do. We're retired."

"We'll go outside on a walking trail for a few minutes," the woman said. "But we know to bring out any trash that we bring in."

"Which makes my job easier. Our goal is to have folks leave the park as undisturbed and natural as possible."

"Then you have a big job," she said. "People leave their human junk wherever they want. And they lug those water bottles around, drop the plastic to the ground with their last sip, and don't give a hoot that it's not biodegradable. They don't have manners or respect for the environment like us old timers."

Her partner pumped his head up and down with applause.

"I can't argue with you two."

"You must be a New Yorker," said the old man as he wielded his cane handle forward.

Jae nodded. "Originally. We northeasterners can't cast away our accents any more than we can remove 'you guys' from our vocabulary."

"Don't worry about it," the woman said. "We're guilty of using 'you all' all the time. Our southern roots are like creeping vines that won't let go."

Jae handed her a pamphlet about the park. She grasped it with wrinkled fingers as he took a long-winded breath and leaned against the counter.

"Young man, your job probably isn't as easy as it looks, but maybe you need a vacation or need one of those young people's energy drinks."

"I'm fine. I'm overdue for a home-cooked meal or a long siesta." He frowned, knowing he had just taken a nap, and realized that working while having a light case of the flu was a stupid idea. However, he could not pull help or a replacement ranger out of thin air.

She eyed him and pointed with a finger. "Then go do it." In unison, she turned with her spouse and they walked away.

Jae sat on a wooden chair next to the varnished counter so visitors would see him. About all he felt like doing was to answer questions and pretend to be hospitable. The late afternoon lagged and no more formal groups came through for a tour. He left after the volunteer closed the gift shop and swung his light jacket over his shoulder as he walked over to his cabin.

Over the sink, he mulled over his almost fully thawed venison. What a stupid idea to think he would have normal taste buds by tonight. He decided to leave it in the bag in the fridge, changed into blue jeans and a T-shirt, and threw an instant oatmeal packet into a bowl. After heating water and managing to slide the Quaker product down with a headache pill, he stepped out on the porch for one last breath of fresh air. He was definitely going to bed early.

He scoured the area for the dogs; he hadn't seen them in hours. Perhaps they were hunkered down for the evening with Patty. Nevertheless, he walked to the tree line checking for them, and to also see the area where he'd found the density of mice burrows and nests. He was sure there was some displacement of small branches and leaves in a few spots compared to before.

With his bare hands, he moved away brush to find a still mouse on its side – dead as the venison meat in his refrigerator. He picked it up by its tail and threw it into the woods.

A rustling of leaves caused Jae to look beside him. Twist plopped himself down to add a few more broken leaf pieces to his coat.

"What do you know, boy? Where's your pal?" Jae shook his head. "If you don't know, I don't know either. I'm leaving, so if you want an invitation to my cabin, don't make yourself too comfortable."

Jae backed out, patted his leg for the dog to follow, and they both went inside. After a quick shower, he nestled into bed. With his fingers, he felt his forehead, confirming another low-grade fever.

Twist settled on a braided rug next to Jae's platform bed. Even the dog wanted to sleep early. What a pitiful, lethargic pair they were tonight, he thought, admiring Twist's simplicity. Nothing special about him. In his prime middle years, he was mostly pitch black except for two splashes of white and brown and he was a medium size. Jae figured he was probably a shepherd mix. His attribute, as well as Curley's, was his friendliness and exuberant greeting to any tourists who came on the premises. The two dogs were free, dependable souls who had secured a home, an outdoor life, and two humans who were attentive to their needs.

Early in the morning as the darkness in Jae's room inched slowly away, the ranger extended his arm to pat Twist on his back. It was too early; his alarm clock had not even gone off.

First, Jae sat up, and with the movement came a wave of nausea. It abated, so he went to the bathroom and then shuffled off to brew a pot of coffee. Before he lost track of the dog for the day, he measured a cup of dry dog food and sprinkled it into one of the dog bowls on the floor. At some point every day, he and Patty coordinated who had fed which dog when.

No way, he acknowledged to himself. Maybe his flu was at its peak because his muscles were sore. If he didn't know better, he'd swear he was stiff and wiped out like after a long plane haul across the Atlantic from Europe; the worst jet lag and from sitting in the most cramped cabin seat possible.

Jae figured he better talk with Patty, take the day off, and get over the flu hurdle once and for all. Otherwise, he'd be of no use to either of them or to the park in the coming days. He poured a half-cup of house blend and went to peek in at Twist.

"Didn't you hear me rattle those kibbles into your bowl? What's taking you so long?"

Twist was poised in the corner of the room. He shot a glance at Jae and then hunched his torso into a dry heave. To no avail, he opened his mouth with several attempts to purge whatever was in his belly. Finally, he expelled a globous mess on the floor.

With much difficulty due to Jae's own sour stomach and desire to wretch himself, he cleaned up Twist's vomit before it ran down in the space between the wooden floor boards and became a permanent odor. As the dawn continued to beam more sunrays into the cabin, he knew neither canine nor human were up for a sunny day. Not one morsel of Twist's Purina in his bowl was eaten and Jae couldn't think of making another packet of oatmeal.

After Annabel's rounds on her own patients, she entered the office where the smell of fresh blueberry donuts was unmistakable. Her student colleagues were present but no round confection was missing from the donut box that sat on the table. Dr. Schott came in and sidled beside her.

"Someone brought you slackers a dozen donuts?" he asked, his eyes bulging.

"We thought we'd do something for you," Bob said. "Not only do you teach us about medicine and our patients every day, but you put up with us too."

"Thank you. You all are hardly a problem."

"Bob takes the credit for stopping and buying these," Annabel said, handing Donn a napkin from a white stack.

Donn sat and pulled his *USA Today* from underneath his arm. He concentrated on taking bites from the donut in his hand and went to the middle of the front news section. The two residents came in and went straight to the open box.

"Help yourself," Donn said. "Compliments of Dr. Palmer." He shook his head. "Um um um. Here's good and bad news about global warming causing a projected rise in sea level. Breeding habitats for salt-marsh mosquitoes will likely decrease, but bird and mammalian hosts living in those niches may be threatened by extinction. Endemic viruses may decrease." He paused and sank his teeth around another fourth of his donut.

Stuart, who needed the donut calories more than Donn, listened attentively. "But over time, that increase in sea level may only result in a displacement."

Dr. Schott furrowed his eyebrows at him and slowed his chewing.

"What do you mean?" Annabel asked.

"New intrusive salt water on land could possibly turn former fresh water habitats into alternative salt-marsh areas, which, in turn, could support prior or new vector and host species."

After Annabel and Bob glanced at each other over Stuart's thoughtful hypothesis, she looked back at their smart colleague. "Sounds like a reasonable assumption to me. I swear, Stuart, I think you'd be brilliant in any field you pursue. Between Bob's thoughtfulness and your Einstein thinking, I'm privileged to be on the same team with the two of you."

Jordan stopped texting, slipped his cell into his pocket, and wrapped his fingers around the donut and napkin he had put on his lap. "You should be glad I'm around too."

Annabel waited for Jordan's explanation as to why, but none came.

"Dr. Tilson," Donn said, "you're as brainy as the best of them. You have proven that to all of us."

"I wouldn't go that far."

Donn finished, eyed the remaining five donuts left in the box, and noted his students' and residents' cheery expressions. "Let's go see patients like we're supposed to." He walked out the door with lazy steps, giving them all plenty of time to gulp down their last bites.

Annabel paired with Bob in the hallway as she tried to sort through her index cards. "Are your legs sore from our run yesterday?"

"I'm not sure. I'm a little lackluster as far as energy goes, but the run and Pete's was worth it."

"Guess who I was just texting with back there?" Jordan asked, butting in from behind.

"I guess you're referring to my little sister. Otherwise, you wouldn't mention it."

"She's not little to me. She has no classes on Friday and she's playing hookey on Monday, so she's coming up for the weekend."

Annabel gulped. As long as Nancy and Jordan didn't get in her way. Studying and silence in her apartment came first. Although she was guilty of scheduling a date with Dustin on Friday night, she could rationalize that; she was more and more looking forward to seeing him and, besides, it would give her an excuse to break away from her own social app search for reasonable flings.

"She must see something in you," Annabel said and exchanged glances with Bob. She rolled her eyes without Jordan noticing.

Donn stopped short and the students scrambled to gather all their patients' charts and stack them. After they rolled the cart down the hallway, they saw Bob's COPD patient, whose difficulty in breathing had improved. Next, they stopped outside Meagan Helm's room.

"Annabel, would you like to give us an update on Mrs. Helm?" Chineka asked.

Annabel nodded. "Dr. Watts helped me to understand mitral stenosis like it was a plumbing project."

"The circulatory system is about plumbing," Donn said. "The blood has to travel to where it's supposed to be to supply oxygen. If there's a leak or a blockage, then the cells suffer from hypoxia."

"Her echocardiogram yesterday verified mitral stenosis and an enlarged atrium," Annabel said, "but labelled as 'mild.' Her ejection fraction, or the amount of blood pumped out of the ventricles with each contraction, is basically normal."

"Explain the plumbing to me, Dr. Tilson."

"Like an obstruction in a pipe, pressure mounts in the area before it, and if it were malleable, it would dilate with the pressure and the volume. So if the valve between the left atrium and ventricle is clogged or stenotic, then the pressure in the left atrium will increase, leading to left atrial dilation … which could lead to pulmonary hypertension, which you alluded to the other day."

"You enlightened us with a commendable presentation," Dr. Schott said. "So we are all faced with thought-provoking questions. What is a big risk for a patient with mitral stenosis and atrial fibrillation? Should Mrs. Helm be treated with anticoagulants? What would be the risks and benefits?"

Donn's glance veered to Chineka, so she spoke up. "Patients with atrial fibrillation run the risk of developing an atrial thrombus, which is a blood clot that remains attached to its place of origin. However, if it dislodges and travels, it's called an embolus. An embolus can then get stuck in a dangerous place, such as in an artery to the brain, pinching off blood flow to needed tissue. That would result in the patient suffering an ischemic stroke."

Chineka held the students' attention as an orderly passed with a stretcher, so she continued. "Anticoagulation reduces the risk of ischemic stroke because it decreases the ability of the thrombus to form in the first place. However, treating a patient with an antithrombotic anticoagulant such as warfarin increases their risk of bleeding."

"Well put for the students to understand," Dr. Schott said. "I'll take it from here. There are tools we can use to assess risk scores to help us determine whether or not to anti-coagulate a patient, but they are not highly predictive. It comes down to us as physicians to assess each patient individually and use our clinical judgment.

"As far as a bleeding risk from anticoagulation, Mrs. Helm's age of forty-seven makes her a significantly lower risk than, for example, a seventy-year-old. And her history makes me lean towards not initiating anticoagulation. She does not have hypertension, diabetes, or congestive heart failure. She does not have chronic atrial fibrillation and has no prior history of a stroke. Also, she's not older than seventy-five. We can iron this all out for her with a layperson's understanding of risks and benefits, but I'm going to suggest no oral medication. We'll follow her in clinic and check her heart rhythm when she comes in for her appointments."

Donn waited for any input from Chineka, since she was the resident on Mrs. Helm's case. Dr. Watt nodded in agreement.

"Let's go in and explain the situation to her," he said.

Mrs. Helms greeted the team with a bright smile when they paraded in and gathered around her bed. "Dr. Watt explained the test results to me," she said. "My understanding of my heart problem is that it could have been worse."

Donn fiddled with his mustache. "Yes, your mitral stenosis is mild and we'll watch you like a hawk in clinic." He sat down on the edge of her bed. "Anticoagulation is always a possible treatment for patients with atrial fibrillation, so I'm going to explain to you why we're not recommending it in your situation. And if you agree, Dr. Watt can write out your discharge orders so you can get out of here and spend time with those three grown kids of yours."

CHAPTER 8

Jae left a voicemail for his partner, caving in to the fact that he shouldn't be working.

"Don't worry about a thing," the petite ranger said later as she stood in his cabin doorway.

"You should have taken off a few days ago," she barked as he leaned over the counter.

"I'm going to call a part-time ranger in for the day as well as another volunteer. This park was functioning well before we arrived here and will continue to do so with or without us. Regardless of any sick days we need to take."

Patty frowned at him like she was scolding an elementary schoolkid. She held her hat and her uniform looked like it had been pressed twice.

Jae managed a small smile and shook his head. "You're right, as usual. Don't mind if I say this because I'm not being sexist. You're my first woman partner and I'm the first to admit that you, or possibly any woman, is more devoted about looking after the health and well-being of a partner than any man would be. A male counterpart would now be wondering why I'm not sucking up to my job no matter how lousy I feel."

Patty nodded. "Women earn the top trophy when it comes down to common sense and practicality."

He popped a slice of wheat bread in the toaster. "I better eat something. Perhaps tea and toast." After turning around, he dumped his coffee down the drain.

Patty stepped over and placed down her hat. She grabbed a tea bag from the cupboard.

"One more thing," Jae said. "Twist isn't feeling well. He vomited this morning and looks like a cat dragged him in."

"I should say." She pushed her bangs off her forehead as Twist's lethargic gaze peered up at them with the mention of his name. Not far from his paws, a full bowl of dog food lay untouched.

The sound of nails on the wooden floor came from behind them as Curley trotted in from the porch. He pranced over to his best friend, but he plopped on the floor when he found Twist not his spunky self.

"I haven't fed Curley yet," Patty said, "so he might as well have a go at Twist's breakfast."

Curley didn't wait for Jae or Patty to give him an "okay." He spotted the kibbles, began chomping them up, and, with little chewing, swallowed one mouthful after the other.

"You are busy enough," Jae said, "but maybe one of us should bring Twist to the vet."

"Not you." She gave him a firm stare. "The animal hospital has a vet stay late every day to 8 p.m. and then he or she stays on call. I'll take him after work."

Jae sighed with relief. "Thanks."

"No problem. The dogs are part of the operation around here. We can't ignore their needs." She crouched down and rubbed her fingers into Twist's coat. The dog opened his eyes and stared at her until she stood back up.

The microwave with a mug of hot water beeped as Jae buttered the toast.

"Text or call me if you need me," Patty said. "If I don't' see Twist this evening, I'll come by and get him."

Patty was the last one out of the visitor's center at the end of the day, so she locked up behind her. She had not heard a peep from Jae, nor had she seen the dogs.

She lightly rapped on Jae's door and inched the wooden door open when there was no answer. Lying on his side on the couch, Jae looked the picture of tranquility with his mouth semi-open; he wore comfortable cotton pants and a T-shirt.

She surveyed the room for Twist and found him beside the wall near the front door. As she walked over, she had to step over another pile of his vomit. She debated whether to clean it up and possibly disturb Jae, but she realized that the priority was Twist's visit to the vet. After wrapping her fingers around the dog's collar, she urged him up and out the door and then lifted him into her truck.

The female ranger and the mixed Shepherd soon visited the local veterinarian's office where a young doctor filled two vials with Twist's blood and recommended that the dog stay over for hydration and for test results, which should be ready by the morning.

Inside the clinic, the students and residents huddled around Dr. Schott, who sat on a plastic chair peeling Saran Wrap off a homemade peanut butter and jelly sandwich. He grinned up at them. "Unlike the six of you, I had a department meeting at lunchtime and missed lunch."

"I heard they sometimes serve food at those meetings," Dr. Burg said, suppressing a smile and admiring her soft leather heels.

"You're not to supposed to know that. But in my defense, the two platters in the middle of the conference table had more donuts. Can you believe it? Just the day that Bob treated us to the same thing. I think I'm going to roll out of here tonight full of bread flour and yeast."

Most of them laughed and Stuart added, "You're going to need milk of magnesia tonight."

"Stuart!" Melody exclaimed. "That's more than we needed to hear."

"I don't mind," Donn said. "He's correct. My GI tract may be devoid of any wavelike movements the rest of the week and the contents of artificial flavors and bread flour may end up sticking to the muscles of my intestines."

"Yes," Jordan said. "This is more information than we need."

Bob grabbed a nearby chair and sat next to their chief resident. Annabel wondered why he wasn't smiling. Normally, he'd also be adding to the humor of their conversation.

"Yes. Let's drop talking about my eating habits. No more donuts for me for the rest of the rotation … except for once. I'll bring them in the last day. Maybe."

A medical assistant peeked her head out from the front desk. "Uh, are you all going to start seeing patients? All the rooms are full and the waiting area is soon going to become standing room only."

Donn sprang up, reattached the plastic wrap around half his sandwich, and placed it on the counter. "Dr. Watt and Dr. Burg will each accompany a student into a room and the other two students can go see a patient and then come report them to me."

Everyone grabbed a folder from outside an examining room. Annabel opened hers next to Bob. "Is something bothering you today?" she asked.

Bob shook his head and glanced at her. "Except for being tired, nothing is wrong."

"Okay, but if you need to vent about something, I'm a good listener."

Since they weren't on call last night, Annabel wondered about him being tired. A busy night, perhaps? A new girlfriend and overnight bed partner? She chanced asking him, as timidly as she could.

"Is there a new girlfriend who wreaked havoc on your sleep last night?"

"I wish. No. I'd be smiling if that were the case."

Bob opened the chart in front of him and Annabel flipped hers open as well. She had picked up her favorite inpatient's chart. May Oliver had been discharged recently; an appointment so soon didn't make any sense.

With a solid knowledge of her patient's personal and medical history, Annabel only glanced at the reason for her visit. She adjusted her stethoscope around her neck, smoothed the waves of hair hanging alongside her white collar, and went into May's room.

"I'm glad to see you," Annabel said after opening the door. "The morning hospital rounds are not the same without you, but I'm happy you went home."

"Aw. That is sweet of you to say so." May sat on the exam table; her hair was still mostly shaven off. It had looked terrible and sparse from chemotherapy for her lung cancer and metastases, so May went ahead and shaved most of it off to make it more sculpted and neater. The end result defined her attractive yet thinned-out face, and large emotional eyes.

May reached out to Annabel's hand and squeezed it. "I am not much use anymore to anyone. But I do tell people how I am helping a young medical student learn all about lung cancer."

"Don't say that. You are more useful than you think and I have learned more medicine because of you, but I would trade it all in if we could eliminate your cancer and suffering."

May gave Annabel's hand another squeeze, let go, and then rested her listless hand on her tan trousers. "Another hundred or two hundred years from now, human cancer may only be in medical history books. Anyway, I'm here now with the diagnosis and there's nothing we've tried that makes it go away. I thought your team could help me, however, with the new cough and runny nose I seem to have acquired."

Annabel glanced at her recorded vital signs. They were fine except for a low grade fever. "Are you still coughing up blood?"

"No. Some of what I'm coughing up is greenish as well as what I blow from my nose. It started the day after discharge."

"Sounds like an infection, but we'll check with Dr. Schott. Your immune system is not up to par with all the chemo and radiation you've had thrown at you, so I wouldn't be surprised. You were also in the hospital, which is not a good place for an immunocompromised patient to be as far as picking up germs."

Annabel examined May: her lungs and heart with her stethoscope, her abdomen by palpation, and her eardrums with an otoscope. She opened the door and peered up the hallway. She signaled to Dr. Schott when he saw her.

"May Oliver is here," she said.

Donn came in, and after listening to Annabel's synopsis of May's visit and her physical exam, he agreed with her tentative assumption. He sent May for an X-ray and confirmed an infection.

They walked back into May's room. "Here," Dr. Schott said, handing her a prescription. "You have an infection, so we're putting you on an antibiotic for ten days."

As May dressed, Donn and Annabel left the chart at the front desk. Donn grabbed the other half of his sandwich. "You handled her visit like a pro," he said.

"I am worried that one of these visits will be her last."

Donn's expression soured. "I agree."

"I said a prayer for her a month ago. I'm going to do it again. I'm not the religious type, but if anyone deserves a blessing, it's her."

Although late-day rounds back at the hospital proceeded like clockwork, Annabel had too much scut work to do. By the time she called for a ride home on her cell phone app, she was impatient to be home. She spotted the scheduled driver outside the revolving doors of the hospital within five minutes and jumped in the back seat.

The GPS started immediately as the driver headed out of the parking lot and glanced in the rearview mirror. "Busy day?" he asked after Annabel let out a big sigh.

"With little exception, every day is hectic."

"Ain't that the truth. I just got off my day job, will drive you, and then attend to pressing matters at home." He wore a leather jacket and a dangling, unilateral earring. Soft, soothing classical music streamed from his iPhone.

"You sound like a hard worker."

"I usually take on a few rides after work for supplemental income. I have a twin brother who lives with me. He's unemployed at the moment, not by choice." He became silent and Annabel became curious.

"Is he an identical twin?"

"Like a mirror image."

"Wow. I bet you both play pranks on people."

"We pull some winners."

"I have young twin cousins – a girl and a boy."

"Unlike my brother and I who are monozygotic twins, your cousins are fraternal twins from two separate eggs fertilized by two separate sperm." He smiled into the rearview mirror.

"Few people know that kind of embryology," Annabel said, surprised. "I guess folks who do are twins themselves."

He nodded. "I was premed for a while and studied my ass off. Had to give up the idea and go to work after college."

"Maybe that was a blessing in disguise. I'm in my junior year and the years still to come are daunting."

He stopped at a light and glanced back at her. "Are you going to become a family doctor like a lot of females or an orthopedic surgeon like most guys?"

"That does sound stereotypic, but I haven't a clue. So far, I'm liking all my rotations."

"I would have become a psychiatrist," he said flatly.

Annabel's eyes moistened. "The psychiatrist I worked with on my last rotation was killed by a schizophrenic patient. It was terrible."

His head bobbed back for a second in disbelief. "I would imagine."

"She was a super lady and teacher. And it was sad that a patient did it. His mental illness was responsible for the awful act and now he's locked away for his own protection as well as society's."

A silence came over both of them. The driver slowed at the end of the I-75 exit and made a left turn.

"My brother is suffering from a significant case of depression. I think of him like a little brother and observe him like a hawk."

"I hope he's undergoing treatment. My place is on this street. You can drop me off wherever." She grabbed her backpack with one hand.

He slowed and stopped the car. "Nice meeting you. Become a good doctor."

"Thanks and I appreciate the interesting conversation and the ride." She closed the door behind her as he rolled down his window and they both smiled at each other. Inside, on the transportation app, she gave him a five-star review like the other drivers she had already used.

Annabel closed the blinds in her apartment and sat cross-legged on her bed. Tonight she was going to spend solely on studying antibiotics, especially after listening to Dr. Schott rattle off antibiotic choices for May Oliver. She might as well do her texting now and then buckle down.

Nancy had not alerted her about her impending trip and, for that, she was annoyed. She texted quickly:

When are you going to tell me that you're coming tomorrow?

Right now, her sister texted back.

Annabel shook her head. *Bring a sleeping bag like last time!*

I will...and I've got a date lined up with Jordan for tomorrow night.

I have a date too. Just don't use my place for something I wouldn't do. She grinned at her statement and waited for a smart aleck response.

Very funny. I hardly know him.

At least Nancy doesn't jump into the sack like I do, Annabel thought. Like the driver tonight, who monitored his sibling, she should look after her younger sister and not be a bad influence.

I'll see you tomorrow night...at some point. Don't forget your key to my apartment, either.

That goes without saying.

Annabel grinned. In her opinion, Jordan wasn't worth the trip. She began texting again. This time to Dustin, her friendly police officer.

Looking forward to tomorrow night.

When she didn't hear back, she pulled over a textbook and opened to a whole chapter on antibiotics. A half hour later, a phone ding sounded.

Me too. A night devoid of police work! And I get to sit across from a bright, pretty young woman with long, silky hair!

You're too kind. See you then.

Annabel smiled but went straight back to learning everything she could about aminoglycoside antibiotics.

CHAPTER 9

Patty Caye woke, showered and dressed, and tidied up her main living area. This morning, Curley followed in her footsteps. She wondered if he was anxious for breakfast or perplexed because his canine best friend was still missing from around the premises.

She stirred instant coffee into a mug of microwaved water and bent down with a bowl of dog food. "Okay, Curley, eat up. Your buddy is not here, but let's hope he comes home today." For the moment, the dog only cared about what was on the area rug before him and lowered his head into the bowl.

Late yesterday, she had made a decision and asked the extra volunteer and part-time ranger to come again for another day or two. Although she had not told him yet, there was still no sense in having Jae back to work so soon. She picked up her cell phone and gave him a buzz.

"Hey, partner. You feeling any better?"

"I suppose," Jae lied.

"Stay put because I've got you covered today."

"It figures. I'll take you up on it. I need all the sleep I can get." He scanned his living room and was glad she hadn't popped in. Empty mugs, bowls, dirty laundry, and unread newspapers dotted the chairs and table. "Any news about Twist?"

"I'm calling the vet. If I find out anything definitive, I'll let you know."

She hung up and eyed the time on her phone. Early staffers should be at the animal hospital by now, so she called.

"This is Patty Caye. I'm calling about Twist."

"Ranger Caye," the vet answered, "your dog's routine lab work is normal except for the slight renal dysfunction, which we corrected with IV fluids. He's anorexic and lethargic, however, so I want to run more tests. The gold standard testing option I'd like to do goes to a special laboratory, has a long turnaround time, and a high cost. That will delay a diagnosis. In the meantime, I can do a serologic screening test."

"You are making me more concerned that his problem may be serious."

After a silence, the vet said, "If the screening test is positive, I will still have the other test in the works to confirm the result. Going further with the dog's work-up is all up to you."

She put her hand up to her mouth. "Of course. Absolutely. I would never contemplate not doing what must be done for an animal's welfare."

"I'm glad to hear that. You are not a ranger for nothing, but you'd be surprised what people don't do for their pets. This job is sometimes full of sorrow and heartache."

Wanting to massage Curley's ears, Patty crouched down in front of him. "Please call me right away when you learn of any test results."

Annabel sprang out of the driver's car and into the rain. She dashed into the downtown internal medicine department's building and stopped at the ground floor cafeteria for a cup of coffee. She upgraded her morning selection to a mocha cappuccino, loaded on her backpack, and carried her delicacy up to the small auditorium to attend grand rounds.

All the students rotating on the service were seated or filtering in as well as most of the residents and attendings. A few rows down, she spotted Bob and Jordan and scooted into their aisle; Stuart followed behind her.

"Good morning, y'all," she said.

"This should be worthwhile," Stuart said while reading the topic of the lecture on the screen. "Wolff-Parkinson-White Syndrome or WPW."

The senior resident lecturer on stage fiddled with the microphone as a tech person adjusted wires.

"What the heck is that?" Annabel asked.

"If you don't know, then the lecture will benefit you that much more," Stuart said.

Jordan sat on the other side of Bob and leaned forward. "You mean to tell me that you are clueless about WPW? And you recently cared for a patient with atrial fibrillation?"

Annabel rolled her eyes. "In that context, now it sounds familiar. Something about an accessory pathway for electrical conduction in the heart."

"You better understand what normal is before you learn what's abnormal," Jordan said. "Normal conduction is through the His-Purkinje system."

Annabel scrunched up her forehead. Since she finished cramming antibiotic information into her brain, she also better bone up on the electrical ins and outs of the heart. Like Jordan mentioned, she obviously didn't cover the subject adequately with her atrial fibrillation patient.

"You better know how to recognize WPW on an EKG," Jordan added with a smirk.

Bob leaned further into his chair as if he was in the direct cross fire between the two of them. Now Annabel's temper was seething hot like her cappuccino.

"Just because you're going into cardiology doesn't make you better than me," Annabel retorted.

"Interventional cardiology," he corrected her.

"Well … excuse me. You may have memorized an index card's worth of heart anatomy and function, but not much more about anything else."

"What a joke."

"You are a joke. Although Bob, Stuart, and I would never do such a thing, you needed to cheat on your mid-term exam."

Jordan's eyes blinked in succession. His mouth opened, poised for a rebuttal. "Liar."

Bob turned his head toward Annabel and his glance fell on Stuart, who shook his head.

Annabel tried to steady her cup as she took a sip. The thick-spectacled resident in the front began his talk and she swore that she would remember his lecture on Wolff-Parkinson-White syndrome.

After the lecture, Annabel and Bob hurried to the elevator.

"Can I hitch a ride with you to the hospital?" Annabel asked.

"Sure. Have you started using Uber?"

"Driving back and forth to the hospital, yes."

"Does it feel weird riding in the back seat of some stranger's car?"

"Not anymore. And if I talk to the driver, so much the better. Everyone has a story."

Bob let her step out of the elevator first and they headed for his sedan. The rain had tapered to a drizzle as they both averted the pools of water in the asphalt. They buckled up and Bob started the engine.

"So," Annabel said, "what's your take on that exchange between me and Jordan this morning?"

"You didn't need that. Just let it go."

"I'll try."

"You saw him cheat?"

"Like his life depended on it."

Bob concentrated on weaving through the parking lot. She wanted to vent some more, but he didn't seem focused on listening to her. Later, Annabel's afternoon went by uneventfully; she was taking care of fewer patients than the other students. She grabbed her taxi service ride at the end of the afternoon and spoke little with the driver, who was also absorbed in his own thoughts. After getting out, she bounded up the stairs to her apartment. She only had an hour before meeting Dustin and her sister might be nearing Cincinnati. The door swung open as she put her key in the keyhole.

Her sister stood there wearing blue jeans and a V-neck sweater. Her hazel eyes squinted after the long drive and her light brown hair was perfectly brushed.

"You made good time," Annabel said, "and you look like you're ready for your date with Jordan."

Nancy grabbed a white paper bag on the counter and handed it to her.

Annabel peeked in. "Homemade cookies from home."

"Compliments of Aunt Mary and Mom." She swiped her hair and grinned. "I'm tired, but I'm so excited about going out that it doesn't matter."

Annabel nodded. "Do you mind if you follow me while we talk?"

"No. Sorry. You've got a date, too."

Annabel picked out casual pants and a button-down blouse. "How is everyone at home?"

Nancy sat on her sister's bed. "Mom is perfectly fine and Dad is slightly stressed about the usual changes in medicine. Electronic medical records and all that. Casey is his usual loveable self and Mary is frazzled that she's not painting as much as she should. I think the twins are taking up more time than anyone thought would be possible, but Melissa and Tommy are an absolute blast."

Annabel slid on silver earrings while listening. "Has Dad heard from Rachel? Anything about Julia?"

Nancy shook her head. "No. Maybe we'll see our half-sister when she's all grown up."

"We may not want to." Annabel turned from the mirror. "I'm out of here. What is your arrangement with Jordan?"

"He texted yesterday. He'll be here by six thirty."

"Don't wait up for me and have fun ... if that's possible," she mumbled. "I'm on call tomorrow so I won't be real late and I also have to get up real early."

"Bye," Nancy said as her sister disappeared out the door.

Annabel pressed the car remote. It had been days since she needed to use her Nissan. She frowned at her current parking space; it would surely be gone when she came home.

She avoided the interstate and drove along local roads thinking about Dustin Lowe. Their history bridged over both their personal and professional lives. Dustin and his partner, Edgar, had arrested a man who robbed her at a gas station; a planned robbery after he lured her in through a social dating app. In her mind, the hook-up was designed to be more than a date ... possibly a one-night stand ... and the crook had divulged that to the police officers.

Dustin, therefore, was privy to Annabel's "dating" indiscretion. Since he and his partner had already been seeing Annabel and her attending doctor in a social context, Dustin had decided to back away from her and not see her in that manner anymore.

However, their lives continued to cross because of Dustin's police work. First, due to a schizophrenic patient, and secondly, due to the suspicious death of a Parkinson's disease patient that she was helping take care of. Annabel proved to be a medical sleuth, and Dustin, quite a law enforcement officer.

She did not think of it before, but the two of them - a med student and a police officer - made a stellar team. They both had put away a psychiatric patient for his violent rampage, but also a medical assistant who did not dispense drugs in the normal way.

It was remarkable they were going out again. He knew her one shady secret and yet realized there was so much more to her than that.

She soon pulled on a side street, spotted Dustin's black Acura, and parked. After moisturizing her lips with lip gloss, she pulled open the door of the diner and spotted Dustin facing her way in a booth. He slid out and they met halfway. He leaned in unexpectedly and gave her a quick hug.

59

"For the dynamic situations and cases we've been part of … together," he said softly in her ear.

As she inched onto the soft bench, she shivered. He had just echoed and hugged her for the things she had thought about on the way over.

"Let's get you something to drink," he said and waved toward the nearby waitress.

Annabel smiled to herself over Dustin's most memorable facial feature. The dimple in his chin could easily fit the tip of her pinky finger. He had never mentioned his age, but he was around her age or slightly older. His thick black hair was slightly receding and the tight ringlets on the top of head weren't styled that way; they were as natural as when he was a little boy. For such a high-stress and responsible job, he did not give off vibes like he was high on adrenaline all the time, but instead oozed mature confidence and tranquility.

"How about bringing a fresh cup of decaf?" Annabel asked when the waitress arrived.

Thin hair grew above the waitress's upper lip and her eyebrows practically covered her upper lids. She took out an order pad and eyed them both.

Dustin moved his water to the side. "I'll take the same. Cream and sugar too."

Annabel smiled when she left and chose her words carefully. "I'm glad you invited me. I know it's just a 'thank you' for helping you procure that medical arrest. You probably rarely need anyone's help, let alone from a med student."

He leaned over the table. "You're welcome, but I also wanted to see you. I was hoping we could date again … or we can reserve that decision until after we finish our food."

She gave him a gentle nod. "I like that idea. That means there's a lot riding on bacon and eggs for dinner."

"Ha! It better be good."

The waitress put down a bowl of creamers and their coffee. "Would you two like to order or spend time with the menu?"

"I'm ready," Annabel said. Dustin nodded and she added, "Scrambled eggs, crisp bacon, and two pancakes."

"A cheese omelet, sausage, and two pancakes as well," Dustin said.

"Gotcha." She grabbed the menus and went toward the kitchen.

"How is your partner?" Annabel asked.

"Edgar is fine. We both find our jobs to be demanding and rewarding at the same time. Sometimes we think the severity of crime is increasing as well as the nut jobs we come across every day. How about you? Are you surviving medical school, the wards, and all that studying you must do?"

"Some days more than others. I think medical students could study their whole life, but unless there are real patients to practice on and learn from, nothing would sink in."

"Ahh … that's why they call it the 'practice' of medicine."

"For sure."

It took time for their orders to arrive, but neither one of them cared. The view and the conversation across the formica table was stimulating.

CHAPTER 10

Dustin sprinkled salt on his omelet and slid the shaker across the table to Annabel.

"Pepper?" he asked.

"No thanks."

"Me neither. These are almost as good as my mom's eggs when I was growing up."

"We must have been born to similar moms, although my parents put cold cereal on the table a lot."

"Which ones?"

"For starters, Rice Krispies and Corn Flakes. And, unlike other kids, I never knew what Captain Crunch tasted like. My parents said they would never feed us ice cream and cake for breakfast, so why should they allow us to go to school after eating a cereal bowl full of sugar."

"Lethargy would have set in by the time the first class started if you ate them. So what was your favorite? Rice Krispies or Corn Flakes?"

"Listening to the snap, crackle, and pop was more fun. More often, I ate rice and not corn cereal. What about you?"

"The usual choices on our breakfast table were Rice Krispies and Corn Puffs." He beamed a smile and couldn't look away from her. "I, too, preferred rice krispies."

"That's a coincidence. However, when we were growing up, the huge variety of breakfast cereals that exist now were not available." She maintained eye contact. "What cereal do you prefer now?"

He put down his fork. "Actually, I can't remember the last time I ate any. I like oatmeal, so I do the quick and easy thing once in awhile and throw together one or two instant packages."

"Get out. Me too. I buy the original without all the added flavor of apples and brown sugar. The non-instant is better, but I'm always in too much of a hurry to make it. I keep granola around too, but only use it to snack on."

"Seems like we both like pancakes too," he said, pointing to her side plate. He grinned a mischievous smile. "Perhaps one of these mornings, we can eat breakfast together at my place."

"Perhaps," she said, flashing a warm smile.

Nancy opened the blinds to Annabel's front window and scanned up and down the sidewalk and street. There was no sign of Jordan and he was fifteen minutes late. If he was running tardy and delayed somewhere, at least he could text or call her. How ironic that he was the one not on time. After all, she had planned and packed, and then driven for six hours from Nashville, keeping the time set for their date. All he needed to do was come over.

However, he was a medical student. Perhaps he had been delayed in the hospital. Maybe Annabel had been luckier and had escaped on time. She stepped away from the window, went into the bathroom mirror, and dabbed on eye shadow.

She tried not to speculate as to why he was late. Now overdue a full thirty minutes, she finally sat on a kitchen stool and texted him. It was the right thing to do, she thought, because there were more legitimate reasons why a person could be held up than explanations that are frivolous. What if he'd been in an accident?

Jordan, I thought you said six thirty.

Nancy continued to turn over the phone with the pink smartphone protection case. How appalling that she received no reply. Her feelings felt more injured by the minute. She swallowed her pride; she needed to know if he was coming or not.

Jordan, I'd appreciate an answer. Aren't we going out? Are you on your way to my sister's apartment?

While she waited for a text reply, she kept a ray of optimism that a rap would sound at the door and off she would go with the smart, future cardiologist. Instead, a ding came from her phone.

We shouldn't go out together. The best thing for me to do is to stay away from the Tilson girls. You can ask your sister. It's all her fault.

Nancy's heart thumped in her chest. The message was loud and clear … he wasn't coming. She believed it was not because she wasn't smart enough for him or pretty enough. He stood her up because of her friggin' sister. Why? How could Annabel have done whatever mean or spiteful thing she had done to him? Obviously, whatever it was had repercussions to her potential relationship with him.

She wanted to scream and she wanted to cry. She had carved out the weekend for him and had made a huge effort to travel all the way up to Cincinnati.

She didn't know what stunt her sister had pulled with Jordan to cause him to stand her up, but whatever it was, her sister qualified as a bitch. With a capital "B."

Lost in their conversation, the time flew by. Dustin finally picked up the waitress's bill and looked out the window.

"May I chip in with the bill?" Annabel started to dig for her wallet.

Dustin chuckled. "This little thing? Not at all. I would like to splurge on an elegant dinner for us in the near future." He tilted his head.

"Is that a promise?" she asked.

"Yes."

"Then I accept."

They slid out from the booth and Dustin paid at the cash register. He opened the diner door and, once outside, he placed his hand lightly on her waist as they headed around the corner. At her car, she turned around and leaned against the driver's door. An old-fashioned street light shined down.

Dustin's hand slid behind her neck and into her hair. Inching her forward, his lips were on hers, and she closed her eyes while taking in the closeness of his body. She kissed him back with the same intensity. It had been weeks since kissing a man; her heart fluttered in her chest. He was a good kisser and his hand performed magic at the nape of her neck.

They separated a few inches. "Should we stop in one of the restaurant bars for a glass of wine or a beer?" he asked.

"I would love to, but I better not," she said, disappointed. "My sister is at my place. She just drove in from Nashville. I'm also on call tomorrow and in for a long haul, so I better get to bed at a decent time."

He nodded. This time, Annabel leaned in and kissed him.

"Do me a favor," he said when they finished. "Text me when you arrive home so I know you're safe. It's a policeman thing." He smiled and she touched his dimple.

"I could not resist doing that." She grinned and added, "And sure, I'll holler when I get home. Thanks for a nice time."

Dustin closed her door after she scooted in, patted the window, and crossed the street to his Acura.

With a bounce to her step, Annabel walked home after parking two blocks away. She frowned because she and Dustin didn't carry on after dinner with a glass of wine. Next time, she thought. And hopefully next time, they'd be doing more than kissing in a more private spot than beside her car.

She leaned forward walking up the incline of her street but practically stopped dead in her tracks when she realized an important observation. When was the last time she seriously thought about her surgery chief resident, Robby Burk? Her daytime ruminating over him and her nighttime fantasizing about him had slowly ebbed away to a trickle. The dates that had not successfully materialized with him and the lack of either of them making an effort to contact each other since then had made all the difference in the world.

She turned into the path to her side door entrance and pumped her fist. Finally, the lust she'd harbored for Robby was gone. It was fun while it lasted, but her energy would be better off spent on more realistic expectations such as her medical studies, and perhaps a more balanced, pragmatic relationship. With Dustin Lowe?

Annabel doubled her steps up the two flights of stairs and turned the key in the door. If Nancy was inside, she wondered how her sister fared with her obnoxious medical student colleague, Jordan Maldonado.

A half bottle of wine sat on the kitchen counter, the only Chardonnay that Annabel had stored unopened in her refrigerator. A plastic cup sat beside it. Annabel poked her head into the bedroom. Her sister opened the bathroom door, stepped out, and startled when she saw her.

Nancy's surprised expression immediately changed to a hostile glare. She pursed her lips, opened her mouth, and let her pent-up words come flying out.

"You absolute creep. You sabotaged my date with Jordan. My own sister. My big chance at starting a relationship with someone more decent than the college fare I go to school with and you ruined it!"

Nancy took a breath without moving her intense stare off of Annabel.

Clueless, Annabel reeled from the accusation. "What are you talking about?"

"He stood me up on purpose," Nancy yelled. "He texted me that he's going to stay away from us. He said it's all your fault."

Annabel bit her lip. "We may have had a heated exchange today, but that never gave him the right to take it out on you. That's immature and vengeful. You're better off without him."

"You can afford to say that because your life is all picture perfect and you're a smart, hot-shot medical student. He was … my date, interested in me, and following up on a previous good time when we met at the café up the block. You did this on purpose. You made sure you steered him away from me."

Now Annabel's voice went up a notch and her heart pounded in her chest. "You're crazy."

"Crazy? I never stood between you and the guys you have been close to. I was nothing but hospitable to David Bell in your senior year of college and to your friend Bob who you brought with you on your last trip home."

"They were different. They aren't assholes like Jordan."

Nancy took a defiant step. Annabel thought her sister might wield a swing at her.

"You think you're better than me. Always have."

"Now you're pulling at straws. I'm not in charge of providing male material for your love life."

A bang sounded twice on the floor. Annabel grimaced and rubbed her forehead. Her neighbor below, not happy about their loud argument, pounded on his ceiling to voice a complaint.

"You creep," Nancy blasted.

"Creep? I did everything I could to accommodate you. Let you crash in my single bedroom apartment again. And, more importantly, I never told you my opinion of Jordan to begin with because I wanted you to figure him out yourself. He is the worst. I witnessed him cheating on our mid-term test. No one does that in medical school! We are all supposed to abide by principled moral standards."

"Bullshit. You're just saying that." Nancy tugged at both sides of her hair, an old gesture to hide her ears which she was self-conscious about.

Annabel took a deep breath. Carrying on any further with her sister was useless. She passed right by her and went into the bathroom, washed up, and changed into pajamas. After curling up in bed, her mind raced. She and her sister never had a fight like that or exploded at each other like that. The words they exchanged wouldn't go away and she churned over them, boiling mad as she tried to drift off to sleep. Not a word escaped from Nancy, who lay sprawled out in her sleeping bag next to the wall.

The alarm clock sounded and Annabel woke with a start. The prior night's events flooded back into her thoughts as well as the fact that she was on call. She almost jumped out of the bed realizing she still needed to put her overnight bag together. Then it dawned on her.

"Shit," she said, as if she couldn't take one more thing going wrong. She padded over to the kitchen counter and picked up her cell phone. The volume was muted. She was supposed to text Dustin last night when she arrived home and now her spirit fell. After such a super night, this would put a dent in him trusting her because she never followed through with their agreement.

Sure enough, he had texted her last night at 11 p.m.

I'm assuming you made it home okay. Please let me know.

She gritted her teeth and immediately typed out a message.

I am so sorry. Yes, I got home just fine but had an unexpected problem with my sister. I really enjoyed our date and hope to see you soon.

She hovered her fingertip over "send." She didn't like apologizing to him via a short text message, but it had to do. She sent it off. If last night was the last she saw of him, there was only herself to blame.

Now she scrambled to get ready and left in record time wearing scrubs for the next twenty-four to thirty-six hours. Heading to the door, she glanced at Nancy burrowed in the sleeping bag. Maybe tomorrow when she comes home from call, and before Nancy leaves to go back to Nashville on Monday, they could smooth things over. However, she doubted it. They had had a hefty fight with bitter words.

Downstairs, Annabel rolled her eyes at her own stupidity. She quickly slipped her cell phone out of her back pocket and signaled an Uber driver, which she forgot to do upstairs. A driver circled the block soon and a gray CRV pulled up.

"Annabel?" the driver asked.

She nodded, hustled in, and belted up.

"How are you today?" he asked.

"I've had better mornings. How about you?"

"Me too. But we're both on this side of the ground. Can't complain about that." He peered at her in the rearview mirror. Some of his red hair swept across the side of his face, but the rest of it hung behind his neck in a ponytail.

"However," Annabel said. "I just thought up a spin on that. I take it you are referring to death and being buried underground. However, a person can be cremated and have their ashes stored above ground."

"Hmm. I see your point. I guess the thing to say is that we're lucky to be alive and still breathing."

"And add to that 'on your way to work with a good cup of coffee.' That thermos you have in your cup holder must be your best friend in the morning."

"Better than a hot shower," he said, positioning the car in the right lane of I-75.

"I have an idea. What if your passengers could select a coffee flavor from a back seat assortment and make a one-cup fresh brew from a little portable machine during their drive? Overall, that would be a big hit."

"Passengers are not supposed to eat or drink in the drivers' personal cars."

"I'm aware. However, the idea could be refined somehow to work and an extra buck or two added to the preliminary fare."

"Your idea has merit. As Einstein said, 'If at first an idea does not sound absurd, then there is no hope for it.' Or something like that."

At the hospital, she slipped out of the car and thanked the young man. A driver who quoted Einstein to her during her ride in was a joy, she thought. It had taken her mind off of the stupidity of her sister and the fact that she had not contacted Dustin last night when she was supposed to.

After passing through the revolving front doors, she headed straight to the cafeteria for her first cup of coffee.

CHAPTER 11

Annabel counted up the names on the team's whiteboard hanging in the office. Since she only followed two patients, she knew that would change fast. Her coffee had cooled so she took a gulp, but that proved to be a disappointment. It was way too strong, like Mississippi mud, and she poured it down the sink behind the nurses' station when she walked by to see her patients. When she went back to the office, she found Dr. Schott on the couch with his newspaper.

"Good morning," she said.

"Mm, back at ya." He rattled the paper and shook his head. "This is bad. This is really bad. A chunk of ice just severed off of Antarctica. Not like a calving event, but a whole massive split from the continent. Now that massive chunk is drifting and bouncing her way along the Drake Passage, breaking up and melting as she goes. This is so huge, map makers need to redraw and republish world maps. I wish I owned land in Florida twenty-five miles from the coast because one of these days it will end up a waterfront property due to the rising seas.

"I wish humans had more control over Mother Earth's planetary events," he continued, "but even if we did, we'd probably foul it up just like we're already messing up the weather in an indirect way.

"We are poor guardians of the earth. It's inevitable that we colonize other planets because we use and abuse everything we touch until we've rendered it unusable. A throw-away society. Native American Indians had insightful respect for the environment; they qualified as the rightful keepers of the planet, in my opinion."

Annabel nodded to appease him and hoped he was finished while his phone dinged.

"It's Bob," he said, narrowing his eyes at the text message.

"I haven't seen him yet." She peered in the corner of the room. "His backpack isn't here."

Donn nodded with concern as he called Bob's number. "It's Dr. Schott," he said.

Annabel listened to Donn's one-sided conversation. "Report your absence today to the secretary in the internal medicine department. They keep track of students' missed days, especially if and when it lasts a few days. Keep us posted."

Annabel stepped closer. "What is it? Is he okay?"

Donn rubbed his hand over his beard. "He said he's clueless about what's come over him, but he's definitely sick and doesn't have enough energy to come in. I didn't want to impose with too many questions. He doesn't believe he has a fever and there's no nausea, vomiting, or diarrhea. He's sorry he's not showing up for call; maybe he's come down with a twenty-four-hour medical student bug that's causing him to play hookey."

"He even jokes around when he doesn't feel well. You know he would never stay home unless he was on death's door."

"Heaven forbid. I hope that's not the case. No, he's a trooper and he sincerely needs the day to rest and get over this."

Donn pushed the newspaper to the side as Dr. Watt and Dr. Burg came in and the two other students followed. Annabel's eyes fell on Jordan and they both suppressed sneering at each other.

"Dr. Palmer won't be here today," Donn said. "That means that three students, not four, will be picking up admissions. Also, you students can help the residents with the patients Bob was taking care of." He ambled out the door without another word.

Along the hallway, Annabel brought up the rear of the pack. Jordan clung to the resident's coattails, brownnosing Melody as he went, and Stuart followed, his quiet self. She missed her coffee rush and her hand settled around the box of chocolate expresso beans in her pocket. She took them out and wiggled a few into her hand. Feeling a loss, she studied their size and shape. Bob wasn't next to her and she couldn't pass them to him. He wasn't there to show his gratitude with a big, wide smile, a chuckle, and some peppy remark. He didn't walk alongside her to start morning rounds.

So far, he was only absent from their day on call for a few minutes and she missed him already.

Patty Caye put on her ranger's hat and opened the door to a misty morning. Curley ran ahead of her, his tail swinging, and picked up speed to chase a squirrel. A film of humidity clung to her face as she walked across the lawn to Jae's cabin. Since she was on the way to the visitors' center, she was going to check on how he had fared since yesterday and to find out her partner's plan for the day.

She knocked on the wooden door and resigned herself to watching Curley. He had apparently given up on chasing a squirrel because he trotted her way with a chipmunk hanging from his mouth. She hated starting the day by seeing that. Or any day, she thought. It was the dog's moral shortcoming which she hated but, of course, the dog didn't know any better. Curley was following his DNA hunting instinct and now she was stuck with lamenting over the poor little lifeless chipmunk.

Patty turned back around and tapped her foot. She rapped on the door again to no avail, so she slid her cell phone out and dialed Jae's number. With no answer, now she didn't like the situation at all.

She tried the doorknob and found the door locked, so she stepped to the last window on the porch. After picking up a loose piece of wood on the windowsill, she grabbed the key to the front door and used it to go inside.

Since the curtains were drawn tight, she flipped on the light switch by the door. Jae was positioned on the coach, facing the back end, and slowly rose his hand to cover his eyes. A bucket sat on the floor and she gagged at the sight and smell of the vomit at the bottom.

"Jae, it's Patty. Come on, let me take a look at you." She crouched over and put her hand on his shoulder, coaxing him to get up.

"No sun," he mumbled, cowering behind his hand.

"The overhead light is on."

As she made progress getting him into a sitting position, he stiffened his posture and grabbed behind his head. "My neck is stiff as a board."

He managed to look at her. "Who are you?"

Patty was so shook up that, at first, her training with medical situations failed to surface. Jae needed medical care and she debated whether to drive him to the hospital herself or to call EMS. She needed to go with him no matter what, to provide information, and she also realized that his illness was a continuation of what he had visited the ER for days ago. Had they missed something? Why was he not progressing along the normal flu timeline for getting better?

At present, there was no life threatening emergency, so she thought it made more sense to transport him herself.

"Come on, Jae. Lean on me to the car because I'm driving you to the hospital."

After settling him in the front seat of her patrol car, she unlocked the door to the visitors' center so the volunteers and part-time ranger would have access after she left, and she put out a bowl of water for Curley.

In Annabel's opinion, rounds were dismal. It felt like a negative force field existed between her and Jordan; the air around them was saturated with bad vibes. Stuart added no enthusiasm like usual. He was always off in his own mind, she thought, like his photographic mind was turning the pages from an internal medicine textbook.

Donn wasn't much better. He deviated between talking about current events to patient care, depending on what area of the hallway they stood, and the two residents talked among themselves like they were planning a party. Except for her, they all acted like Bob's absence was a normal occurrence.

After rounds, she hunted down lab work, wrote progress notes on patients, and then finally sneaked away to the ICU for a real cup of coffee. It made a mockery of the previous cup from the cafeteria and she sipped with pleasure as RNs came in and out of the kitchenette.

A sip of the brew slid down her throat when her phone dinged with a text from Donn.

You're up first. Come to the ER for the first admission

Annabel thanked the last nurse in the room for letting her steal their coffee and left. Outside the automatic doors of the ER, she chugged down the last sip, pushed the Styrofoam cup into the waste container, and revved up her eagerness for a new patient.

Dr. Schott and Dr. Burg's heads were clumped near each other at the end of the desk like they were in collusion over a plan. Annabel parked herself next to them as Donn shook his head.

"We all make mistakes," he said. "We over-diagnose certain situations and sometimes we underdiagnose. Hindsight is easy, but I wish the ER doctor had chosen the more cautious approach and admitted him overnight when he showed up for help. After all, they hydrated him late into the evening and could have called us for a consult. It would have been no sweat to finish his fluids on the medicine floor overnight and then reevaluate him in the morning."

Melody glanced at Annabel. "Your new patient is in Room 2. You can go in and say hello, but when Dr. Schott and I finish this discussion, come with me to the waiting room. The person who brought him to the ER is out there. We need to ask her more questions."

Annabel waited a moment. "The ER doctor took a decent enough history," Donn said, "mostly from the woman outside, and they are handing him over to us for an internal medicine admission."

Annabel backtracked to Room 2 and pushed on the semi-open door. A man lay flat on the stretcher in a hospital gown, a hand towel draped across his upper face. The room was silent as she approached the side rail and stood inches away from his right bicep.

There it was again ... a sight she had seen on an ER patient in the recent past: an impressive tattoo of a native American Indian and an American eagle and flag. It was him – the man she had rescued from the submarine sandwich shop and driven to the ER.

"Jae," she said. "Remember me? I'm Annabel Tilson, the medical student."

"Jae Nixon is the man I told you about last week," Annabel said to her senior residents at the ER desk. "The man I gave a ride to."

Donn narrowed his eyes.

"You gave me grief about it because I drove a stranger to the hospital from the sub shop when we were on call and I picked up our sandwiches."

"How about that." Donn looked surprised. "You were justified bringing him in."

"However, he vaguely remembers me."

Melody nodded. "He's confused."

Donn slipped in behind the desk and began writing orders.

"Follow me," Dr. Burg said to Annabel. "We're going to talk to the woman who brought Mr. Nixon in ... this time. She's a park ranger and she'll probably be leaving soon to go to work."

"A park ranger?"

"Yes, a national park ranger, just like your patient."

"Really?"

"That's a fact."

The two women strolled over to Patty Caye in the waiting room. She stood out like a red rose in crabgrass. The small woman got up from a chair. She held her hat in her hand and her crisp uniform made Annabel's white, short jacket seem crimped.

"You must be Ms. Caye," Melody said, extending her hand. "I am Dr. Burg and this is Annabel Tilson, one of the medical students. I wanted to ask you a few questions in case you're leaving."

"I'm going to hang around for a little while. I have work covered for the time being; perhaps you doctors will have some answers about Jae within an hour or two."

"Then we'll be sure to give you an update. He seems mixed-up right now, so the ER doctor and my chief resident didn't get much of a history from him. We do have the information about his recent ER visit and that he was diagnosed with the flu, hydrated, and sent home. Can you tell me what's happened with him since then?"

"Each day has been a slippery slide of him getting worse rather than better. Increasingly, he's in his cabin with nausea, vomiting, and a headache. And having to nap, which isn't like Jae at all. He scared the hell out of me this morning because his memory was foggy, and he had such light sensitivity, I had to put a towel over his head in the car." Her look of concern intensified and she fiddled with the brim of her hat.

"Has he travelled anywhere lately or eaten anything unusual that you are aware of?"

Patty shook her head slowly. "No. He hasn't been on vacation for a year. Just the usual days off, which he basically spends in Ohio. And nothing odd to eat. He has venison in his freezer, but he hasn't eaten any recently. He didn't have the taste for it because he feels so crappy."

Melody contemplated the information. "Luckily, we have his medical and surgery history he reported when he was here last. No real problems in the past. As far as you know, that is correct?"

Patty shrugged. "He's a fit guy leading a healthy lifestyle and is often outdoors. A way of life many people would trade for in a heartbeat."

"Thank you for the information. Please give me your number so we can contact you when we learn something or when he gets transferred to a hospital bed."

Patty told her while Melody plugged it into her cell phone.

"By the way," Annabel asked, "where do both of you work?"

"The William Howard Taft National Historic Site."

Puzzled, Annabel crinkled her forehead.

"It's the usual thing," Patty said. "Unless you're a tourist, you aren't aware of the sights in your own backyard. We oversee the 27th president's birthplace, education center, and a park only a few miles north of here. Come on over. Volunteers, Jae, and I love to give tours and there are hiking trails as well."

"Thanks. I'll try."

Annabel and Dr. Burg went back into the ER. Now that Jae Nixon was being admitted, he should recover quickly.

CHAPTER 12

Annabel stood poised over Jae with her stethoscope, his heart thumping regularly as an orderly came in to wheel him to the CT room. Hopefully, imaging of the young ranger's head would shed light on the origin of his problem.

Jae's vital signs were normal except for a low grade fever. He did indicate a stiff neck, but otherwise, his physical exam was unremarkable and he showed no focal neurologic signs.

A spark of recognition came over Jae's face. "You look familiar, which makes sense, because I was here before."

"Yes, you were. I met you, and then drove you here last time. We're trying to get to the bottom of your illness, starting with a CT of your head. You'll have to be still while the loud machine snaps pictures."

The orderly threw a blanket over the sheet and placed his chart next to his legs. Jae closed his eyes and Annabel took a moment to examine his face; good-looking facial features with full lips and eyebrows, a tan skin color, and more important, no asymmetry between the right and left side.

She followed the stretcher out of the room and then wrote her H&P, a more difficult chore than normal because Dr. Burg's and Dr. Schott's H&Ps were on the transported chart and she couldn't peek at theirs. She had to write an "assessment" and "plan," but so far Jae Nixon remained a mystery. And, obviously, the "flu" diagnosis was as erroneous as false answers on a test.

Her iPhone, sitting next to her paperwork, dinged an alert. She opened up text messages and sighed with relief upon seeing Dustin's name. Even if he answered with a negative remark, it would be better than not hearing from him at all. She scrolled through their conversation, starting with his from the night before:

I'm assuming you got home fine. Please let me know.

I am so sorry. Yes, I arrived home just fine but had an unexpected problem with my sister. I really enjoyed our date and hope to meet you again soon.

She narrowed her eyes at his new, longer message:

Apology accepted. Okay then, what night should we see each other "soon?" And ... this time, You pick the type of food and how about a movie afterwards?

She smiled at the concept; a date which would fill up a whole evening. She didn't know what that felt like anymore, although that would be a big chunk of time away from studying at night.

For me, that is like going on two dates! Thai food. And you pick the movie (which is not of an epic length!).

Thai place over by your end of town is superb. If need be, we can decide on skipping a movie.

Thank you! What night? Tuesday or next Saturday would work for me. Tuesday then. What time?

Can we text each other? See what time I get sprung from the hospital, etc.?

Sure. I'll be working day shift so we'll have a similar schedule.

Annabel leaned back. She felt like a kid planning a birthday party.

I'll poke you a line in the interim. I'm starting my day on call with a challenging case.

Glad to hear it. I bet your patient is lucky to have you. Edgar and I are working a domestic abuse case.

Those must be sad situations to see. TTYL?

Looking forward!

Annabel went back to her home screen as Dr. Burg stopped in front of her.

"We have a room for Mr. Nixon. He's being admitted to the medical floor once they finish with his CT. Perhaps you can start hunting up his lab work."

"I'm on it," she said, getting up. "Can't wait to see what shows up."

Jordan Maldonado carried his lunch tray through the cafeteria towards the back end where tables were not occupied. It was the peak time for the lunch crowd, and an aisle over, a woman in a light brown uniform also walked with a plastic tray. He made a right to the last three or four tables. The woman ahead of him sat as he put down his food on the table behind her.

It was smart that he grabbed lunch now, he thought, because Annabel and Stuart had already gained a new patient each, so he was up next. Dr.

Schott could call him any minute or any hour from now. He hated the anticipation that caused nothing but suspense and dread when any phone message came in. Sometimes he felt so uptight on call days that he developed a small skin rash on his arms. Luckily, it was hidden by his white jacket and no one else knew of his childish physical reaction.

The team was going downhill fast, he thought, and he couldn't wait for internal medicine to be over. When his dream becomes a reality and he became a practicing interventional cardiologist, he would have little use for it anyway.

Today, the most undeserving, likeable male of the group, Bob, was absent, so that meant extra work. Sick or healthy, he would enjoy pulling a stunt like that someday, too. One entirely free day off would be like tuition money falling from the sky.

And Annabel. She was a bigger joke. He thanked his lucky stars that he had not rotated on the same psychiatry or surgery service with her, because apparently, she ended up stealing the show. He would surpass her in the future, however, because, like most women, she would probably only become a measly family practice doctor or a pathologist reading pap smears all day. Or better yet, she would end up as the only doctor staffing a small-town physician's office in a shopping mall!

Jordan sampled the coleslaw next to his hamburger and realized it needed to be pushed through a strainer to remove the excess, watery mayonnaise. A phone rang behind him and he glanced to the side.

The woman in uniform fumbled on the empty chair beside her and picked up her cell phone. Now he recognized her outfit from magazine pictures. She was a law officer with the cushy job of monitoring peoples' activities in government public parks.

The woman put down her fork with her other hand. "Hello? I am so glad you called," she said after a pause. "I am worried sick about him, and my colleague, Jae, as well. I'm at the hospital because my partner's being admitted. The two of them are both in different hospitals! But how is Twist and what did you find out?"

Jordan pushed the slaw away and cut his hamburger in half. He couldn't believe the lady's bad luck dealing with two people needing medical care at the same time.

A long pause ensued. "Lepto...spi...rosis?" the woman repeated slowly from the conversation. "I knew something was terribly wrong. That sounds awful. What is it anyway?"

Jordan kept eavesdropping. Nothing like passively learning about a unique disease over lunch; or at least he thought it was rare. He never heard of it.

"I feel blessed that I brought him in so soon and that you skillfully made the diagnosis. Yes, keep him there for IV antibiotics. Like you said, they need to be given early in the course of the disease."

Jordan peered to the side and saw her swipe a forming tear off her eye.

He dug in his pocket for the "Handbook of Internal Medicine" and flipped to the index. Leptospirosis was not listed. He pulled his iPhone from his other pocket and googled the word. A screen full of sources pulled up. It was pretty bad, he thought, if he could find a disease online but not in a medical book.

He read all the signs and symptoms of Leptospirosis, which also mimicked other diseases - fever, headache, vomiting, etc. - and learned there are often two phases: a first phase with the more common symptoms and a second phase more severe, with kidney or liver failure or meningitis.

The culprit, he read, was a Gram-negative bacterium. One that can be carried by all sorts of wild and domestic animals: horses, cattle, dogs, and most commonly associated with rats and mice. The carriers may not even show symptoms of the disease, which would make the disease harder to track down.

He read on, wondering how a human could acquire it, and found out it was through contact with certain body fluids or with water or soil, particularly through broken skin from a cut or a scratch. Contaminated food could cause it as well.

Jordan scratched his head. He wore a moderate crew cut; he preferred the short cut to hide his hair, which would grow out too frizzy if he allowed it. The woman moved her dishes back on her tray and slid out from the table as he read that the risk of exposure for Leptospirosis was higher in people working or participating in outdoor activities.

Since he still had the information open, he wondered how doctors diagnosed it. It was complicated and over his head, but he read it anyway. Diagnosis was based on screening tests and serology at certain labs. He shook his head and gloated. Fortunately for him, he didn't work in a hazardous occupational job related to Leptospirosis; like a farmer, or a vet, or like that woman, a ranger in a park.

Donn clutched a Saran-wrapped pb&j sandwich over the office desk while Annabel pulled up a chair beside him.

"Jae Nixon's CT scan is done," she said. "It's not read by the radiologist yet, but I put a medical student express result request on his desk."

A puzzled look spread across Dr. Schott's face and Annabel laughed.

"You almost had me believing that," he said. "You're filling in with humor since Bob isn't here."

"No one makes a situation light-hearted like him. Anyway, I'll go check again. In the meantime, they wheeled Mr. Nixon straight up here. I also have some of his blood work results." She pulled out her index card for him and turned it over.

"CBC, Chem 7, U/A, LFTs," he mumbled while looking. "Nothing is glaringly abnormal."

They frowned at each other and Donn shrugged his shoulders. He turned his attention to his sandwich and took a bite.

"I better snatch lunch as well," she said softly. "I wish I brought something from home like you."

Annabel stood up and approached the door. Jordan came around the corner and almost smashed into her. They stood facing each other, too close for comfort.

"Obstructing the doorway," he said, thick with sarcasm. He stared her down and held his position.

Donn still huddled in the room, she contemplated, sitting straight behind her at the desk. She knew Jordan hadn't seen him yet because she blocked his view. She tried to hold her temper and she hated to create a scene, but Jordan asked for it.

"That was a cheap trick you pulled on my sister last night."

"A 'cheap trick?' I consider it pay-back for your trumped up allegation against me in the lecture hall the other day. In front of Stuart and Bob."

"Nancy had nothing to do with our spat the other day. She drove six hours for a date with you, which didn't materialize!"

"You lied about me in front of our teammates."

"Ha! Lied to them? I won't mention your proclivity to cheat on a test to anyone again since you will only take the aggressive posture and call me a liar." Her tense muscles relaxed, knowing Donn must be listening.

"You even gloat about being a slanderer. You better stay away from me for the rest of the rotation."

"And stay away from my sister."

"That's a no-brainer!"

Annabel tried to gain control over her heartbeat, which was running away like a racehorse. She inhaled a deep breath and stepped to the side, revealing Dr. Schott.

Donn swiveled his chair around, dropped the sandwich plastic wrap in the waste basket, and stepped past them out the door.

The fury on Jordan's face made Annabel duck and zip out the door like the room was on fire.

Annabel tracked down the radiologist like a bloodhound on a scent. She was especially compulsive about hearing the specialist discuss a CT scan of the head, zeroing in on the snapshot slices of Jae's brain. Even if her patient's scan was normal, it proved fascinating. The ventricles, the sinuses, the sulci, the brainstem all came alive for their viewing pleasure as well as any lesions, hematomas, or shifting of tissue.

She snapped the gray, large envelope from the front desk, timidly knocked on the radiologist's door, and entered the dimly lit space.

"Would you mind? This patient of mine was just admitted. We are perplexed over his diagnosis and my chief resident thinks it may be a central, I mean a brain, problem."

The elderly radiologist beamed. "Come on over, young lady. Let's take a gander. What are his symptoms? You share his medical background with me and I'll share an imaging lesson with you." He put the films up on the only empty viewfinder.

Annabel rattled off Jae's history and added with a smile, "My dad's a neurosurgeon in Nashville, so I'm making sure I don't flunk out due to a lack of knowledge about the brain."

The radiologist took a sip from the paper cup to the side. "We'll make sure that doesn't happen." He wielded a pointer forward to the images. Annabel had a fine grasp of the textbook knowledge; making the connection to the images was more important.

"And here is CSF surrounding the medulla oblongata," he added in the end.

She shook her head. The brain is like a well-oiled machine, she thought. A closed-compartment, the skull, was where the fluid, the blood vessels, and the tissue took up only the space allotted to them. If they went over and above their normal occupancy, dangerous things like increased pressure, began to happen. She again considered her dad - an expert when it came to dealing with those situations.

"So," she said with emphasis, "nothing glaring pokes out at my novice eyes, and you have not mentioned an abnormality."

He read the name tag clinging to her breast pocket. "Dr. Tilson, the CT scan of this patient's head is negative. The scan was not particularly useful except for giving you a radiology lesson."

She sighed. "Thank you for that. I suppose this is good news for our national park ranger, but it still leaves us in a quandary."

"Let me dictate the report, and then you can bring these materials to your team."

Annabel waited, bought a premade turkey sandwich from the cafeteria, and headed upstairs. Before gobbling down her sandwich, she found Dr. Schott hunched over Jae Nixon's chart at the nurses' station.

Before she could say a word about the CT in her hands, he pointed to the chair beside him and she sat down.

Her chief wore a serious frown; she worried about a repercussion for what he overheard in the office.

"I was not supposed to hear that private argument between you and Jordan. So I am going to pretend like I never heard it. What transpired is between you and him and for the both of you to work out. Don't let it interfere with your clinical duties."

He sighed and gave her a sympathetic look. "Also allow yourself the satisfaction that most unscrupulous acts by certain people come back to bite them in their arse. Hopefully, his day will come."

Annabel nodded and anxiously bit her lip. "Thanks, Dr. Schott. I have found your observation to be spot-on in the past. I'll continue to do my best on the wards." She placed the envelope on the counter. "Here's Jae Nixon's CT ... straight from the radiologist after hearing his interpretation and dictation. It's negative."

"That takes any glaring anatomical brain problem out of the picture and leaves us where we started. However, in your absence, Mr. Nixon is being transferred yet again. To the ICU. He's lapsed into a coma."

CHAPTER 13

Annabel and Dr. Burg hustled into Jae's ICU room where anesthesia had intubated him with an endotracheal tube; the ventilator next to him cycled oxygen and air into his lungs. The swooshing sound was overshadowed by the EKG and pulse oximeter beeps coming from the monitors above.

She grimaced; he had again deteriorated … into a coma.

Melody placed a lumbar puncture tray on the rolling table and, in a cordial tone, barked orders to Annabel and Jae's nurse. "Roll him laterally on his side and don't displace his breathing tube. Bring his knees up a bit and slide off the back of his gown."

The resident slid off her white coat and, with sterile gloves, washed Jae's lower back with antiseptic solution and skin swabs. After it dried on his back and she placed the drapes, she prepared the needles and tubes.

"Annabel, based on Mr. Nixon's clinical presentation, you must realize that a spinal tap is the next step in his workup."

She nodded and carefully watched Melody go ahead with the procedure. The resident injected local anesthetic in his lower lumbar area in case he reacted to the next needle stick and then she inserted the spinal needle between a disk space in the middle of his back. Clear cerebrospinal fluid flowed back from his spinal canal and she let it flow into four plastic test tubes.

"You made that look easy," Annabel said.

"Because it was. He's in the perfect position for alignment, but the bigger factor here is his age and body size. Older patients are usually more difficult because they have vertebral bone changes and obese patients are another challenge because of their size."

Melody finished, appropriately labelled all the necessary samples for the lab, and they settled Jae back in a supine position.

"I'll go write the orders," Melody said as she slipped back into her coat and tidied her hair in the mirror over the sink. She turned to Annabel. "Your job is to hand deliver the LP samples to the laboratory. On the way out, we'll talk to his partner, who is waiting for an update."

In the waiting room outside the ICU, Patty Caye's eyes grew big and she stood quickly as Melody and Annabel approached.

"Ms. Caye," Dr. Burg said, "we attended to your coworker expeditiously, but we're sorry it took this long."

"The nurses told me downstairs he was sent here. He is in serious condition, isn't he?"

"Yes. At the moment. He'll receive supportive care in the ICU while we try to get to the bottom of his illness. The CT scan of his head was normal and we just did a spinal tap." She frowned. "You know ... he's been unconscious."

"But while we all wait, isn't he just rotting away with whatever he has and not getting better?"

"The tap results should shed light on his situation no matter what. But try not to worry as we wait on further lab results and cultures. We'll empirically start him on IV anti-bacterials."

Her dazed expression began to fade. "Thank you. Please keep me posted. I'll help contact his parents and try and visit again tomorrow. In the meantime, I must hurry back to work."

All three of them scurried away ... Annabel for her scut work, Melody to see another patient, and Patty Caye to staff Cincinnati's National Historic Site.

As the ranger drove away from the hospital, the frown on her face registered her disapproval that, besides Jae, she had been absent for the visitors, volunteers, and temporary ranger on a Saturday afternoon.

As the sun went down and the lights in the hospital blared brighter with intensity, Annabel finally snuck away with her overnight bag to a call room. That was one perk of this hospital, she thought. A separate sleep room all to herself. A luxury. She put toiletries in the adjoining bathroom inside the room and then sat on the bed with her iPhone in her hand.

She lamented over the argument she had with Nancy. Not seeing her sister all day and leaving her alone at her place didn't feel right either. If only Nancy understood how contemptuous Jordan really was.

Sorry we argued, Annabel texted, *especially over dating material. Men aren't worth it for us to exchange heated words with each other.*

She lingered only a second, sent it, and then brushed her teeth and washed her face while she had the opportunity; she still needed to grab some kind of dinner.

Annabel left the call room as Stuart was coming the other way, seeking out a place to bunk down for the night like her.

He held a Styrofoam cup and stopped. "I just overheard scuttlebutt in the ER. A previous patient from our team just came in by ambulance. A nurse peeked at the old chart and mentioned seeing Dr. Watt's, Dr. Schott's, and your name."

"Do you think he or she will end up my patient again?"

"Makes sense since you're up next anyway."

"Thanks for letting me know."

Annabel continued, but now skipped a trip to the cafeteria and went to the ER. She sauntered in, curious why Dr. Schott had not paged her yet. Patients' stalls were draped closed, a tech pushed an X-ray machine, and a loud conversation could be heard somewhere closer to the admitting door. Her upper level teammates were not in sight.

She glanced up and down the whiteboard, but no patient's name looked familiar to her.

A muscular orderly came her way, wheeling a stretcher past her and shaking his head. Their gazes met.

"Some man is firing off ballistics at a doc down there," he said. "I'm parking this somewhere else."

Annabel tilted her head towards the back of the hallway as he passed. Although there was no major trauma room down there like ones found in a university hospital, a designated room for emergencies still existed. She padded that way in her comfortable clogs, the yelling growing louder as she went.

A tall man stood agitated, half-in, half-out of the doorway to the primary room for stat emergencies. She recognized him - the son of the woman who they had treated for atrial fibrillation - the man who had twin sisters.

The man shouted into the room.

"Death is the ultimate mistake and outcome. She was too young for this and she came to you for help. You needed to be proactive with her discharge medications and not leave a possible sequela of her diagnosis to chance. You, your team, and this hospital can't take back your negligence. It's too late for that."

Annabel trembled with fear. She guessed it was Donn Schott or

Chineka Watt inside taking the verbal beating. "Mr. Helm," she vaguely heard Donn say from inside, but he was verbally cut off.

"I can tell you this," the man screeched. He flung his arm out and pointed defiantly. "I'll need a year to grieve over this, but I won't be through the initial shock before I hire a malpractice attorney. If I have anything to do with it, your career is finished before you start. You'll have no more road to drive on."

The man turned and stormed out the automatic doors. It happened so fast, Annabel finally remembered to breathe. She treaded a few steps and peeked into the room.

Donn stood against a stretcher with a body on it, covered to the shoulders with a sheet - a woman's body - Mrs. Helm. Dr. Schott's eyes, glazed over, stared straight past Annabel.

Off to the side, huddled against counters, was one paramedic and a nurse. There was the lack of a usual mess after a trauma patient comes in with massive injuries and there was no chaos after a non-trauma medical resuscitation. No extra carts, equipment, or uncharted documents or paperwork littered the area. It was like the woman was transported to the hospital by the paramedics ... already dead.

Annabel sneaked away without speaking to Dr. Schott. Not that he would bother with her anyway. This was one of those instances, she recognized, where medical students were impotent of any importance in the scheme of things. Donn had "senior" tasks to take care of and she didn't envy him. Paperwork and a death certificate were one thing, but the tirade directed at him was not justified at all. She shuddered, wondering how any chief resident would or could get over that.

She guessed, at some point, the team would hear about the case. Meagan Helm's atrial fibrillation must have been a time bomb. But who could predict what would happen to her when she left the hospital, or any patient, for that matter? Despite the current standard of care being implemented, a patient could disprove the odds for improvement, or for that matter, be struck accidentally by a car in the parking lot.

Must someone always take the blame or be responsible for an unforeseen event? she wondered.

Annabel headed for the cafeteria but changed her mind and ambled back to the call room because she didn't feel like eating. With a sigh of relief that she didn't bump into Jordan, she went in and glanced at her iPhone. No return message from Nancy. Maybe her sister was giving her the silent treatment.

She slipped under the sheet, resolved to get some sleep, and thought about Bob. She had a lot to tell him but, more importantly, she wondered how he was feeling.

The alarm clock buzzed in Annabel's room, making her more startled to realize she had slept through the night. Post-call rounds were scheduled with Dr. Mejia, and after the busy work, she'd be sprung from the hospital for a real and long afternoon off.

She showered, changed into clean scrubs, and headed to the ICU. The usual morning nurse smiled at her next to the coffeemaker and Annabel poured them both a cup of vanilla roast.

"Who's your patient in here or are you stealing our coffee like everybody else does?"

"I do that as well, but I'm the student taking care of Jae Nixon."

"Family members and friends filtered in yesterday. Didn't stay at his bedside very long. It scares lay people off when they see someone lying in a coma, on a ventilator, and hooked up to machines that seem to be the only barrier between them and death."

Annabel nodded. "So true. I don't blame them. Do you know if there are any spinal tap results back on him?"

"The secretary's been filing lab work on all the patients, but I haven't seen them."

Annabel finished and went first to evaluate Jae. Saddened by his condition, she peeled her eyes off of his facial features, where the tape across his lips held the endotracheal tube in place. His picturesque tattoo didn't move with the normal flexion and extension of his biceps. She sighed and carefully noted every one of his vital signs - all normal and without the need for pressure support IV drugs.

After listening to his lungs and heart, she went to the desk. She found more regular blood work results, but nothing back on the spinal tap. She knew … she would have had another patient this morning except that Mrs. Helm didn't make it.

In the office, Annabel said good morning to everyone and sat next to Donn. He was mentally conflicted and stared at a bloodstain on his scrubs. Stuart was flipping pages in his medicine handbook, and the two residents wore circles under their eyes. When Jordan came in, he lived up to her expectations and avoided her with a wide berth.

No one said a word and, finally, Dr. Mejia poked his head in. "Time for rounds. This morning isn't getting any earlier." He smiled and pulled at the lapel of his sports coat. He held his eyes on Donn for a bit longer and Annabel gathered they'd been in contact … maybe he knew about the Meagan Helm situation.

As they set out, Dr. Mejia talked softly with Dr. Schott. The attending's head shook back and forth more than Donn's and once he patted his colleague on the shoulder. Annabel trotted behind them and strained to hear the conversation.

"Donn," Dr. Mejia said, "lawsuits in practice are inevitable. I'm just so sorry your first one is going to happen so soon."

"I'm not even an attending yet," Donn said despondently. "And I, or we, followed accepted protocol and our clinical judgment."

Dr. Mejia stopped, had the students fetch charts on patients, and then signaled them into a circle.

"As a team," Dr. Mejia said, "we were inflicted with an incident last night. I bring it up because this type of situation is a reality for all of us, now and in our entire future careers. Whether or not legal ramifications are deserved or not, you will all suffer from a medical lawsuit.

"Our patient, admitted and discharged recently for atrial fibrillation," Dr. Mejia continued, "was brought in by paramedics late yesterday and was dead on arrival. We suspect that her atrial fib came back, with a rapid ventricular response while she was home alone.

"As we know, we found out she had mitral stenosis secondary to rheumatic heart disease. We believe she developed acute pulmonary congestion. Her son found her and called EMS too late. She could have also had a major stroke."

He let the group think about that.

"Is there a question about the care she received?" Jordan asked.

"That's part of it. We had discussed at length our decision for her discharge. Chronic atrial fibrillation warrants anticoagulation since it minimizes the risk of embolization and stroke. She wasn't your patient,

Dr. Maldonado, but you should know the risk-assessment tools we used for our decision."

"Yes," Jordan beamed. "Multiple factors made her a less likely candidate for oral anticoagulation: her younger age, her lack of hypertension, diabetes, and history of stroke. She also didn't have a history of atrial fib which categorized her as 'chronic.'"

"Well done. You are paying strict attention to your area of interest. Anyway, the family is boiling mad. They probably went to the internet, read a little bit on the subject matter, which makes them experts, and are hiring an attorney to sue Dr. Schott, me, and the hospital for negligence."

Chineka Watt winced. She could be involved as well.

"Maybe the family will reconsider," Annabel said, "once the reality of the situation sinks in. Perhaps with the shock of their mother dying, the grown kids are displacing their emotions on the care she received rather than their loss."

Dr. Schott sighed and rubbed his beard, but he continued to stand inches back out of their circle.

"And you could make a good psychiatrist," Dr. Mejia said, glancing at Annabel.

"In any case, besides following the standard of care, always do what your clinical experience and hearts tell you to do for the benefit of your patient. The chances of a bad outcome when you do all those are small. What happened with Mrs. Helm is a one in a thousand probability.

"We must keep our wits, not change our perspective, on how we treat our patients, and handle legal battles with courage and truthfulness."

CHAPTER 14

Dr. Mejia glanced into the window of Jae Nixon's ICU room as the team continued on Sunday morning post-call rounds.

"I heard," he said, "we admitted a national park ranger in a coma."

Jordan Maldonado's ears perked up. Often, rounds were the first time he would hear about the other students' patients. He thought back to yesterday when a female ranger in the cafeteria talked on the phone about her partner being in the hospital. Chances are, he thought, this patient must be her partner. The woman's discussion had also covered someone else in her life who was ill and had been diagnosed with the unusual disease he had indexed and read about.

"Dr. Burg and Dr. Tilson are on his case," Donn said. When he added no more information, Dr. Mejia looked at Annabel.

"Dr. Tilson, go ahead."

Annabel swallowed her nervousness and began her presentation of the patient.

"Jae Nixon is a thirty-five-year-old white male who came into the ER about a week ago and was diagnosed with the flu. He returned yesterday, brought in by his partner, complaining that he was not getting better. His partner also shed light on his history. Mr. Nixon's malaise and overall flu-like symptoms were worse. His headache was still there, he had a low grade fever, nausea, vomiting, sensitivity to light, and he had developed confusion and some stiffness in his neck.

"Mr. Nixon has no allergies, doesn't smoke, drinks occasionally, and works as a national park ranger here in Cincinnati."

She shifted her weight to the other foot. "His past medical and surgical history are both negative. Not even a strep throat or a tonsillectomy.

"On physical exam, he presented with a low-grade fever and a mildly elevated heart rate in the eighties. He was hunched behind a towel to shield his eyes from the overhead light. His lungs were clear and his heart had a regular rhythm. The mini-neuro exam showed no facial droop or fundoscopic abnormalities, but he did talk intermittently with mental uncertainty.

"I have some testing results on Mr. Nixon, but I need to update what

happened by the time he transferred to the floor yesterday.

"His mental sluggishness and sickness grew worse.

"He lapsed into a profound lethargy and coma.

"And since his respiratory rate declined and his ABGs and oxygen level were diminishing, anesthesia came by and intubated him. Now here he is in the ICU."

Annabel sucked in a deep breath. She felt too much pressure, especially since Dr. Schott was keeping quiet.

"Keep going," Dr. Mejia said. "Test results should be revealing."

"Mr. Nixon's CT scan was negative."

"We'll jump ahead, then," Dr. Mejia said with a serious tone, "to the assessment that was made. Why did you all order a CT of his head?"

"Due to an ongoing, worsening headache, light sensitivity, and a fever," Annabel said but knew there was more she needed to divulge.

"That could be from a migraine headache. We don't usually do a CT scan on someone with a suspected migraine. Do we?"

"Perhaps."

"In this case, the entire clinical picture was quite detailed, making your chief resident's decision warranted. What was it he was concerned about?"

"A central origin for his sickness, such as meningitis or enchephalitis, or maybe a space-occupying lesion."

"And the CT turned up nothing. What came next?"

"A spinal tap. The results aren't in yet."

"And other labs?"

"His CBC, Chem 7, LFTs, U/A are mostly within normal limits."

"We are up a creek, then." Dr. Mejia's hand brushed his sport's jacket collar and he considered. "However, what is your assessment? Working diagnosis?"

"Enchephalitis or meningitis, sir."

He nodded. "We think our high tech CT machine can tell us everything, but here's the truth. He can have one of those despite a negative scan."

Annabel nodded. "He is receiving antibiotics."

Dr. Mejia stole a glance at Donn, who nodded his head. Annabel hoped she was off the hook.

"The antibiotics are empirical," Donn said, "so there is the possibility that this young man continues to deteriorate if we don't find out what we're dealing with."

Jordan took one step forward, ready to divulge a storehouse full of information. He had nothing to lose. He was dead certain about the situation because of what he'd heard yesterday from the female ranger.

He puffed up his chest, ready to regurgitate exactly what he read yesterday.

"The history of this patient that Ms. Tilson just told us about," Jordan said, sounding like the attending, "sounds like a textbook case to me."

"Pray tell," Dr. Mejia said, furrowing an eyebrow. Annabel shifted position. Jordan called her "Ms."

"First, the patient presented with classic symptoms of many diseases, but in his case, there are two distinct phases. The first, in which he had the common symptoms of headache, fever, and nausea and vomiting. And then a week later, a second, severe phase with apparent meningitis.

"Jae Nixon most certainly has Leptospirosis."

Silence ensued. Either Jordan Maldonado was the smartest med student ever to figure out a rare diagnosis or he was a crackpot to bring it up.

"Leptospirosis?" Dr. Mejia asked. In the past, he had heard the name of the disease but knew nothing more.

"Yes, sir. It makes sense. Even because of his job. It is caused by a bacterium carried by rats and mice, dogs, and wild animals and it takes contact from water, soil, or body fluids into the skin to acquire it. Annabel's patient is probably outside a lot working, or involved with outdoor activities being a ranger so, again, it makes sense."

Jordan looked at Annabel, his smugness penetrating her.

"Your studying is going forward well beyond your interest in cardiology," Dr. Mejia said crisply. "What else can you tell us? What about diagnosis or treatment?"

"The disease is caused by a Gram-negative bacterium. Since he's on antibiotics, he's probably going to get better. The illness can last from a few days to three weeks or longer, but there is better success the earlier the treatment is started. But without antibiotics? Recovery may take several months."

"Okay, Dr. Maldonado," the attending said, their roles clearly reversed, "can we make sure about the diagnosis?"

Jordan nodded emphatically. Annabel thought his head was going to fly off.

"There are screening tests and specialized labs can do the serology."

Dr. Mejia turned to Melody. "Dr. Burg, you are the resident taking care of Mr. Nixon?"

"Yes."

"Be sure and talk with Dr. Maldonado after rounds for any more information."

The attending took a step back. "Also," he said, "write an order for the infectious disease service to come by and do a consult on Jae Nixon. We're most likely dealing with a rare disease, one that our own bright medical student has brought to our awareness."

In the front of the hospital, Annabel dropped her overnight bag and backpack with reading material on the sidewalk and called for a ride home. She never thought she would feel this, but she was super glad to break away from her team. Right now she had a stronger attachment to her patients than the doctors she'd been working with for the last several months.

She correlated the information on her phone app with the Toyota slowing down in front of her. "Hi," she said and scooted in the back seat when the driver stopped.

The man in the car was barely tall enough to align with the head rest. "Today's a beautiful day. You a nurse?"

Annabel figured wearing scrubs and being female made her a nurse. She shook her head. "No, I'm taking the more sadistic approach and I'm training to become a doctor."

The drive home ensued in silence as she figured out her plan for the rest of the day. The driver was right. Lots of sunshine, so a run along the Ohio might brighten her disposition. And besides wanting to take Nancy out for brunch, she wanted to call and visit Bob.

The driver stopped in front of her apartment and with a "thanks," she scrambled out. She fumbled to find her apartment key. Noisy footsteps came down the staircase from above and then a young man with lanky limbs appeared on the last steps. His alert eyes settled on her.

"I'm your neighbor on the second floor. I see you come and go. You a nurse?"

"A medical student."

"Oh."

"Sorry about the noise the night before last."

"Yeah, well, it was the first time I had to bang on the ceiling to make you pipe down."

"It won't happen again. It was a sibling squabble."

"I guess not. It looked like she cleared out this morning."

Annabel frowned. "I wasn't expecting that. She was supposed to leave tomorrow."

He shrugged his shoulders. "I've seen you up at Pete's."

"The Café is the only place close to eat which doesn't require a ride in the car."

"I don't cook much, if at all."

"You a student?"

"Going to college. Got fed up with dorm life the first two years so my parents are footing this rent bill, which doesn't hurt them in the least."

"You're lucky. I better get going. Sorry again."

"No problem."

Annabel climbed the stairs and went inside to an empty apartment. Her sister had not even left her a note.

Annabel ditched the scrubs and put on a Cincinnati Reds T-shirt and sweatpants. She sat, pulled on her sneakers, and smiled while thinking about her previous run with Bob and his lesson about lock laces. He must be feeling better after taking a whole day off, she guessed. Regardless, she wanted to help him out in any way she could. She popped his number up on her phone and called.

After a few rings, Bob's sluggish voice came on. "Hey. You home?"

"Yes, off from call. You sound terrible."

"Thanks."

She shook her head. "Can I come over? Maybe bring you some food?"

"I'm not hungry."

"But I think I better check on you."

"Hell. You're a pain."

"I'm coming over."

"You don't even know where I live."

"Which is quite appalling ... after all this time we've known each other. However, I know the area where you live and I'll GPS your exact address."

"I'm not up to entertaining you and, if you take your own car, heaven forbid, you'll lose your parking space."

"To hell with the parking space and I'm not coming unless you roll out the red carpet and prepare me shrimp scampi. When was the last time you ate anything?"

"Uh … yesterday morning."

Annabel clenched her mouth. She didn't like the sound of his situation at all. "I'll be there as soon as I can."

"The door will be unlocked."

Before getting into her car, Annabel walked to the neighborhood Café where she was happy to see Pete's thriving Sunday after-church crowd. The food on the tables made her mouth water as she stepped to the counter.

"What would you like, Annabel?" Pete asked.

"A take-out. How about packing up two containers with scrambled eggs and toast? My friend is sick and that may be bland and light enough for him to eat."

"Is it your male med student friend?"

"That's him."

"I have fresh blueberry muffins right out of the oven. Why don't I pack two of those instead of toast?"

"Perfect. Thanks."

Pete came back with the order and Annabel took off.

Knowing that Bob lived northeast of her, Annabel avoided the interstate and drove the side streets. She pulled into the ample parking lot of his apartment complex; he didn't have a parking problem like she did. She walked through the ground floor of the two story buildings looking for his apartment number and found it between the street and a covered pool.

Clutching the bag of food, Annabel knocked and then poked her head in. "Bob?"

"I'm in here."

She passed a simple walk-in kitchen space to the combined eating nook and living room area. Bob was on a thick burgundy couch against the wall and only swiveled his head to see her from his supine position. She sat on the cocktail table next to him.

"When you call in sick, you're not kidding, are you?"

He managed to curl up one side of his lip.

"What is going on anyway?" She placed the bag on the table for the time being.

"I have no energy. It's like there's a pipeline inserted in my vein, draining me of adrenaline, testosterone, and thyroxine."

"What about other symptoms?"

"Besides mild body aches, I don't feel like eating, and I'm suffering from a growing energy deficit." He took a deep sigh.

"No GI symptoms, fever, or neuro symptoms?"

"I don't think so, Dr. Tilson."

Annabel rolled her eyes. "Maybe Dr. Maldonado should be here taking care of you. He's become quite the clinician. I'll have to fill you in on our team. But first, I brought you the perfect food." She foraged in the bag, opened one container, and a utensil pack. "Come on, sit up."

Annabel crouched over, put her arm around him, and helped him to a sitting position. "This is fresh from Pete's Cafe."

Bob stayed leaning over and, while Annabel made him some tea, he did his best to eat. She came back and placed the mug in front of him and began eating from her container while sitting cross-legged on the floor.

"Thanks," he said. "It is a good thing you brought me something." He sank back into the couch. "Tell me about call."

"I'll give you the highlights," she said. "Our fearless leader, Dr. Schott, is not himself. His gumption to teach was sucked out of him by a patient's family member who came in and hurled insults at him along with the threat of a lawsuit. The man's mother died after we discharged her, my former atrial fibrillation patient.

"Also, the man I drove into the hospital a week ago came back and is now my patient, but he fell into a coma and is in the ICU. Although we couldn't figure out his diagnosis, know-it-all Jordan seems to have figured it out. I think Dr. Mejia is so star struck, he's going to bequeath Jordan a trust fund.

"And remember Nancy came up on Friday to go out with Jordan? Well, because of our fight about his cheating the other day, he stood her up. Now my sister isn't talking to me because it was apparently my fault. She left today without a word."

"Is that all?" he mused.

Annabel laughed, split off a piece of muffin, and put it in her mouth.

"I have to lie back down," he said.

"Is your condition bad enough to bring you to the hospital?"

"No way. That would be overkill."

Annabel fluffed up his pillow and he eased back down. She looked around as he closed his eyes.

"Your furniture is sure nicer than mine. This place is pretty comfortable."

"I salvaged stuff off of Craig's list."

"I'll remember that for next time."

"Appreciate your coming over. You don't have to stay any longer."

"How about I study for both of us? I'll get your internal medicine book and read out loud?"

"I'm worried I may not be able to keep up with the rotation."

"Please don't say that. No way. I will read-study out loud. Just listen up."

She plucked his medical book off of the kitchen table. After thumbing through the index, she selected a chapter on "Adrenal Insufficiency" and began.

"Primary adrenal insufficiency refers to adrenal failure or …"

Annabel peeked at Bob every few minutes. In a half hour, he was fast asleep. She got up, stretched, and walked around. It was the framed photographs on the shelves that caught her attention the most. A wide-grinned, bright young Bob held a fishing pole near a shore line, and a college graduation picture with, more than likely, his parents. Their expressions registered sheer joy over their son's accomplishment.

Bob resembled his father, but, she thought, he inherited his sense of humor from his mother. She even looked mischievous. Other pictures were of him and his sisters, posing in restaurants and on hiking trails.

Annabel made herself a cup of tea and sat on the floor again. After an hour, she closed the book.

"Bob, I'm going to head out. I believe you won't be well enough to show up tomorrow. Give me the name of your primary care doctor."

With coaxing, Bob gave her the information. She called and left a message on the weekend recorder asking for an appointment for the next day.

"They should call you back tomorrow," she said.

He shook his head once. "I doubt I'll want to drive there if they schedule me."

"I'll check with you in the morning; I'll arrange an Uber driver to be here if you get an appointment."

"Yes, Mother."

"Don't 'yes, mother' me. If we don't look after each other, then who else will?"

Bob rolled slightly to his side.

"Will you be able to sleep?"

"Sleep is like a cat. Ignore it to make it come."

A smile graced her lips.

"Thanks," he added. "I'd give you a hug if I was standing."

"Here, then." She leaned over, gave him a small embrace, and left a glass of water and a textbook within reach.

CHAPTER 15

As Curley ate from the bowl on the front porch, Patty Caye stretched her arms over her head. "I'm going to pick up your buddy this morning," she said to the dog.

Curley finished eating and Patty clicked her tongue for him to follow her along the nearby trail; Monday mornings she always made sure the walking path was free of litter and tree limbs. She passed the brush line where Jae had cleared out the recent mouse dwellings and thought heavily about the coincidence of Jae's and Twist's sicknesses. Although she wasn't a vet or a physician, it dawned on her that the illness in both of them may be one and the same.

Patty unlocked the visitors' center after the hike and told the paid and unpaid staff that she was off to the vet's office. After a short ride, she was the first customer in the brick building. The vet called her into an exam room where Twist gave her the cheeriest greeting he was capable of by licking her hand.

"You sweet thing. I missed you." She wrapped her arms around his chest despite his hair clinging to her uniform like Velcro. "Forgive me for the cage and the IV. How scary for you, but you're going to soon be your old self."

The vet sat on a customer's chair. "He's good to go home. However, keep him out of trouble and inside for a week because he's still recuperating. His IV antibiotics are now switched to pills, so be sure to camouflage them in his food."

"I will. My partner and I got more than we bargained for by letting two strays hang around the park."

"I hate the word 'stray,' which makes me think of an animal which lacks a definite plan or purpose. No living being is accidental or unintended."

Patty locked eyes with the man. "We believe the same way. I won't use that term anymore. Being sick, the dog made me realize how precious he is. From now on, the two dogs around my cabin will be my steadfast family members. I bet I can speak for my partner too."

The vet tousled Twist's coat while she stood.

"I've been wondering," Patty said, "about Leptospirosis. You told me quite a bit about it, but my partner is very ill and is on life-support in the hospital. Do you know if people can acquire the same thing?"

"Absolutely."

"Besides the dogs, my ranger partner has been close to mice and their nesting areas lately. It makes me wonder ..."

"Sure thing. The rodents may be carrying the responsible bacteria. Your partner and Twist could have been infected from the mice, especially from mice urine, which goes unnoticed wherever they are scurrying about. Or the dog became infected by the mice and your partner infected by the dog."

Patty slowly nodded. "I'm glad we spoke. I will share this information with the doctors taking care of Jae."

The vet opened the door. "Sometimes communication between different health care staff solves or averts a lot of problems."

"Thank you. You did more than treat one of my best pals."

"I visited Bob yesterday," Annabel said to Dr. Schott as she stored her backpack in the office. "Chances are, he'll be calling you any minute to say he's not coming in."

Donn leaned against the desk and rubbed his chin. His newspaper was nowhere in sight.

"We're approaching the tail end of the whole rotation. He's risking a 'not complete' for the course."

"He doesn't have a choice. It's like there is nothing wrong with him, but there is."

"That doesn't make any sense."

"I know." She squared her shoulders. "I left a message at his doctor's office, so he should get an appointment today."

"A few more absent days and he may need to redo some, if not all, of the rotation."

"That's what he's worried about."

The rotation was already dismal without him. If he didn't finish, it would probably disrupt them from being together on the next specialty. She swallowed hard. Since the third year of medical school had started, they had been inseparable and the situations they'd shared were unforgettable.

Donn soon waved the team into the hallway. His cell phone beeped with a text message and he looked over his shoulder at Annabel. "It's Bob. Like you said, he's not coming."

After rounds, Annabel stayed in the ICU. She wrote her notes on Jae Nixon and waited. The infectious disease consultant had not been by on Sunday. She was due any minute.

The coffee she sipped on was fresh; she had made it herself. She popped a chocolate espresso bean into her mouth, let it melt with the hot brew, and thought of Bob.

What's going on with a doctor's appointment? she typed on her iPhone to him.

They are booked today, but they stuck me on the schedule for tomorrow at 4 p.m.. I'll see Dr. Raymond and he's worth the wait.

Didn't you tell them you were a medical student?

What difference does that make?

I don't know. I'm just saying.

Are you worried about me?

As worried about you as you were about me when you drove me to TN because my dog died. You didn't want me driving myself!

Oh.

She smiled at his minimal response. *Can I bring you food tonight?*

No. You need to study.

I can still do that. I'll study out loud at your place.

Okay. A smile emoji popped up.

I'll be over, she responded.

As Annabel slipped her phone away, she sensed a figure in front of her. A woman wearing a long, white physician's coat beamed down at her with a warm yet authoritative expression. Her cheekbones sat high on her face and her skin wore age spots. Her peppered white and black hair was pulled taut into an old-fashioned bun.

"May I?" the woman said.

Annabel's hands rested on Jae Nixon's chart. She grasped both ends and handed it over without a word. The physician nodded with approval and opened the chart on the counter as Annabel observed her name tag – Shania Enno, M.D.

"Medical student Tilson," the woman said with a smooth voice, as if she oozed yoga from her vocal cords.

Annabel held her gaze.

"Tell me everything you know about this bereft man on a ventilator. I am the infectious disease doctor, Dr. Enno."

Annabel hesitated, wondering if the woman would continue to stand. She appeared to be in her early seventies and her bumpy-boned hand rested on a cane.

"Alejandro will take care of me," Dr. Enno said.

"Alejandro?"

The woman raised her cane off the floor and waved the handle, which was patterned with natural dark and light wood. A turquoise stone or inlay was embedded in the end of the handle and the wood of the long shaft was striated like Mother Nature had painted her herself. Polyurethane coated the whole piece, no doubt smoothed and coated by a master craftsman.

"Oh," Annabel said, realizing the woman had named her walking aid. Her mind was now clear of her patient and solidified on the infectious disease specialist before her.

The woman planted the cane back down and practically read Annabel's mind. "I can do without sitting right now. I make sure I stay on my feet for a portion of the day. The veins in my legs must work harder and stay in better shape pumping that blood clear back to my heart.

"Tell me about your patient."

Annabel presented Jae Nixon's entire case to the elderly physician. In the end, she paused and then said, "However, after all the uncertainty of Mr. Nixon's illness, one of the other medical students came up with Leptospirosis as the working diagnosis."

Dr. Enno's expression stayed the same; she registered no wonderment at the mention of the disease. Meanwhile, the ICU doors slid open and a woman wearing a park ranger's uniform went straight to Jae Nixon's room.

"One of Mr. Nixon's visitors," Annabel said, pointing past Dr. Enno. "I should go talk to her."

"Let's both go."

Annabel walked at Dr. Enno's speed into the stark room. Patty Caye turned with frightened eyes at both of them.

"I'm Dr. Enno," the physician said, "and perhaps you've met Annabel,

Mr. Nixon's medical student on his case. I was called in for my expertise in infectious diseases."

"And I'm Patty Caye. I work with Jae. I just came back from picking up one of the dogs that Jae and I take care of, and I have very important news which may help. Our dog was diagnosed with Leptospirosis and is making a fine recovery, but I learned that people can get it too. It's possible Jae picked up the same thing as the dog. Both of them may have acquired it from the mouse population we're plagued with or Jae got it from the dog who still picked it up from the mice."

"Thank you so much," Dr. Enno said. "It is a working diagnosis on the table for the time being. But tell me more about the area you work in, what you do, and this mouse population. Infectious diseases are notorious for specificity; their geographic distribution, their hosts, the time of year, and the life cycle of the infectious agent."

Patty gave Dr. Enno a vivid description of life at the park and Jae's tasks with the trails, the wildlife, and exterminator duties with rodents.

"Since our dog is better," Patty said in the end, "I'm assuming Jae is also going to pull out of this." She put her hand to her mouth, hoping for a positive response.

"We can never predict what comes tomorrow," Dr. Enno said. "Right now, I need to examine my new patient and check his chart and test results. After I do my consult, I am sure that Dr. Schott will contact you."

Patty's eyes were fixed on the woman as she patted Jae's arm. "I'll go grab breakfast and go back to work. I needed to come in and see him today for myself. I hope I helped."

"Yes, dear, thank you."

Patty left and Dr. Enno walked to the top of the bed. She stared at Jae's tattoo.

"That is magnificent body artwork," Annabel said, taking a chance that Dr. Enno also appreciated it.

"I agree. I am half American Indian, so I admire the subject matter as well as the colors." She proceeded to pull medical gadgets out of her pockets and examine Jae. Annabel watched the woman's methodical physical exam and then walked back to the desk with her.

"Alejandro, your cane," Annabel said. "What does that mean?"

"'Defender' or the 'protector of mankind.'" The lines around her eyes crinkled. "Obviously, my cane is most useful to me rather than the entire human race."

It was early afternoon, often when Annabel would find Donn in the office eating his pb&j sandwich, especially if he hadn't gone to the cafeteria. She poked her head in, only to receive a haughty stare from Jordan. After crossing the pedway to the call room area where Donn had his own private office, she rapped on his door.

"Come in," she heard. The shelves were stuffed with textbooks and paperbacks. An unopened cellophane-wrapped sandwich sat on the end of his cluttered desk.

Donn stifled a sigh. "What brings you over?"

"Sorry to disturb you. I have a request … if I can leave tomorrow by three o'clock so I can drive Bob to the doctor's appointment he has at four o'clock."

Donn crossed his legs. "Tomorrow there is no clinic or call. Consider it done. Who is he going to see?"

"A family practice doc named Dr. Raymond."

Donn raised his eyebrows. "I know family practice and internal medicine doctors who are stumped with unusual illnesses and their patients are sent off to big name institutions. But Dr. Raymond? He's diagnosed conditions that even the Mayo Clinic couldn't figure out."

"Really? Bob said he was worth the wait to see him."

"I have bad news, however. The department said if he doesn't come back by the end of the week, he'll need to make up the time."

"Can he take the final exam?"

"That may be up to him, but he stands the risk of failing."

Annabel fixed her eyes on his desk. Not if she could help it, she thought.

"Can I tell him what you said?"

"Yes, it would be best if you do."

Annabel ran her hand through her hair; the waves settled on the front of her jacket. "One more thing. The infectious disease doctor just saw Jae Nixon. A Dr. Enno."

Donn's eyes widened. "We're striking home runs. They don't get any better than her."

"I wondered about that. She certainly is different."

"She has years of experience and, despite her age, knows of every new potentially dangerous organism that breathes, crawls, swims, or has anything to do with humans. She's like a one-man CDC. She can be unnerving with all that knowledge except for the fact that she emanates calmness like a spiritual goddess."

Donn extended his arm and grabbed a nearby soft drink. His pensive expression returned.

"Dr. Schott, I'm really sorry you're dealing with the threat of a lawsuit." She turned to leave. "And thanks for letting me leave on time tomorrow."

CHAPTER 16

"Did you manage to sleep at all today?" Annabel asked when she went to Bob's that evening.

"I rested on and off. At least I'm in a chair for your visit and not on the couch." His legs were straight out on the recliner and covered with an afghan.

"I brought you something tasty, light, and bland - stone cut oatmeal - and I had Pete drizzle honey on it. The contents are still warm." She dug in the bag she brought and handed him a Styrofoam container and a spoon.

"What would I do without you?"

"You'd manage. I bring good news too. Dr. Schott is making sure I'm out on time tomorrow to bring you to the doctor's. I won't be calling you an Uber driver."

Bob slid down oatmeal and shook his head. "You don't need to do that."

"But I will."

Annabel pulled out a sandwich from her own take-out order. "I'm going to read to you again after I eat."

They ate in silence and she glanced at her phone. She was overdue to text Dustin back from earlier in the day, so she went ahead and typed.

I'm looking forward to tomorrow night as well. How did the domestic abuse case work out?

I hate them! he responded. *Most of the time, whatever the situation is, it grows worse over time.*

Not good.

"Are you texting Nancy?" Bob asked. "Are you back on speaking terms? You can't let some idiot like Jordan influence the both of you."

"No. She's ignoring me. This is from Dustin Lowe. We're going out tomorrow night."

Bob attempted a half-hearted smile. "Your schedule tomorrow is packed with men. One enjoyable and one nothing but a burden."

"You're not a problem. Plus, you don't know and I'm not telling you - my life regarding men right now is totally toned down. Compared to normal."

Bob tilted his head. She wasn't going to divulge any more, so he continued eating.

Another message popped up on Annabel's phone. *Text you late tomorrow for a definitive time.*

I have a little chore to do which may or may not delay me, but we're on no matter what!

Bob crossed his ankles as Annabel put down her phone. "Did Dr. Schott say anything more about my finishing the rotation?"

"Yes. If you're not back by the end of the week, you'll have to make up any lost time on another internal medicine rotation. However, you can take the final exam if you want. If you pass, it'll count. If you fail, you must repeat the entire length and testing of the rotation."

Bob squinted his eyes. Getting through the rotation was one thing, but he realized that if he didn't get back on the wards soon, he would be out-of-synch with Annabel. The possibility of rotating next with her on ob/gyn or pediatrics would be lost.

"You're not saying anything," Annabel said.

"Actually, they are being fair with me."

"I think so too. There is only so much you can do about getting yourself better in a hurry, but if that doesn't happen, you can tackle the final exam if you think you stand a chance of passing. And, there won't be that much time to make up on another rotation. One of the problems I see is that all your timings will be messed up."

He wondered if she meant between the two of them. "Yes, that's unfortunate. But, no matter what, despite being so tired, I must try and study like a madman."

"You already are a madman, so you're on your way to passing."

Bob closed his eyes and shook his head with a grin. When he opened them, Annabel leaned over and took his empty container.

"If I have anything to do with it," she said, "you are going to pass. We both are. Unless I'm on call, I'm going to help you out every night. And each day, I'll tell you the clinical stories from the wards."

She unwrapped her tucked-in legs. "Tonight, let's take a crash course on hepatitis."

The next morning, Annabel sat behind a talkative driver on the way to the hospital. She wanted to tape his mouth shut. She had become such a regular customer of the transportation service that she could write out a preference list. The cars were never a problem because they were clean and the back seats roomy. Every driver streamed music; the genre was usually okay with her. She wasn't picky, but the volume made all the difference in the world. Too loud made for a nerve-rattling drive, which she didn't need at the crack of dawn.

In essence, the most important aspect came down to the driver. Once in a while, she'd hit the jackpot when a conversation began with an unusually interesting person and she'd hear interesting aspects of their life. At those times, she wished she could stay in the car and listen to more.

Overall, a respectable friendliness from the driver was the key, and a little light chit-chat was perfect. Too little or too much sapped her energy away from whatever it was she really wanted to think about.

And this morning, she thought about Bob and her date with Dustin that night. And as they pulled off the interstate, she wondered about Jae Nixon still in a coma and the woman who was holding all the cards for him to get better. If she ever considered infectious diseases as a specialty for herself, there would be no one better to shadow than Shania Enno. It was in her best interest to absorb as much as she could from the elderly woman.

She darted into the office, left her things, and headed to the ICU. In Jae's room, she stumbled on the changing shift and heard the tail end of the night nurse's report to the a.m. replacement. "I just changed out his Foley catheter and replaced a bag of IV fluids," the husky nurse said. "This young man's condition is depressing and I can't wait to leave."

Annabel nodded at them. She looked at the nurse's clipboard at the bottom of the bed. Jae's twenty-four-hour urine output was adequate. His vital signs were less robust than the day before, he still ran a fever, and she worried about his lungs. The longer he stayed on the ventilator, the greater chance that he'd end up with a respiratory infection. She knew ... one thing could lead to another.

She finished a routine physical exam and spotted Dr. Enno at the main desk.

"Go grab your morning java," the woman said, "and come back here and take a seat."

Annabel filled a cup to the brim and came back. The woman rolled back the chair and crossed her ankles. Alejandro leaned against the counter between them.

"What is your personal thinking," Dr. Enno wondered, "about the chosen antibiotic that Mr. Nixon is on … days ago and now?"

"It was done empirically, so it was justified," Annabel responded truthfully, hoping the woman wasn't annoyed at the team's decision. "However, his condition has not changed, so it's obviously not working."

"Correct. In general, it takes at least three doses of an antibiotic to reach a steady therapeutic blood level, so if the correct agent is being used, a patient's condition shouldn't worsen after that but should begin to improve."

Annabel pulled in closer and crossed her hands.

"He's on an antibacterial and I don't think Jae Nixon's infection is coming from a bacterium." She squinted her eyes at the open chart next to her. It was open to the lab work section.

"The rest of the LP results are back?" Annabel asked.

"Yes. The spinal tap shows a modest CSF pleocytosis count with predominant lymphocytes. This young man? It appears a virus is the catalyst for his profound illness. He most likely has viral meningitis."

"Wait a minute," Annabel said, dumbfounded. "I just realized … I thought, or we presumed, he had Leptospirosis."

"No, my dear. Far from it. I wish he did."

Annabel sipped her coffee while Dr. Enno wrote a note in Jae's chart. She needed to read what the doctor said so she could report it on rounds, but she hoped Dr. Enno would share more knowledge. She thought about Patty Caye and Jae's dog. It had been reasonable to strongly consider Leptospirosis in Jae because of the dog's diagnosis. They both shared similar symptoms and an environment ripe to pick up the disease.

Shania clipped her pen back on her upper pocket and wrapped her arthritic hand around Alejandro.

"Let's talk about viral meningitis," Dr. Enno said. "As always in medicine, we start with probabilities. What is most common. Do you have any ideas?"

"I believe I heard it this year. It stuck with me easily because my dad is a neurosurgeon and he's mentioned it. The usual group of viruses would be groups of enteroviruses, notorious for many infections like colds and flu-like illnesses."

"Remarkable," Shania said. "Your dad's knowledge rubbed off on you."

"Dr. Enno, more remarkable is that you became a doctor way back when women in medicine were as rare as February 29th. What was that like?"

Her eyes shined and the wrinkles around them smiled. "Dear, it was difficult for them – the men – I mean. I was a nurse already, a born caregiver who earlier learned much from the American Indian ways of my father. I landed myself into a formal medical education with Alejandro at my side. Both of us are old."

She leaned forward a bit and tapped Annabel. "I figured I was as smart and able to be a physician as any other person. Double the discrimination was hurled at me, but my skin was thick and tough. You know, the greater the struggles you go through, the stronger you become."

Annabel agreed wholeheartedly and nodded. "You had your cane before you needed it?"

"Yes. Other people were not aware of it, but Alejandro made them take me more seriously. Somehow my piece of art, crafted by a Chippewa Indian, took them off guard. I also literally believed in the wise words of Teddy Roosevelt. 'Speak softly and carry a big stick.'"

Annabel smiled. She wished she could sit with the woman all day.

"But back to viruses. Yes, enteroviruses are the common critters of viruses. There are two others you are aware of, I'm sure, but you may not know that they can cause meningitis.

"First, deserving of many people's disgust, are the herpes or HSV viruses. Type I herpes simplex virus is responsible for the fiendish cold sore, the contagious oral virus we pick up as a child. It's spread by infected saliva or by kissing your favorite aunt at a family reunion."

Dr. Enno's passion for her specialty rose from her small voice. "The virus travels inside the nerve cells into the cluster of nerve cells or ganglion and goes to sleep in a dormant state. When it wants to, it starts multiplying again and travels back along its previous path to the skin where it artfully creates blisters on a person's lips."

"People don't like wearing Herpes I to a party," Annabel quipped.

"If they can help it. Type II is also deserving of our loathing, but at least it stays out of sight."

"Genital herpes," Annabel said.

"Yes, *that* sexually transmitted disease - the one many people are walking around with and don't know about. Last CDC statistics are that there are three-quarters of a million new cases per year in our country. Both viruses can cause encephalitis and meningitis, but Type II is more often the cause of meningitis." Dr. Enno stopped and let that sink in.

"Secondly, another cause of viral meningitis comes from HIV. The human immunodeficiency virus can cause inflammation of the meninges during the early stages of the disease. We are clueless as far as Mr. Nixon's sexual history or history of blood transfusions, so this is something we must consider. And, interestingly enough, viral meningitis sometimes is the first sign of an HIV infection, so if we identify it early, treatment can begin right away to thwart off the patient's possibility of acquiring full-blown AIDS."

Annabel nodded, grateful for the private lesson. For sure, she would share the information with Bob.

"I did read somewhere about tuberculous meningitis. I suppose that isn't a possibility?"

"My index of suspicion is slim. Patients in that case may show up with nerve palsies and their CSF findings show an extremely low glucose, high protein levels, and a fairly meager white blood count. His CSF findings are not suggestive at all."

Annabel marveled that Dr. Enno could summon up the exact lab profile of a disease just by mentioning it. It made her want to consider the specialty. However, Shania wasn't the first attending she wanted to emulate.

"So," Dr. Enno said, breaking into her thoughts, "I just ordered HIV testing, especially since one of my mantras is 'adults with viral meningitis due to an unknown etiology should undergo an HIV test.'

"And, regarding herpes or HSV, a treatment exists, so like what we did before with the anti-bacterials, we will start empiric treatment. The drug is acyclovir, so we will begin that immediately. I advised your medical team in my note."

Annabel felt like now a substantial search was beginning, especially since Leptospirosis and a bacterial cause was out of the picture. "My chief resident will be starting rounds soon. I will relay your assessment and plan to the resident, Dr. Burg, and Dr. Schott."

"Yes," she said and frowned. "Dr. Schott. He's suffering from the shock of hearing 'see you in court' for the first time."

"He's pretty freaked out."

"For him, and if it ever happens to you, the best advice to think about is from Robert Frost. 'The only way out is through.'"

Annabel nodded. "I'll be off this rotation, but I hope he has a good outcome or that the lawsuit goes away."

"I will speak with him privately. Now, back to our task at hand." She sat straighter and ignored Alejandro. "Dr. Tilson, I gave you my clinical summation. However, the viruses we discussed usually cause a bout of meningitis in a patient, the patient is treated to ease their symptoms, and they may or may not have a recurrence. In other words, these viruses rarely cause a patient to end up on life support."

She tapped Alejandro on the floor. "Jae Nixon spiraling into a coma makes me uneasy."

Dr. Enno's last remark made Annabel shudder as she left for rounds. She wished she knew more about the ranger, but she may never get the opportunity if he doesn't wake up soon.

CHAPTER 17

"Dr. Mejia is joining us for rounds this morning," Dr. Schott said over his shoulder as the team took off down the hallway. "Annabel, we'll start in the ICU with your patient."

"I have a lot to report about Jae Nixon," she said. "I don't want you and Dr. Burg to be blindsided. Would you like me to tell you first?"

"No," he said curtly. "It can wait."

Annabel and Stuart walked side-by-side. "Where's Jordan?" she asked.

"Good question. Our team is shrinking by the day. However, I bet you can do without him. Seems to be bad blood between both of you since that lecture when you mentioned his cheating."

Dr. Schott abruptly stopped and spun around. "The cheating he did … now I want to know the details."

Stuart remained silent and Dr. Burg and Dr. Watt stood clueless.

Annabel swallowed hard. "I don't think I should talk about it."

"Come out with it. There will be no repercussions for what you tell me, that I can promise. And more than likely, no consequences for Jordan. My footing as chief resident is already shaky. Besides cheating being wrong, there should be no reason whatsoever for someone on this team to be doing it."

Annabel closed her eyes for a second. She was no snitch, but she didn't have a choice. The team waited for her response.

"Jordan had an open medicine handbook in his lap during the mid-term exam."

"Are you saying that because he figured out Jae Nixon's disease?" Donn's cheeks flushed and he exhaled forcefully. "Is there some kind of rivalry going on here?"

Annabel reeled with his outburst. "No, I …"

"Society's cream of the crop – medical students – behaving like kindergarteners?"

Donn's voice was too high for the hallway and a woman visitor distanced herself as she passed.

Annabel held her tongue while her heart pounded. He asked her to come clean, she did, and now she was being penalized for it. She didn't dare try to defend herself again. In fact, she thought, there was nothing at all that she should be defending herself for. Anger started to rise from her gut while Dr. Schott's glare became less intense.

Donn turned around, and with a heavy foot, walked ahead through the ICU automatic doors. The team stayed so close they almost collided when he stopped within eyesight of Jae ... lying motionless on the bed in the middle of all the medical equipment.

The swoosh of the doors sounded again and Dr. Mejia and Jordan Maldonado came prancing in. The attending wore a bold maroon tie and Jordan had his hand wrapped around his cell phone. Annabel wondered how Jordan managed to be with the attending.

"Good morning," Dr. Mejia said, rubbing his hands in front of him. "Dr. Burg, why don't you present an update on Mr. Nixon."

"Sebastian," Dr. Schott said, "the student is privy to the latest on Jae Nixon, if you don't mind."

Everyone turned to Annabel. She didn't want to sound haughty about announcing the fact that her patient didn't have Leptospirosis; she wanted them to figure it out themselves. Dr. Schott didn't need any more fodder to lump her into a kindergarten class or "I told you so" type of behavior.

"Mr. Nixon's condition remains the same," she said, "in a comatose state, with a fever, and with less robust blood pressures. His lungs are staying clear. There's no sign of a urinary infection with the catheter and urine output is just adequate. I want to bring up nutritional support, so I don't forget, with something like TPN. If that will soon be a possibility?"

She didn't wait for an answer and no one interrupted.

"Mr Nixon's CSF results came back with a modest pleocytosis count with predominant lymphocytes. Along with the fact that the antibiotics were not working, Dr. Enno D/Cd them, and started him on acyclovir for the possibility of HSV and she also wants to rule out HIV."

Dr. Mejia patted his comb over one time and maintained his seriousness. Jordan's face registered puzzlement and his mouth fell open.

"That means he *does not* have Leptospirosis?!" Dr. Mejia said. "We barked up the wrong tree?"

"Barking is the correct word," Annabel said. "It was the rangers' dog at the national park who came down with a serious case of Leptospirosis. However, it was a strong possibility that our patient could have acquired the responsible bacteria as well - either from the dog or because of the environment and the rodent population where they live."

Jordan's iPhone plummeted from his hand. A loud thud sounded on the durable, institutional floor, and then a crack. Everyone looked down. The device was lying facedown. Dr. Maldonado made a pathetic sound as he crouched down and picked it up.

Jordan Maldonado couldn't believe it. The female ranger's conversation he overheard in the cafeteria was about a dog! How could he swallow that he'd jumped to conclusions and assumed it was also the male ranger? Worse than that, the brownie points he had earned with the attending, whose profession and recommendation he'd give his right arm for, may be demoted.

And shit, he thought, staring into his hands at his seven-hundred-dollar iPhone where he lived on social media when he wasn't studying. It was cracked like a pane of glass straight across the front face.

"Well, well," Dr. Schott said. "Looks like two things have been eliminated this morning. Although there were similarities, like Jae Nixon having a biphasic history of symptoms, Leptospirosis and a bacterial infection are stricken from his possible diagnoses. And, secondly, Dr. Maldonado's GD phone, where his thumbs are always planted, has died."

Annabel never read one word of medicine all day. She made sure she revisited all her patients in the afternoon, all her notes were written, and she acquired every possible lab result.

Even though he blew up at her before, Annabel assumed Dr. Schott had not changed his mind about letting her leave at three o'clock. She did not find him in the team's office which meant she had to traipse over to his private room. She had to confirm and tell him she was leaving, but dreaded talking to him alone.

When she arrived at his office across the pedway, his door was ajar. She rapped, pushed it all the way, and found the room empty. He must be around, she thought, and decided to go in. She stepped to his desk for a piece of paper to write him a note.

She feared what she saw when she eyed the open documents on top, a torn official-looking manila envelope next to them; it was a stapled cluster of court papers.

Walter Helm, Sally Helm, and Susan Helm, Plaintiffs vs. Donn Schott,

M.D. and Sebastian Mejia, M.D.

Annabel glanced down the front page, reading bits and pieces.

Said doctors treating our mother, Meagan Helm, mismanaged and failed to prescribe her the appropriate medications for her discharge after an uncomplicated short hospital stay. Lack of such medications caused, directly, the death of Meagan Helm, who had no chance of resuscitation after dying a swift and horrid death. Only Dr. Schott and Dr. Mejia had the knowledge and the ability to avert said occurrence and they failed to act responsibly or with diligence and care, and, instead, acted with overt negligence.

Annabel read another paragraph and shuddered. It all sounded horrendous, like the two doctors were wanted criminals. Were all medical lawsuits like this one?

She knew firsthand about Meagan Helm, her atrial fibrillation and the careful care she received; the situation portrayed in the legal papers was distorted and histrionic.

Was this what she had to look forward to later in her career? Accusations of negligence when none existed? Accusations of carelessness and indifference which might make her throw in the towel?

No wonder Dr. Schott was being snippy and short-tempered, she thought. He knew the lawsuit had arrived and his mood had changed. Seeing this would make any doctor panic.

Footsteps approached. Donn walked in, he stopped, and his eyebrows went straight up.

Annabel startled and stood up straighter from the desk. "I ... I was going to write out a note and leave it on your desk."

"You must have seen the lawsuit. Some uniformed man served it on me like he was going to handcuff me and take me away."

"I'm sorry."

"No need to be sorry. It's the attending's and my problem. Dr. Mejia just has more experience with something like this than I do."

Annabel nodded and stepped back from the desk.

Donn frowned and sat on the armrest of a small couch. "There should be a doctor's support group or a continuing medical education series on how to deal with lawsuits. Medical school and residency doesn't prepare us for this."

"I hope you deal with this the best you can and that it never happens again." She twisted her hands together. The minutes were ticking by and she hated to be late for Bob.

"Listen, I'm sorry for today," Donn said. "I insinuated that you tried to get back at Jordan after he shined on the rotation because of Jae Nixon's diagnosis and that you had lied about his cheating. He was wrong about the diagnosis. Another lesson to take away is that, until all the possible data and clues are in, we shouldn't jump to a diagnosis. Many disease states mimic each other."

"It certainly seems that way. I'll remember."

"Did you really see him with a medicine handbook during the test?"

"Yes, but I don't feel comfortable telling you."

"I understand."

Annabel bit her lip. "Do you mind if I go now? I'm supposed to drive Bob to his doctor's appointment."

Donn scratched his chin. "I forgot all about that. Get out of here. Tell him good luck with his appointment. I hope Dr. Raymond finds out what's wrong with him, and that he gets better. We all miss his smiling face. God knows, we've lost all spirit and the team atmosphere is dismal, mostly due to me ... your despondent chief resident. I can't fake my moods or my teaching style to act like everything is okay. It's going to take me awhile to get over my initial reaction to these papers.

"Anyway, I didn't mean to bring it up again. Go ahead."

"Dr. Schott, your lawsuit came up this morning when I was talking to Dr. Enno. She's a very nice and comforting lady. I think she wants to talk to you and be of help if she can."

"Her soothing voice is enough to inspire me to meditate, which is a ridiculous thought, because who has the time for that? At least I'll be bumping into her since she's consulting on your patient."

Annabel jumped into her Nissan in the parking lot and drove straight to Bob's apartment, slowing down through the school zones. His complex was family friendly with kids getting home from school and scrambling out of their parents' vehicles, entirely different from the business and college types in her own neighborhood.

Bob's door opened after she knocked and he stood there still wearing the pasty color he'd acquired since falling ill.

118

"How are you feeling?" she asked without moving.

"Partly cloudy."

"I bet you're exaggerating just to appease me. You're more like fully overcast with thunder rumbling in the background."

"If need be, I'd protect you under an umbrella." He looked past her at what the weather was really doing. "Do I need a jacket?"

"You'll be fine without one unless Dr. Raymond's office has no heat on at all."

"Forget it." He stepped out and closed the door.

"Tell me where to go," Annabel said when they buckled up in her car.

On the way, Bob directed her while she spilled out details about the entire day: Dr. Enno and Jae Nixon's case, Dr. Mejia and Jordan, and Dr. Schott blowing up at her and then his lawsuit and apology.

"I hate to say it," she said in the end, "but if you had to be absent from the wards, now is the time to do it. Out team has too much conflict."

"On the contrary. You're making me jealous I'm not there. Your patient is an intriguing case, the likes of which you may never see again. You're finishing up the rotation with a superficially pleasant team that is secretly dysfunctional with a backstabbing, self-righteous medical student; a dog-whisperer of an infectious disease consultant; a depressed, angry chief resident; and a gullible, flashy attending. There are two female residents who keep their personalities in check and a brilliant other medical student who would come out of a burning building unscathed."

Annabel glanced over at him quickly and then laughed. "If anything is missing, it's you."

"Yeah." He smiled back at her. "The biggest personality is missing."

Bob handed over his insurance information and filled out the paperwork in Dr. Raymond's waiting room. Without much of a wait, a nurse called him back and Annabel stayed put. A man with an artificial leg sat across from her, the metal evident below the hem of his trousers, and a few seats down an old couple held hands and intermittently talked softly to each other like they were telling secrets.

Annabel placed her *Internal Medicine Handbook* on the table next to her and texted Dustin.

Looks like I'll be ready by about 7, but I'll keep you posted. I don't want you waiting on me.

Annabel held her phone waiting for a response while the woman nearby talked to her partner. "I hope this doctor is older and wiser than that one last week. He was young enough to be my grandson."

"Anyone is young enough to be your grandkid," her spouse said.

Annabel and the man across from her smiled at each other as a ding sounded on her phone and Dustin's response popped up.

As long as we continue to communicate, I'll wait on you!

Thank you. Where are we going?

A restaurant downtown with a New Orleans flare. Do you like Cajun?

You bet. Is it dressy?

You always look dressy.

That's not always true. You should see me sometimes.

I hope to.

She stifled a chuckle. His flirting via text messages was way more fun than reading medicine.

The nurse left Bob's room without telling him to take off his shirt and to put on any type of patient gown, so he considered himself lucky. He stepped up, sat on the white paper cover on the exam table, and glared at the certificates on the doctor's wall: CME documents, resident certificates, and a state license. Not interesting reading material for most patients. The activity of simply coming in for the appointment made him feel extra tired, so he pulled out the footrest and lay back.

The door opened with a little swat and a big bald man with flat ears and a slow smile walked in. Bob pushed himself up and the two men shook hands.

"I'm Dr. Raymond. You've come to the right place. There is no room for illness when you're a medical student."

CHAPTER 18

Bob wrung his hands as he sat on the exam table in front of his new physician.

"Dr. Raymond," Bob said, "I'm losing days on an internal medicine rotation, so I hope you're as good a doctor as they say you are."

"Who said that?"

"That's the general consensus over at the V.A. Hospital."

"Never trust what you hear." He winked, read Bob's vital signs, and pushed in the table extension so Bob could sit up. "Now, tell me what brought you in here to be poked and prodded on."

"I am so tired, I can barely function. I've been knocked out on the couch for days. Along with that, I have mild body aches, but that may be because all I'm doing is lying around."

"When did this start?"

"About one or two weeks ago."

"Any major upsets in your life that could have catalyzed a depression?"

Bob shook his head slowly. "Nothing out of the ordinary and I am not depressed."

"Any fever, headache, or chills?"

"Once in a while I run a low-grade temperature."

"Nausea, vomiting, or diarrhea?"

"No, sir."

"Confusion or a rash?"

"No, sir."

Dr. Raymond deviated and asked him for a full family, social, and medical history, just like the students asked of their patients.

"Believe me, I'm a healthy guy," Bob ended.

Contemplating, Dr. Raymond rubbed his ear and looked over Bob's head. "Any of your patients come to mind that you could be mimicking their symptoms?"

"Not really. Before I left, I had the usual COPDers, diabetics, and cancer patients."

"Besides the fact that you can pick up anything nasty in a hospital, were you anywhere suspicious or out-of-the-ordinary lately? And where do you go for recreation?"

"The last time I went out of town, it was to Tennessee with the female medical student in your lobby. She's fine and the time line doesn't fit. I haven't been to the gym in a month. The only other place I went was for a run in a park garden and along the river with my same friend." He scrunched his forehead. "That was two weeks ago."

The doctor pulled an ophthalmoscope from his pocket and shined it in Bob's eyes. "Have your eyes been red?"

Bob shook his head, Dr. Raymond went on with his examination, and then sat on a stool. He leaned over and ticked off little boxes on two lab sheets. "Follow me."

Outside, he handed the sheets to a lab tech, and pointed Bob into their room. Bob rolled up his sleeve and a woman drew a couple of vials of blood. He went back to the exam room and waited.

Sitting there with nothing active to do, Bob worried more about Annabel being late for her date than what the doctor would say when he came back. If he had a say in the matter, he thought, he wished Annabel didn't have a date, and that her relationship with Dustin Lowe had not resurfaced.

Twenty minutes later, at the close of office hours, Dr. Raymond came back in. "I think I know your diagnosis," he said confidently, "but I don't think you'll be finishing your rotation. You need rest to gain back your strength and, based on clinical signs and symptoms, I will not withhold treatment to wait on confirmatory tests. I'm starting you on antibiotics."

Bob's shoulders sagged with the thought of being pulled from medicine. And did Dr. Raymond really know the diagnosis and treatment?

"Antibiotics for what?"

"Ehrlichiosis."

Bob squinted and shook his head. "I never heard of it. What is it?"

"You're carrying a disease caused by Ehrlichial bacteria, of which there are at least three species known to affect humans."

"Any ideas about how I got it?"

Dr. Raymond's wide chest heaved with a sigh. "From the bite of an infected tick. Specifically, the lone star tick."

Bob stared with disbelief. "This is crazy. What I mean is … I am not aware of being bitten by a tick. And don't they only come out in summer?"

Dr. Raymond sat on his stool. "Half of the infected people who develop Ehrlichiosis never find a tick on themselves and never remember being bitten. The victim can be clueless because the bite can be painless, the little bugger can be brushed off, or it falls off. But the damn tick takes a nip out of you. Not all ticks end up clinging onto human flesh like a rock climber to a summit."

Bob scratched his neck just thinking about the beastly little things. His eyes grew wide as he sensed a strong deja vu.

"Wait a minute. I mentioned a recent run. I did a stupid thing and sat down on the ground - right against tall weeds along an embankment down by the river. I remember being itchy with something bugging me on my upper back, behind my right shoulder."

Dr. Raymond grinned. "I bet the weather was unseasonably mild too."

Bob rolled his eyes and nodded. "I guess my fortunate luck finally failed me."

"Not yet. We're going to get a handle on this before you suffer a more severe course with life-threatening symptoms. Or a prolongation which requires hospitalization and IV antibiotics. There is even up to a 2% fatality rate with this disease."

"Dr. Raymond, you're scaring me to death. What did my lab work show?"

"I made you a copy." He handed over the CBC with a differential and all the chemistries.

Bob scanned it with dismay, and reread it again.

"Thrombocytopenia, leukopenia, and elevated LFTs," Dr. Raymond said. "Classic, especially that deplorable platelet count, in the context of everything else."

"Only if someone smart and perceptive like you puts this whole clinical picture together," Bob acknowledged. "I can't believe these numbers are mine. What antibiotics do you suggest? And will it be a definitive treatment?"

"The first line of treatment is Doxycycline - for seven to fourteen days. I expect you'll start showing clinical improvement, but you may not be up to your old self for a few weeks. The stamina you need right now for the rest of your rotation will not exist."

"I can't believe this," Bob pouted.

"I took an extra vial of blood for specialized laboratory testing. Your immune system should be producing antibodies to Ehrlichia by now if that is what's streaming around in your circulatory system. Like I mentioned, my index of suspicion is high, so I will not withhold treatment. Also, by the way, Ehrlichia cannot even be detected by blood cultures."

A shudder ran up Bob's spine. The more Dr. Raymond talked, the more he wanted to purge himself of the awful bacteria zipping through his bloodstream.

"Thank you," Bob said, "for your help. I'm fortunate I came in to see you. I better not take up any more of your time."

"No problem." He tapped Bob's chart in his hand and opened the door as Bob stepped down.

The front office was quiet as most of his staff had left. "By the way," Dr. Raymond said, "you are correct. I see one or two Ehrlichiosis cases a year and they show up in June and July. However, cases do pop up during any month of the year, especially with the slow northern progression of this tick population from the southeastern and southcentral United States. Due to global warming."

Bob nodded while clutching the lab results.

"Make a follow-up appointment in a week," the doctor said and poked his head into the front office window. "You two ladies leave when you've checked out Bob Palmer. I'm going back to my office. I need to contact the CDC with a reportable case of Ehrlichiosis and confirm it when the remaining labwork comes back."

Annabel paced the office waiting room after sitting too long. Finally, Bob came out and he tried to force a smile.

"Uh-oh," she said. "What did he tell you?"

Bob twisted his face with disapproval. "You know what a normal platelet count is, right?"

"Sure. 150 to 400 in the usual reference range units. Thrombocytopenia, a low platelet count, is less than 100. And susceptibility for hemorrhagic bleeding conditions is a count less than 50. Why?"

"My platelet count is 40."

"What! Are you serious?"

"No kidding." He handed her the yellow sheet with all his lab values. In dark capital letters next to his platelet count was the word "LOW."

"Oh no," she mumbled. "This is awful."

She handed the paper back to him and sank into a chair. "Don't bump into anything. You'll bruise or crack open your skin and bleed to death."

"I agree. Now is your opportunity to punch me, make me bleed like water from a hose, and get away with murder."

"I don't think so, and don't mention or even think about such a thing. Does he have any concrete suggestions about your diagnosis?"

"Ehrlichiosis."

"Ehrlicy what?"

"A disease caused by ticks."

"No way. Impossible."

"I thought the same thing, but I probably had one crawl into my shirt the day we went for a run. Down by the Ohio. From the weeds."

She shook her head, not wanting to believe it, and dragged out her *Internal Medicine Handbook.* After checking in the index, she shook her head more emphatically the second time. "Your disease isn't in our book."

"Ha! Because Ehrlichiosis is rare and doesn't make the cut for a standard student's textbook."

"I should say."

Annabel realized … she was the one who dragged him for a run. "This is partly my fault."

"No way. Shit happens."

"Only to me. Not you."

Bob pointed to the exit door, she stood up, and they ambled out.

"Is there a treatment?" she asked.

"Yes, doxycycline, but I'm not going to feel better overnight. I'm off the rotation for sure. However, I should still try and pass the final."

Annabel thought about it as they stopped in front of her car. "I can help you to the end. We can study the same stuff. Are you open to me half moving in with you? Crashing on your couch so I don't have to go back and forth?"

Bob raised his eyebrows. "That's too much to ask."

"No, really. It could work. I would even have available parking in your complex, so I don't have to call Uber to take me back and forth. We can pack in the studying and try and do better than Stuart. We just have to make sure you don't overdo it, take breaks, and get adequate rest and sleep. Look at it this way … it would help me focus too."

"Okay. I won't argue. When your mind is made up about something, I doubt if it will budge. Plus, I'd love your company."

"So the arrangement is settled. Let's go fill your prescription. Tomorrow the team's on call, so I won't be over until Thursday."

Annabel dropped Bob at his place after they stopped at the pharmacy and then she drove home to change for her date. She texted Dustin.

I'm running a half hour late. Sorry about that.

I'll pick you up. Not to worry.

See you soon, she replied.

Annabel looked on her bed, grateful she had already picked out what to wear. After slipping into a dark orange dress, she topped it off with a complementary matching brown jacket. She didn't spare the jewelry on two fingers, her wrist, and earlobes: all warm amber resin in silver settings. After applying a smidgeon of makeup, she brushed her hair and highlighted its shine with mousse.

Her seldom-used doorbell rang. Annabel slipped on flat brown shoes and opened the door. Dustin's head turned from looking down the staircase and he broke out into a smile.

"Don't you look fantastic."

"Nothing too special."

"On the contrary. You're glamorous no matter what you wear."

Annabel stepped out and they went single file down the stairs as Travis came up two steps at a time and stopped at his door.

"It's too early in the week for a date," Travis said as Annabel passed.

"Maybe so," she laughed. "But we're going to do it anyway."

"Have fun."

Downstairs, Dustin pointed down the block. "My Acura's around the corner."

She walked alongside him on the narrow sidewalk. "So what happened with the domestic abuse case the other day?"

"Edgar and I sometimes go back and forth to the same homes. For the same calls. For the same recurrent situations. We call them 'frequent flyers'; the domestic abuse is so routine. Last week was our third time going to that woman's home with three kids. After our second trip there, she got a restraining order against her ex, but some good that did. Apparently, however, he got locked up yesterday for another offense."

"At least you won't be making a fourth trip any time soon."

"So true."

Dustin opened the passenger door for her and they headed downtown. As he changed CDs, she thought ahead about the evening. She'd been so busy with the wards and with Bob that she had neglected to guess or fantasize about her date with Dustin. She absolutely liked him but failed to consider. Would they end up in bed together?

Neglecting to think about that possibility was not like her at all. Was medicine starting to rule her life? She deserved a social life on the side; maybe not as active as her Findar app past history, but certainly she needed a little hanky panky once in a while.

Dustin settled on a top country CD, which she also liked, but what was she going to do about later, if sleeping together came up as an option? It was already late enough to be going out to eat and she had a long call tomorrow. Staying up late would have repercussions for tomorrow. Yet, with all the dates the two of them had been on, they still hadn't bunked down together.

For the benefit of her medical education, getting to bed on time, and not rushing through sex with him, she thought, it would be best not to sleep with him tonight. On the other hand, they were overdue. Wasn't sexual compatibility and likability in bed important to find out about before investing more time with him? For sure, since meeting him, she'd grown to like him more and more, regardless of knowing if he was a good lover.

He hummed along with the music as he parked and then lightly steered her into the front door of a vibrant restaurant with short white tablecloths. They walked to the right of the head waiter and cash register. Dustin pulled out a chair for her and slid to the other side of the table, facing the entrance.

"Don't mind me," he said. "My background training and career puts me on alert all the time. I always take this side of a table … to observe people as they come in."

"To monitor for unusual situations or suspicious behavior?"

He nodded and she realized he had done the same thing when they went out before. They both took menus from a waitress and listened to her spiel on the jambalaya special of the day. The two of them smiled.

"What do you think?" he asked. "A little gumbo up front?"

"And share a big platter of jambalaya?"

"Sounds like a winner."

Dustin nodded his approval to the waitress for both items. She filled their glasses with ice water and left.

"How's your partner?" Annabel asked.

"Edgar's fine. I'll tell him you asked about him. He makes my job a lot easier and, I believe, a lot safer. We watch each other's back. I'm fortunate to work closely with someone I trust and get along with."

"He seems like a nice guy. It's that way with me and Bob Palmer, the medical student. He's been sick and missing some ward time, so, presently, there's an uncomfortable void for me."

"Hope he gets better. I suppose neither one of us can ever afford to be sick, especially you. What you do and the service you'll provide in the future doesn't leave room for you to be the patient."

"So true." Annabel picked up her glass for a toast.

"Would you like an alcoholic drink or wine instead?"

"No. I'm on call tomorrow and never drink before that long haul."

"Water it is, then." He clinked her glass. "To the beginning of the second part of our relationship ... with finer food, a more intimate conversation, and who knows?"

"Yes, to round two," she said with amusement in her eyes. "I think the dimple in your chin just turned mischievous."

As they became more engrossed in conversation and Dustin studied the people around them, the waitress returned with their dishes.

"I brought it all out at once," the waitress said. "Be careful. The dish is piping hot, so the food won't get cold anytime soon." She placed the jambalaya and gumbo in the middle of the table and two separate dinner plates in front of them. "Need anything else at the moment?"

"No," Dustin said. "Thanks."

Annabel used a big serving spoon to wiggle some of the rice dish onto her plate while being amused at the couples sitting at the table next to them, across the spacious aisle. The two middle-aged couples were eating their main course. One of the men kept joking; every few minutes the other three of them burst into laughter.

Annabel and Dustin glanced over and then smiled at each other. She tried the jambalaya and motioned up and down with her head.

"This jambalaya," she said, "makes me wonder how fantastic their beignets must be."

"Why don't we find out later? Take a few home to your place or my place?"

There it was, she thought, a clue for later, but lousy timing. "I'm sorry I delayed us this evening. If not tonight, then please, let's do a rain check next time. I'll even appoint myself the gopher and pick them up."

A shadow of disappointment crossed his face while one of the women at the adjoining table laughed at her husband's joke. Annabel glanced over. They were all shelling and eating shrimp topped with a generous helping of spices and herbs. The female's chuckle faded and it turned into a distressed cough.

The woman leaned forward over the red crustaceans and then suddenly stood. Her coughing turned into choking and, although she tried, she couldn't speak. Her hands went up above the collar of her blouse and tapped her throat. She was unable to take a breath. With a backward thrust of his chair, her spouse jumped up.

"Martha! Martha!" the man yelled.

The woman's face reddened.

Her husband stood stricken with panic, unable to move.

Annabel dropped her fork and scrambled out of her chair.

CHAPTER 19

As the commotion at the table next to Annabel and Dustin escalated, the restaurant staff and other customers in the restaurant glued their attention towards the woman holding her throat and her husband barking her name in panic.

Not a sound escaped from the middle-aged woman's vocal cords as she gave up trying to dislodge the shrimp hung up in her trachea. No one at the table did anything to render first aid, including her husband, who finally stopped yelling "Martha."

With four big steps, Annabel was beside the woman, who was shorter and heavier than Anabel's five-foot eight-inch slender build.

Martha signaled for help, her airway obstructed and suffocation an impending threat.

"Can I help?" Annabel asked, wanting permission before touching the woman.

The woman gestured, waving one hand towards her neck.

"Hurry," her husband yelled.

Annabel stepped behind her. Martha wore a checkered blouse tucked into a skirt, which made it easy for Annabel to wrap her arms around the woman's upper abdomen. She applied a sudden upward pressure without any luck.

On the second attempt, the woman's foreign object came spilling forth – a decent-size chunk of a curled shrimp.

Martha tried to regain her breathing back to normal as her husband put his arm on her upper back. "Are you all right?" he asked.

She gave him a slight nod and grabbed Annabel's hand, holding on to it like her life still depended on her. The head waiter stood behind the husband, waitresses paused nearby, and all customers had their eyes planted on the victim and Annabel.

Martha squeezed Annabel's hand.

"Why don't you sit down?" Annabel guided her into her previous chair and crouched down.

The woman sat, cleared her throat again, and took a deep breath. "Thank you. What would I have done without you? What's your name?"

Dustin watched the alarming scenario unfold at the restaurant table next to him. He wondered about the poor woman customer's outcome because her situation grew worse; he feared she could become unconscious if her airway obstruction continued.

His apprehension diminished when Annabel scooted over and began assisting her. Martha's husband and the other couple at their table appreciated her presence; they made space for her to perform a Heimlich maneuver.

He decided to stay put as folks gathered nearby to gawk while other customers stayed at their tables. The manager left the cash register at the front entrance and stood close, mouth open with concern. Past the manager's and maitre d's high-top desk, the men's bathroom door opened and a man in his early twenties exited.

The man wore a simple blue T-shirt and brown jeans and stepped gingerly while observing the developing commotion. He did not go back to his spot at the bar. Instead, he eyed the entrance area, devoid of staff or customers.

The young man slinked slowly towards the cash register. His eyes scanned the restaurant area where Dustin sat and Annabel performed her medical student magic. Dustin shifted his gaze towards the medical emergency and then quickly looked back.

The young man now had his back to the front window, and he had the front drawer of the register open. From the side, his hand paused over it and then it sneakily inched in and pulled out bills.

Dustin did the same thing as Annabel had done and scurried out of his chair. His long legs took him past another two tables, no one giving him a second glance, and he ended up abutting the tall desktop at the front entrance.

Without any forewarning, and with the element of surprise, Dustin grabbed the young man's hand. In the palm of his hand, the man's fingers clasped large denomination bills, which had been stored underneath the register's main money compartment.

"I bet you don't work here," Dustin said.

"Mind your own business," the fellow retorted.

"What's going on here?" the manager asked, stepping back to his post.

"You have a robbery in progress," Dustin said. "I'm an off-duty policeman, so I'm calling my station."

The manager took a step back. "Two incidents at the same time. This is disruptive for business. If I'm ever going to have a heart attack, now's the time."

"I strongly advise you not to do that. My date's got her hands full at the moment."

Dustin put his hand on the young man's shoulder, signaling for him to sit on the bench where customers waited. He took the cash out of his hand, counted it in front of the manager, and handed it to him. He scanned the front entrance and was relieved to find security cameras.

"You're busted," Dustin said. He pulled out his cell and called his local station to report the crime.

At the Heimlich maneuver table, Annabel gave reassurance to her newfound patient after she was sure the woman was clear of any breathing difficulty.

"Even though you may be in the clear," Annabel said to Martha, "I think you should seek medical care before going home ... to make sure you have no residual physical damage to your throat or airway."

Martha stared into her eyes and nodded. "You saved my life, young lady. How can I repay you?"

"By having a doctor check you out and look down your throat. Okay?"

"Do you have medical experience?" the husband asked.

"Kind of. I'm a medical student, in my third year."

"Thank God you were here."

The manager abruptly turned, several other customers shifted their gaze to the entrance, and Annabel also looked over. A situation had developed and Dustin seemed to be in the thick of it.

She wondered what he was doing. Were they both practicing extracurricular work duties when they should be enjoying their time together?

A cop car with bright swirling lights came by and stopped out front. When two uniformed officers came in, they greeted Dustin and made out a report. Dustin relayed the robbery he witnessed while everyone else's attention had focused on the choking customer. The manager mentioned the doorway security camera and the thief decided not to plead his innocence.

"So this is how you spend your off-duty time?" the older officer asked Dustin with a grin.

Dustin shrugged. "I wish not. In essence, I'm on a date."

Annabel walked up with the Heimlich-maneuvered customer and her husband. The woman turned and gave Annabel a slight hug and her husband grabbed her hand and gave it a kiss.

"Thank you again," they both said in unison.

"I'm taking her to the hospital on our way home," the man added, "so she can be checked out like you suggested."

"Good luck." Annabel turned to Dustin and tilted her head. "What on earth is going on here?"

"There was a little thievery going on while you were expelling crustacean exoskeletons from a lady's windpipe. Meet Officers Trent and Billows."

"Hello. Nice to meet you."

"Likewise," Trent said. "Can't say I've ever seen or heard of such an intriguing date. Are you two always this fascinating?"

Annabel laughed. "Come to think about it, we do seem to attract trouble."

Trent shook his head and tapped his fist into Dustin's arm. His partner grabbed the man wearing the T-shirt and escorted him out the door.

"Stupid ass mothafucka," the thief mumbled.

"What did you say?" the officer said as the door closed behind them.

"We'll call any of you if we need more information later," Trent said. He tipped his head at the manager, followed Billows out to the car, and hit the stealer in the back of his head for his foul language.

Annabel and Dustin headed back to their table to their food, which was now cold. The manager was on their heels.

"We'll take this away," the manager said, "and serve you again. Needless to say, your dinner is on the house, and order whatever you'd like. That is the least I can do. I can't repay you both enough for your Good Samaritan service tonight in our restaurant."

"How about a once-a-week coupon for twelve months for a free dessert?" Annabel suggested.

The manager nodded emphatically, happy to get off so easy.

"I guess that takes care of our beignets for tonight," Dustin said. "Should we keep our same entrees and let the kitchen staff warm them back up?"

"Yes, for sure."

The manager took the jambalaya and gumbo away while the friends of the departing couple from the next table got up and came over. They stood in the aisle.

"We appreciate what you did for our friend," the man said to Annabel. "We were scared to death that she was going to fall on the floor and choke to death. I thought about slapping her in the back, but that wouldn't have helped like what you did. Can we buy you a drink?"

The couple lingered and the man nodded at the empty spaces at their table.

Annabel shook her head. "No thank you, but I appreciate the offer."

"Where did you learn to do that?" the woman asked.

Annabel stole a glance at Dustin. He furrowed his forehead, waiting for them to leave like she was.

"An instructor talked about it in a CPR class I took," she said, not divulging that she was a medical student.

"I thought you were a nurse or something."

Annabel shook her head.

The manager, with a waiter, stepped alongside them and set down their food, including an extra dish of mixed stir-fried vegetables. "You both must be hungry and overdue for dinner," the first man said.

Two bearded old timers left another nearby table and also stopped. "It was befitting to see two youngsters stepping forward to render help tonight," one of them said. "It's been two counting decades since I'd seen that with my own eyes."

"Here." The waiter grinded seasoning over one of the platters. "Some extra Cajun flavoring." He stuck the bottle back in his apron.

The second old man scrutinized Dustin. "You be in the military like I was?"

"I bet he is," the man with his wife said.

"No," Dustin said. "Although I would be proud to serve if the need arose." He glanced at Annabel and then at the food. She raised her eyebrows.

"Actually," Dustin said to the waiter, "we need to be somewhere else. Would you mind packing up our food?"

The waiter scrambled to bus the platters to the kitchen. "Don't be late on our account," the manager said. "We hope to see you again soon too."

The first old man licked his lips. "Your mouths are gonna water for more once you savor that stuff."

Two waiters came back this time with a paper bag stuffed with Styrofoam containers. Dustin wrapped his hand around the handle and they both rose. "Sure I don't owe you anything?"

"No, no, no," the manager said.

The cluster of customers still managed to be dead weights next to their table and Annabel and Dustin peeled around them. They picked up their pace as they neared the front door.

Outside, as they piled into Dustin's black Acura, Annabel burst out laughing. Dustin raised his eyebrows as he put the key in the ignition.

"We sabotaged our own date!" Dustin exclaimed.

"I'm to blame."

"You can't help saving someone's life."

"And you can't help sticking your nose into police work." She continued to chuckle and had to clear a happy tear from her eye.

"Maybe she would have been all right," he said, "after her husband pounded on her back."

"I don't know. Choking is the fourth leading cause of unintentional death. I wasn't going to feign stupidity and watch that unfold."

"Did they take your name and number? Are they going to send you a reward?"

"I wish. You fared better with our free dinners."

"And you sabotaged us with free dessert for a year." He smiled over at her. "I guess that means we're strapped to each other for twelve months."

"Hmm. It will depend on how tasty those beignets are."

He rolled his eyes. "Where are we headed to eat our dinner? Your place or mine?"

"I'm on call tomorrow. If it's okay with you, let's go to mine."

"You bet."

A half-moon graced the night sky as Annabel and Dustin walked two blocks over to her place after they parked. They held hands and still joked about their evening. They argued in jest over whether it was a failed dinner or not. It depended on how they looked at it.

Annabel put her finger to her lips as they passed Travis's door on the second floor. Inside her apartment, she grabbed dinner plates from a cabinet while he pulled the containers out of the shopping bag.

"My apartment is not exactly spacious for company," she said. "Although my sister has stayed here, I never entertain."

"You have more important things to do."

They both opened up the three larger containers. Annabel rested her hand on top of the last one.

"This must be dessert." She pried it open and they both grinned.

"I know you're dying to try one," he said. "You're one of those people who doesn't save the best for last."

He picked up a beignet with one hand and caught the powdered sugar with the other as he guided it to her lips.

She leaned forward and took a small bite. "Correct," she mumbled. "Tonight, the best is coming first."

He pulled a fraction of the doughy fritter for himself, letting it practically melt in his mouth.

"This is delicious," he exaggerated, "but you're going to taste better."

They leaned close and, as their mouths met, the powdered sugar on their lips dissolved from the kiss. Dustin's hand went behind her neck and Annabel's hand locked into the small of his back. With parted mouths, their tongues explored slowly ... then intensely.

Annabel felt a needed desire surge through her from her mouth, to her breasts, to between her thighs. She hung on to every passionate kiss like she couldn't get enough. Dustin did the same as they stepped around the stool in their way, and the bulge in his trousers grew against her.

He picked her up. "Where to?" he asked.

She pointed to the other room and their mouths joined again. Dustin carried her inside where they toppled onto her bed.

CHAPTER 20

Annabel and Dustin's clothes were strewn on the floor and the bottom of the bed. She propped herself up on her right elbow and laid her hand on his bare chest.

Dustin shifted his eyes toward her. "I heard somewhere that sex can be satiating."

"We just proved it. You wore me out. I don't know if my legs are going to work tomorrow."

He inhaled a deep breath. "Me too. I better be stuck in the patrol car most of the day."

"I won't be so lucky. I'm on my feet most of the time." She tapped his lower lip. "Should we eat our dinner? Then I better go to sleep."

"Sure." He gave her a kiss and walked straight to the bathroom while she enjoyed the view. She rolled off the bed, threw on a T-shirt, and scooped Cajun food on two plates. Dustin dressed and came out while the microwave beeped.

"Just enough to quench our appetite," she said, taking out the second plate. "I'm going to appreciate the leftovers too." She put the Styrofoam containers in the fridge and soon they polished off their food.

Annabel grabbed her cell phone. "I'm arranging an Uber drive for the morning."

"I hope you're not cursing me out tomorrow for sabotaging your needed sleep tonight."

"On the contrary, I'm going to be smiling all day thinking about both aspects of tonight."

He carried their dishes over to the sink. "One of these days, I'll make dinner for you. I'm not too bad of a cook."

She used the app while watching him clean the dishes. He wiped his hands on a towel and motioned her up off the stool. "Get to bed. Save more lives tomorrow."

They kissed tenderly and he was out the door. She scrambled into bed. As she turned to get comfortable, she realized she had never invited a man to her own bed before. There was a first time for everything and it had definitely been worth the wait.

Hours later, after her trip to the hospital, Annabel hunted around the cabinets in the ICU for the tallest cup she could find. She found a small stash of sixteen-ounce cups in a drawer and pulled one out. Although feeling guilty for taking so much of the unit's hot coffee, she poured as much as she could and left a little room for cream. It went down smooth and velvety, and she told herself the caffeine would succeed in making her alert for morning rounds.

She also tried to wipe the silly grin off her face – the "morning-after glow" or the "I just got laid look." She was glad that Bob was currently absent because she bet he would sense her elation and question the hell out of her.

Annabel put the half-finished cup and Jae Nixon's chart next to each other on the main desk and went into his room. Even though she was only in her first year of clinical rotations, a pattern was beginning to develop. Jae wasn't her first ICU patient; the ability to anticipate a patient's needs and problems was beginning to form. His baseline blood pressures trended lower than before and his heart rate a little higher. Urine output was also less robust. Like usual, she admired his tattoo, and then examined the rest of his arm. His IV probably needed changing, and if that were the case, a larger one should replace it.

After listening to Jae's heart and lungs, she walked back to the desk where Dr. Enno flipped through his chart. The infectious disease consultant was seeing her consults earlier than her own attending and chief resident made rounds.

How could the senescent woman be that dedicated, interested, and attuned to her patients and the world of medicine and manage such long hours? She shook her head. Shouldn't the woman be retired and lounging on a cruise deck overlooking the mighty blue ocean where she could watch dolphins cascading further out from the perimeter of a ship's hull?

Annabel wrapped her hand around Alejandro to move it out of the way and sat down. The cane felt comfortable and polished, so she lingered her fingers on the bend of the handle.

"Good morning, Dr. Tilson. One of our results is back on Mr. Nixon."

Annabel wondered if it was the HIV test. Medical students were the ones who scooted around the hospital and found results faster than anyone else, but not so with Shania Enno.

"He is HIV negative," Dr. Enno said. She patted the shaft of Alejandro like she was petting a dog. "If Nixon's HIV status was positive, I would be sitting here telling you my next teaching points."

"Will you tell me anyway?"

"Of course. What would be essential is that we estimate our patient's level of immunodeficiency with a CD4 or T4 cell count. Normal adult levels range from 600 to 1500 cells per cubic millimeter. When levels decline to less than 500, the immune function of patients is compromised, and they become more and more susceptible to obscure and rare infections.

"The clinically sneaky part of HIV is that seventy percent of patients remain asymptomatic, the disease undergoing up to a ten-year latent period before they are clinically immunocompromised."

"What about the other thirty percent?" Annabel asked.

"They present with a sudden, acute HIV syndrome, which is one consideration I had for Jae Nixon."

Annabel nodded, trying to commit the information to memory.

"I'll leave a note for your team, but tell your chief on rounds that our patient is HIV negative." She grabbed a progress note sheet and began writing with her slow hand as Annabel held Alejandro.

The cane had been with the old woman to diverse medical settings over the years and Annabel wondered if it was a physical substitute for a meditation mantra. She eyed the woman's pulled back gray and black peppered bun. She didn't have a doubt that the woman practiced meditation – most likely the reason for the tranquility which spilled out of Dr. Enno like crystal clear water flowing through a mountain pass.

Donn leaned against the desk, his unused newspaper folded behind him, as he waited for the last of the team to trickle into the office. Since finding out about the Meagan Helm lawsuit, he had not read to the team from his paper. Annabel missed that aspect of their morning routine. She never had time to read like that and she only saw highlights about current events when they popped up on her iPhone. The state-by-state information that Donn usually relayed to them on a daily basis was news she never heard of anywhere else.

Annabel sat between Melody and Chineka on the couch. She was still on a high, or a drunken stupor, from being with Dustin only ten hours ago.

The entire evening's tryst with him was difficult to forget. She took a deep sigh and Melody gave her a questioning glance.

Jordan arrived, oblivious that Dr. Schott was waiting for him.

"I thought you'd be here first," Donn said. "Without a cell phone, you have no distraction inhibiting you from performing your clinical duties. Unless, of course, you already bought a new one."

Jordan twisted his mouth. "I'm picking one out tomorrow after call."

"Great. I hope they sell you a lemon." Donn shifted his gaze to Annabel. "What did you and Bob find out at Dr. Raymond's office?"

"He is sicker than either of us imagined. His platelet count is 40!"

Donn's eyebrows shot up. "How in tarnation? What does he have?"

Feeling giddy and mischievous, Annabel looked at Jordan.

"What are you looking at him for?" Donn asked.

"I thought since he diagnosed Jae Nixon with Leptospirosis, he still thinks of himself as a genius and is ready to diagnose Bob."

"But he was dead wrong."

"Exactly. Maybe he can redeem himself."

Jordan's eyes narrowed in anger as he backed up against the book shelf. "I don't know his symptoms like you do."

"Annabel," Dr. Schott said, "even if he did, I would no longer give Jordan the benefit of the doubt. What did Dr. Raymond say?"

"He has Ehrlichiosis."

Donn scratched his beard. "I read about that months ago from an article in an internal medicine journal." He looked at the residents. "What about you two?"

Chineka and Melody shook their heads.

"Dr. Tilson," Donn went on, "I must make other announcements, but sometime on rounds, you are going to teach us a thing or two about Bob's diagnosis. We're on call today, so let's look sharp and ready. We also have clinic hours this afternoon. You students will take all guidance from the residents and Dr. Mejia, if he shows up. I'll be gone early this afternoon for a deposition. Time consuming legal matters have begun." He lowered his eyes to the floor.

Before they trotted into the unit, Dr. Schott gathered the team next to the panoramic window of the empty ICU waiting area.

"Tell us everything you know, Dr. Tilson, about Bob's illness. I take it he's grounded for the rest of the rotation?"

"Yes," Annabel scowled. "But he plans on sitting for the final exam."

"I will let the department know. Now, tell me about Ehrlichiosis as if you are writing a succinct, one- or two-paragraph description. Cover all the basics like a pro."

Even though Donn's attitude was in a wad, Annabel thought, he still knew how to get them to think on their feet. She planned her description carefully.

"Ehrlichiosis is caused by bacteria. That bacteria is transmitted to a human by the bite of an infected tick and flu-like symptoms occur within one or two weeks of being bitten. In our country, there are about three different Ehrlichial species, but Bob's disease most likely came from the lonestar tick." She stopped to think about how to continue while all her team members stood stunned on hearing how he acquired it.

"Symptoms can include a fever, headache, fatigue, and muscle pain."

"Perhaps this disease is 'going around,'" Jordan boldly interrupted. "It could be the one affecting your ranger since he doesn't have Leptospirosis."

"Leptospirosis and Ehrlichiosis are both caused by bacteria," Annabel said, "but we already determined that bacteria are not the cause of Jae Nixon's illness or meningitis."

Donn nodded, pleased with Annabel's report and reasoning. "Give us a quickie on diagnosis and tell me what Dr. Raymond ordered for Bob's treatment."

"It seemed to me that a high index of suspicion for thinking outside the box was necessary for Dr. Raymond to consider this disease. Blood tests were necessary; thrombocytopenia, leukopenia, and high LFTs are usually present, which was the case with Bob. Further, special testing is used to detect the presence of antibodies against the disease and if it isn't correctly diagnosed, it can be fatal.

"We stopped on the way back to Bob's apartment yesterday and picked up Dr. Raymond's prescription for doxycycline and the serologic testing, the indirect immunofluorescence assay, is pending."

"Thank you," Donn said. "How Bob acquired this gem must be a mystery."

"We have an idea about that, sir."

"Rare diseases are often unexplainable." Donn said. "Which brings us to Mr. Nixon. Let's go into the unit."

Melody Burg stepped forward outside Jae Nixon's ICU room and gave the update on his medical condition, sparing Annabel being on the hook again.

"And his HIV result came back negative," Annabel added to Melody's summary. "Dr. Enno happened by earlier when I was here."

"What do you two think needs to be done with your patient today?" Donn asked.

"Continued and more supportive care," Dr. Burg said, "including a mild dopamine drip for his renal perfusion."

"Does he need a central line?" Annabel asked.

"Your peripheral IV skills have improved," Melody said and looked at Donn. "How about I guide Annabel through her first central line? I'll gown, glove, and step in to take over if needed."

Annabel's heart raced a couple of beats. She couldn't believe what Melody said. If Donn agreed, it would be her biggest procedure yet; something she didn't expect to do until she was a resident. She held her breath, waiting for Donn to make a decision.

"I'm not personally in a good mood to say 'yes,' but I can't take my attitude out on Annabel. Her skills and conscientiousness are noteworthy enough. The two of you put in a right subclavian line. However, do it before lunch and clinic so that if you have any doubts or need help, you can call me. I'm leaving around twelve. Plus, admissions will probably start rolling in later."

Annabel felt like yelling from a rooftop. Remarkable fortune was following her; maybe she needed to go out with the police officer and grasp Alejandro more often. "Thank you. I'll be careful and successful."

"Good luck," Stuart said. "I'm envious."

Donn motioned for the team to move on and Jordan and Annabel brought up the rear of the pack.

Jordan's mouth narrowed and his eyes glared at Annabel with resentment.

"Don't forget," Jordan said softly. "When you stick the needle in under his clavicle, the apex of his lung will be right there. That's a minor detail you slept through during gross anatomy. Don't puncture his lung and cause a pneumothorax."

Annabel wanted to smack him, but no way was she going to let him downgrade her elated mood.

"Jordan, you have your *entire* life to be a jerk. Why not take today off?"

CHAPTER 21

After rounds, Annabel and Dr. Burg grabbed a central line kit and other materials from the supply room.

"You're on," Melody said as she hastily began opening the kit on the tray table next to Jae's bed. Annabel took a deep breath but watched every move her resident made while the nurse turned Jae's head and breathing tube to the left.

"What are the two biggest contraindications to placing the central line?" Melody asked as she prepped Jae's upper chest area.

"An infection at or around the site," Annabel said, "and, for sure, a coagulopathy."

"That goes for many invasive procedures."

After they gowned, gloved, and masked, Melody showed Annabel how to prepare the contents of the kit. They did a more thorough prep, and applied a sterile drape.

"We're going to use a triple lumen catheter instead of one big bore line," Melody said. She ran her finger along Jae's clavicle, stopped, and demonstrated. "This is the best insertion point to try and hit the subclavian vein."

Annabel noted the landmarks, and with a finder needle, aspirated venous blood. After another needle and placement of the guidewire, she slipped in the triple lumen catheter and sutured it in place with Melody's constant supervision. Her sense of accomplishment soared. Jae Nixon needed the line for important medications and fluids and she had needed the experience. She could cross off another "first" in her training, she thought, and made sure, that the dressing went on properly and the needles went into the sharps container.

"What comes next?" Melody asked. "Super important after a central line."

"A chest X-ray. To make sure I didn't drop Mr. Nixon's right lung." Annabel thought about Jordan's snarky remark. It was apparent he wanted her to fail with her first ICU procedure.

"For sure," Melody said. "Especially for Mr. Nixon. An awake patient may exhibit symptoms and difficulty breathing, but Jae is on a ventilator and signs and symptoms of a pneumothorax could be camouflaged."

"After the film is taken, I'll follow up with it myself in the radiology department."

"If his lung looks fine, then we start him on dopamine for his renal perfusion." Dr. Burg walked away from the beeping monitors while slipping on her resident's jacket. "By the way," she said, "nice job."

"I had a good teacher."

After Melody left, Annabel grabbed her white coat and listened to Jae's lungs, which still sounded clear. She thought about her first encounter with the ranger at the sandwich shop. He was too young, healthy, and robust to be lying in an intensive care unit with a breathing tube jutting out of his mouth.

At least Dr. Enno had eliminated HIV as a cause, but was HSV out of the question as well? The acyclovir was doing nothing for him. Without any clinical improvement for Jae, the infectious disease specialist would probably stop it.

As she stood sadly looking at Jae's tattoo, she realized the team's efforts with supportive care were currently the basis of getting Jae through whatever had invaded his body. Even though they had no idea about the etiology of Mr. Nixon's sickness, their medical treatment was keeping him alive.

Annabel waited in the radiology department for Jae's chest X-ray and then stole it out of the "to be read" box. She rapped on the radiologist's door, hoping he wouldn't turn her away. She was becoming a pest.

The door to his long reading room opened. "It's you again."

"Sorry. I have a chest film on the same patient who had the CT a few days ago. I just did my first central line on him."

The radiologist stepped back to his chair while holding a sandwich.

"Sorry to disturb your lunch."

"No problem, young lady. I'll help out an exuberant medical student any time." He took the film out of her hands and slipped it into the viewing box. "No pneumothorax and you've done a fine job with placement." He pointed to the tip of the catheter down the subclavian vein.

Annabel looked carefully; there was no evidence of even a subtle pneumothorax. She broke out in a smile.

"This patient of yours, he's becoming more complicated, isn't he?"

"Yes. My rotation ends soon. I fear that he'll still be in the unit when I leave. I hope not."

The radiologist pulled down the film. "Throughout your training, patients will come and go like lightning. There is something to learn from every one of them. Since there are residents and an attending dealing with patients, it is the rare student that leaves a positive impression on a patient. Be that student."

Annabel gulped. "Thank you. I'll try." She softly closed the door behind her when she left and had a warm feeling of achievement.

Like the radiologist, Annabel grabbed lunch from the cafeteria. She hoped to eat it in clinic before or between seeing patients. First, she told Dr. Burg that Jae's chest X-ray was clear. Melody called the nurses to approve the use of the triple lumen catheter while Annabel unwrapped a chicken sandwich. She glanced at the first patient's chart and cringed.

"What's wrong?" Stuart asked, stepping next to her.

"May Oliver is here for an extra appointment."

Stuart crinkled his forehead.

"The metastases from her lung adenocarcinoma are spreading rapidly and we've done all we can for her."

"There's still palliative medicine," he said.

"So true. Jae Nixon's situation is the same. We're treating symptoms and not a diagnosis."

Stuart gave her rare eye contact. "By the way, how is Bob today? Have you two texted yet?"

"Not yet, but we have come up with a plan. I'm going to stay with him at his place, starting tomorrow. He's so wiped out, but I'll help him study."

"You are going above and beyond to help him out. If I can be of service, let me know. I'd be a wreck if I were him ... not finishing medicine right now."

"You're so smart, Stuart. You could handle anything."

"I may be test smart, but that doesn't mean I'm going to be the best clinician. You may outdo me with that."

Annabel waved his comment off with her hand and walked into May's exam room while peeking at the note on the chart. The reason for her visit

146

was "more coughing up blood."

Thirty-two-year-old May Oliver sat hunched over on the exam table while her mother, Louise, stood behind the black-topped upholstery. Annabel greeted them both, the obvious sadness on their faces making her dread talking to them. May's breaths were deep, her breathing labored.

"Here I am again," May said. "I'm so glad you're here."

Annabel gave her a sincere half-smile. "I see your primary lung symptom has returned."

"Yes. The hemoptysis. See ... I've learned the terminology for my own medical problems. That's how much time I've spent with doctors in all these past months." May's hand, frail and white as toothpaste, cupped Annabel's.

"I'm finished seeing the cancer doctor," she continued. "After treatments and the continuation of the brain and bone metastasis, I'm calling it all quits. I'm here for that reason. Not for you and your team to prescribe me antibiotics, or another bronchoscopy to stop the bleeding, or to put me in the hospital and pump in liquid nutrition."

Annabel gulped and glanced at May's mother. Louise fought to keep back a tear. May signaled for an emesis basin and Annabel handed her one from the counter. Her patient coughed up a wad of blood as well as green sputum.

"Let me listen to you," Annabel said. "It looks like you've caught a lung infection as well."

"I'm sure of it. Most likely pneumonia."

Annabel listened to the front and back of her noisy chest, which made her think of a death rattle. She clipped a pulse oximeter onto May's index finger and it registered ninety-two percent.

"May, you're not getting enough oxygen. You should really be in the hospital."

May shook her head as emphatically as she could ... which wasn't that much. Her eyes spoke for her. They enlarged and glared at Annabel.

"No."

Annabel pulled over the stool, sat down, and fought back sad emotions. She had been part of May's care team since she first showed up with her symptoms and was diagnosed. They'd shared similarities, including going through their pets' deaths, and now May was calling it quits.

Annabel could not fault her and decided not to try and change her mind.

May had been a trooper and had given trying to stay alive her best shot. It was time to let go and go out with grace, dignity, and acceptance of her final fate. Her adult life, at only thirty-two years old, had been full with a military deployment and as a manager of a coffee shop.

Annabel started to talk but had to stop and breathe deeply; the situation was anguishing. May's mother slid a tissue out of her purse and dabbed her eyes.

"Then what can we do for you?"

"I need to make it easier on my mom. I want to go back home and die there. Can you prescribe narcotics for me?"

Annabel faced her directly without judgment and kept silent as she thought about her request.

"Dr. Tilson, I do have some pain pills. Not enough. I'm being honest."

"And I appreciate that. Dr. Burg will be in here; this is not something we condone. However, did you contact hospice yet?"

May shook her head.

"You have the right to die pain-free, May, and with dignity. That's what hospice is all about. It would be perfect for you because of the limited time left for you. It is a team approach and those compassionate people will help both you and your mom and dad get through this. They can prescribe the correct pain medication dosages that you will require to be pain-free and comfortable. Spiritually, I also believe their care will be important."

Louise Oliver took her daughter's hand. "We did hear about it some time ago. All the doctors lately, however, focus on getting rid of May's metastases and symptoms, not on the actual end of life."

A small rap sounded on the door and Melody Burg entered. She glanced at all three of them. "You all appear gloomy and grave, but life can't be all that terrible. What brought you in, Mrs. Oliver?"

"Hemoptysis again," May said. "However, Dr. Tilson just addressed my concerns and wishes. I am going to leave now with my mother and don't want any other suggestions or care. May I please have a prescription to call on hospice care?"

"The pulse oximeter registers ninety-two percent," Annabel said, "and here are her vital signs." She gave Melody the chart. "And she finished all treatments suggested by the oncologists."

"Are you both sure?" Melody asked May and Louise.

"Yes," May said.

"Then we won't stand in your way. The prescription will be at the front desk on your way out."

Melody left, but Annabel lingered. Simultaneously, May and Annabel leaned forward and embraced.

"I'm so sorry," Annabel said, choking on her words.

"Don't be. The cycle of life is different for each of us."

As Annabel stood straight again, she nodded at Louise. If she looked again at May, she would not be able to contain her tears. She stepped out without glancing back and knew she'd never see the ninety-five-pound woman again.

Annabel carried a dinner tray to a cafeteria window table where Melody and Chineka sat with Stuart. Dr. Schott was close behind and they both took the end chairs.

"Thanks for breaking away at the same time," Donn said to everyone. "We can kill two birds with one stick. Talk about patients and get our meal over with."

Jordan appeared and nestled next to Donn. "Too bad we think of food that way – getting it over with."

"So true," Chineka said. "The only eating I ever really enjoy is outside of the hospital."

Annabel peeled the top bread slice off her sandwich and frowned. "This is supposed to be a BLT sandwich, but I need a microscope to see the lettuce. It's a good thing I ordered a side salad and cole slaw."

Donn imitated her frown. "These green beans are boiled down to mush. As the hours of the day increase, the food quality decreases."

"The food in the morning doesn't start out too palatable either," Stuart said.

"Food aside," Donn said, "how was clinic?"

"We survived," Melody said. "Everything was manageable, so we didn't need to call you. Better yet, how did your deposition go?"

"I hope that was my first and my last. Every word out of my mouth was typed by the reporter at the head of the table. It was nerve racking and most of the questions by the prosecuting attorney were accusatory, mean, and nasty."

"Sorry," Melody said. "We all think your treatment of Meagan Helm's atrial fibrillation was appropriate."

"Thanks. You know, hearing other docs say that is important to me. Otherwise, I'm really questioning what I did."

Annabel shook her head. "No way, Dr. Schott. You and Dr. Mejia give stellar care." She paused her fork. "By the way, May Oliver came in today and we referred her to hospice."

Donn grimaced and shook his head. "She's way too young, but you did the right thing. And how did Jae Nixon's central line go?"

"Annabel nailed it," Melody said with a smile.

"I'm glad to hear that. I'm going through a crisis and I appreciate a team that doesn't need to be micromanaged."

CHAPTER 22

Jae Nixon's experience lying in the ICU bed with something painful in his throat wasn't always the same.

He had no idea how long he'd been in the present situation. It seemed like such an incredibly lengthy amount of time that sometimes he thought this was his whole life. Sometimes he couldn't even tell if the visions in his head were fake dreams; made up for his entertainment.

Maybe the main character in them wasn't really him; maybe he had not experienced the events depicted in his concocted mirages.

Overall, when spotty segments of lucidness crept into his brain, he wrapped his mind around the fact that he was in some kind of a medical situation and that the events which rolled across his thoughts were like some kind of YouTube video and were indeed a segment of his past.

Maybe the streaming content had some significance, but it remained difficult to figure out or to make sense of it at some higher brain level.

Was he being drugged? Or experimented on? Like right now ... three women in pale blue cotton outfits busied themselves around him. One of them tilted his head to the side, which made the hard thing in his throat get slightly yanked. That hurt.

It became more difficult to see the other two as they poked around in a container on the tray table. One of the young women seemed more familiar to him. For some reason, her fingers slid along his right collarbone while the other woman did most of the talking.

Ouch, he thought as he felt pressure and pain where she stopped moving her fingers on his right upper chest. She forced something into his skin. Why were they torturing him? He wished he wasn't having one of his rare mentally clearer moments; he could do without this. He tried to divert his brain to something else and not be with them in the present.

Jae drifted further into himself. A combination of past knowledge, events, and situations formed in his brain. In certain clumps of time while the two women hovered immensely close to him, he travelled deeper into his mind with more intelligible knowledge about who he was and what he did. He replayed recent events from his past:

Hunting was one of Jae's passions outside of his work as a national park ranger. For him, it combined multiple purposes into one. His deer hunting with a bow and arrow was a substantial and skillful sport and the whole ordeal took place out in nature, where he felt most at home.

Of course, he never overhunted for venison he wouldn't eat; hunting let him put his own needed food on the table. None of the venison went to waste. At times, hunting deer also helped cull the species population when officials determined their density in an area had become too thick.

Jae was super methodical with his gear checklist. He stood on his wooden porch between the front door of his cabin and his Silverado, which he'd backed up to the front step. He was ready to begin his arduous process.

He considered his checklist the forerunner to packing every possible piece of essential gear. As he well knew, there was nothing worse than getting out to a deer stand and realizing he'd forgotten an important knife, or a deer scent, or God forbid, water. In his opinion, being unprepared was a sign of an immature, half-cocked, impulsive hunter. For him, those days were gone.

Besides, this was the very end of the deer hunting season and he depended on his empty freezer space being filled with venison for the rest of the winter after this trip. He could taste it now, and, no matter how he prepared it, he enjoyed what he thought of as his "man meal."

Already dressed out in his hunting boots and insulated parka, he checked off his stacked items and carried them, stored or un-stored in gear bags, to his pick-up truck. The big stuff went in the back cargo area. He packed the smaller items, such as binoculars, a compass, and flashlight, on the seat and floor of the cab.

Jae double-checked his archery equipment in the pickup bed. Present and accounted for, he thought. He locked his cabin door, strolled over to Patty's place, and petted Curley and Twist, who had already come out to seek the fresh air. He beamed when she opened the door. She woke earlier than usual because she told him to stop by before leaving.

"I'm out of here before dawn like I planned," he said. "I'll be back no later than late afternoon. If you don't see me cruise in by then, send out the cavalry. I'll try not to be grumpy at work next week if I wasn't successful and have nothing to show."

"You'll be fine. I have faith in you." Dressed for work, she held a mug of coffee. "Need a cup for the road?"

"Thanks for asking. I'm good." He turned and waved like a kid going off to summer camp.

Because Jae followed a dependable protocol, he was a successful bowhunter. Prior to this late-in-the-season expedition, he had scouted out his hunting area in the woods early and often.

He was no amateur.

He practiced archery often and simulated real conditions by outfitting himself fully in the heavy gear he used during a real hunt. The dry run imitated military boot camp ... you had to practice in ungodly simulated conditions to be effective on the real battlefield.

As Jae drove the last back road into his hunting area, he smiled. He exuded confidence because of his preparedness; not one hunter he knew studied the habits and life cycle of these whitetails like he did. Their movements and body language were as familiar to him as a nursing baby to a mother.

When Jae arrived, he was well prepared in the woods as far as his tree stand placement because he had previously trimmed necessary branches from a few trees. It assured a clearer view from his stand of certain lanes where the deer travelled. That needed to be done beforehand, otherwise, the whitetails would know something had changed and be leery to pass through or around the area. Deer were cleverer than most humans gave them credit for.

As he positioned himself by six a.m., he also grinned because he had not over hunted before from his perch. Since his last visit, his scent was long gone.

Now it was time to outsmart the wind, play it to his favor. He calculated the wind direction and made sure he was outwitting the olfactory glands of any whitetails in his effective kill range, which for him was twenty-five yards.

He took a subtle deep breath, waited, and watched. Two grazing deer passed after two hours, but they strolled too far away from his comfortable range. He kept quiet and still and they never looked in his direction.

By mid-morning, Jae hit pay dirt. A mature buck ambled into his eyesight from the right and stopped. At this time of year, the animal's primary food item was browse plants; he stared as the buck's long tongue reached in between branches. It grabbed twigs and stems and chomped on the nutritious treats as he then made slow progress forward.

Jae's crossbow was loaded, arrow ready. No obstacles stood in the way between him and his prey.

He held his breath. He waited for the exact moment. His shot would count.

With stringent accuracy, he pulled his "trigger." His deer didn't have time to move and Jae made the perfect shot.

At first, Jae approached the buck slowly and cautiously to make sure there was no life left to it; otherwise, he'd be the one to suffer the damaging consequences. The deer was dead; still dead.

He counted ten points on the antlers; each point was over one inch. He was legal and Jae had no problem regarding the bag limit because, for one thing, it was his first hunt for the new year.

He finally allowed himself a huge smile and a deep congratulatory breath. Next, he slipped out one of his two sharp knives.

Without puncturing any of the major internal organs, Jae began gutting his kill. He cut out the gastrointestinal tract and the liver, and then went on to the lungs and the heart. He did a thorough job of slicing out the windpipe.

After working up a sweat under his camouflage, he removed his parka and stared down at the mess all over the ground. A long-sleeved camo shirt was the only article left on his chest to now transport the buck to his vehicle, but he didn't care. With still so much to do, global warming made this winter day like a sunny day in paradise.

With the field dressing over with, he scouted out the cleanest path on the ground to drag the buck over to his Chevy so as to not dirty the meat any more than he should. After hoisting it up, he assembled the rest of his gear in the bed of the pickup truck as well as in the front cab.

Jae listened to country music on the drive back to his cabin at the national historic site, occasionally peering in the back as if pinching himself that he was going home with a blue-ribbon. Even Patty would be impressed with his success for one single morning. Of course, it was a payoff for all his previous careful planning.

A happy man, he pulled next to his cabin. He sprang out of his Silverado and first went inside to wash his hands after all the Purell he had rubbed into them.

After drinking a bottle of an energy drink and chewing on a granola bar, he went back out and began the job of hanging the buck on his meat pole between the cabin and the woods. Man-handling the large animal, its carcass and fur next to his body, was a primitive experience. It was a muscular workout as well and he enjoyed every minute of it.

His preferred method, Jae hung the deer with its head down. Strung high up enough, it was not at all close to the ground. After going back and forth to the shed for more equipment, Jae opened up the rib cage more thoroughly with a saw, propped open the space with a designated piece of wood, and then uncurled the long hose and dragged it over.

"Wow!"

Jae turned and there was Patty dressed in uniform, wearing a smile, and holding a small bag of peanuts.

"You are something else, Jae Nixon. Well done."

"Thank you. I try." He stood back and admired his work as well. After throwing a smile her way, he turned on the hose nozzle and began rinsing the deer's cavity. "He's going to be delicious and you'll be the second one to savor him after me."

"I can't wait. You process the only hunter's meat that I trust. You're so damn thorough and careful about stuff."

"Of course, you're being kind. I'm the only hunter you know."

Debris and blood rinsed out of the carcass, but Jae took a step forward to peer inside, particularly for any hair which may have found its way inside.

"This water will cool him down a little bit, too, besides washing him clean."

"I better get back to work," she said. "Just wanted to come over and say hello. Get some rest later."

"Thanks. Nothing like working on a day off ... doing what I adore doing."

She agreed and stepped away. The center was extra busy with tourists. Even the gift shop had folks browsing in every aisle.

With particular attention to the inside, Jae gave the carcass one more rinse. Then he again checked his knife for sharpness. It was time to skin the hide.

After hours and hours – after awakening and up until now - Jae was ready to put the big tasks behind him; ready to pamper his own body, which was spent, tired, and fulfilled. He had enough in one day of what he called his "love and labor of hunting."

Inside his cedar door, Jae went straight to the laundry room and peeled off his clothes. They went straight into the washing machine and he started a cycle with extra sudsy detergent.

Now, instead of clothes sticking like Band Aid adhesive on his skin, clean air swept over him, which made him feel that much more grubby. In his birthday suit, he padded to his bedroom and stepped straight into the bathroom. He opened the shower door, turned on the water to let it warm up, and slipped a bath towel in the door handle.

But before he made his decision to step in, Jae was aware of a new sensation. As if his leg smarted from the sting of nettles, he swiped his hand over the skin of his right ankle.

The prickly sensation didn't stop, so he looked down at the wispy hair on his lower leg and saw a dark diminutive creature crawling like a bulldozer up his shin.

Holy shit. He hated those things.

But he didn't *just* hate those things.

He hated them with such zeal, such intense fervor, that his panic against them was worse than if a rattlesnake threatened his hand.

It took at least a half a minute before Jae had the little monster between his thumb and forefinger. Its legs thrashed and yanked forward like there were a hundred of them instead of eight. And in his opinion, eight were too many, but at least that number helped distinguish them from insects … which only have six legs.

It was a tick.

And as Jae carried it over to the sink, the damn thing finally contorted its legs closer into the side of its body as if playing dead. He eyed a small glass bottle of cologne next to the sink and decided that would be his weapon.

He tried to drop the critter on the counter, but the thing clung to his finger like it was ready to eat his last meal. Jae harshly flicked it and it landed on the tile countertop.

He grabbed the bottle and rammed the bottom edge into the flat, dark body until he was satisfied he'd crushed the living life out of it. Being thorough, he knocked the little beast into the toilet bowl, pushed down the handle, and watched the swirling water pressure flush it into the depths of his underground septic tank.

CHAPTER 23

Annabel and Dr. Burg still hovered over Jae. From the medical team's perspective, they believed that Jae Nixon rested in an unconscious state, a medically diagnosed coma, which was true for the most part.

Especially during periods of stimulation, like now when the two women poked and prodded on him to insert a subclavian central line, he arose from his more profound mental sluggishness to replay or dream snippets from his recent past.

The ranger had replayed his entire last hunting expedition when he cross-bowed a ten-point buck and processed the deer where he made the kill. Then he lugged it home in his pickup truck and completed the arduous task of hanging, washing, and skinning the thing.

The most intense memory, however, was not the large hoofed mammal he'd bagged, but the tick no bigger than a pinhead crawling on his leg.

His thoughts continued onward as the student doctor sutured the central line into his skin and applied a dressing to ward off an infection. In a few minutes, a technician entered his room and they all helped to position him for a chest X-ray. He hated being moved, but by the time they all left, he was deeply involved again with hunting memories ... now post-hunting memories of getting ready to shower. His recollections about some events were as vivid as if he were inside a live reenactment.

Jae was still in his cabin's bathroom. After crushing and flushing the damn tick from his leg down the toilet bowl, he let out a sigh of relief. That was one arachnid he could have done without.

As much as he hated the thing, he loved seeing it whiz around in the swirling water and disappear into the bowels of the commode.

He backed away from the toilet bowl and stuck his hand into the shower stall where he had turned on the nozzle. The water temperature tested perfectly, so he stepped in. For what seemed like a magical eternity, he stood still and let the pure warm water flow on, and run off, his body. Like the buck he had just rinsed off with the hose, grime, dirt, and hair became dislodged and ran off him into the circular drain.

Now he needed to focus on the significant impurities clinging to his body.

He picked up his man soap from the resin soap dish mounted in the wall and scrubbed and lathered his hands. His legs came next because he wanted to wash off the physical, as well as the mental, idea of the tick who had just darted up his right leg a few minutes ago.

After he lathered below his knees, and his legs felt reborn, he again took the cleanser and massaged the bar of soap into his thighs. He took a moment to let the dirty water runoff and away.

Still holding the musk-scented soap, Jae washed his penis, scrotum, and the generalized region of his crotch. He clutched the soap tightly while he pressed laterally toward his right hip.

But starting out from his groin, he could swear his fingers swiped over a bump.

He lowered his head, dropped the bar of soap, and parted the dark pubic hair obscuring his view.

"Fuck!"

It was another tick.

Worse than that, it was attached.

Which made sense.

Just like Jae had hunted in a likely area where he caught venison for his next meals, the tick had burrowed in a warm, moist area of Jae's body where he hid as obscure and covert as he had lived in the foliage of the Ohio forest. After all, he wanted a meal as well.

Jae's anger, as well as his fear, ramped up along with his heartbeat. He turned off the water and tried to quell his rapid pulse. The little buggers carried diseases, but he guessed the odds for contracting one with one bite from one tick was probably low.

It was the tick itself and now it's vampire-like duty of sucking his blood that repulsed him. The parasite had sought him out - a warm-blooded vertebrate – to dine and feed on to continue his life cycle.

He grabbed the flattened, tear-shaped body and pulled.

But for fear of its own life, the tick held on with a death grip.

The blooksucker had drilled too far into his flesh!

Between Jae's thumb and index finger was only a part of him - a dark brown remnant of his butt end.

The tick's snout was still gripped in a jaw lock ... sucking near the vein running through Jae's private parts. Maybe even a vein or an artery to or from his penis which helped sustain the reproductive act. What horrors!

Wanting to get the ravenous head out of him immediately, Jae stepped out of the shower and over to the countertop. Right to where he'd just taken care of the first tick, which he'd found before it had latched on. He opened the top drawer and grabbed a pair of tweezers. Enough of the arachnid still sucked on him for the tweezers to hold on to, but pulling outward didn't work.

Jae's strong anger continued.

He could fell a buck, but he couldn't extract a tick.

From the same drawer, he pulled out a plastic container of petroleum jelly. He dried his groin thoroughly and then put a clump of the Vaseline on what was left of the protruding beast. That'd smother it and lubricate it, he'd read, making it easier to extract.

As a hunter, it wasn't like he never had them crawl on him before, but those experiences with them was one reason he hated them so much. They were unnerving sons of bitches and he didn't want even one encounter with them. It was, however, a rare event for one to make himself, or herself, at home and become one with his body.

The sun set as Jae tidied up the front seat of his pickup truck. This was the easy and last task of the day – gathering and disposing of wrappers, napkins, and a portable to-go cup – and giving the floor carpet a light vacuuming. He needed to go to bed soon and, undoubtedly, he would sleep like a baby.

Better yet, maybe he'd sleep like a torpid bear. Especially since he had finally tugged out the tick's head with tweezers after lubricating it for an hour with petroleum jelly.

He shoved closed the driver's door as Patty came walking home from the visitors' center.

"What are you still doing out here?" she asked.

Jae shook his head. "I'm a glutton for punishment, but I'm done. Finished. I'm going inside and will be sleeping before Curley and Twist decide who they're going to spend the night with."

"Here they come," she said, upon seeing the two dogs jump up when they heard their names.

"I found two ticks on me while showering," Jae added. "I practiced surgery to carve one of them out of me."

Patty shuddered. "Really?"

"I'm exaggerating. It took patience and tweezers to get the job done."

"I don't know of any rangers coming down with Lyme disease, but there's always a first time for everything. Please be careful."

Jae nodded and ruffled Curley's ears. "Goes without saying. You watch it around here, too."

They both took a few steps in the same direction with the dogs sprinting in front.

"I'll walk the trails in the morning before opening up the visitor's center," Jae said. "Have a good night."

"Congrats again on your catch."

The two dogs split up. Curley jumped onto Jae's porch and Twist sprang ahead of Patty.

Exhausted, Jae went inside and fell into bed. Curley curled up on the washed-out bedspread at the foot of his bed.

With Bob physically out of the internal medicine rotation, Annabel, Stuart, and Jordan theoretically picked up his admissions. Their call night was busier than usual and Annabel ended up with two new patients.

That meant she never slept. At two a.m., it seemed like she would get to bed, but they called her back immediately to the E.R. before her head hit the pillow. The middle-of-the-nighter was a ninety-seven-year old who had tripped over his cat on his way back from the bathroom. EMS brought him in for evaluation. Not only did the residents want to monitor him for any adverse sequela, but they discovered his diuretic dose needed an adjustment.

Fortunate for the team, Dr. Mejia didn't show up for group rounds in the morning. No one wanted his extra teaching after a sleepless night.

After the group dispersed and all the scut work for her floor patients was finished, Annabel went back to the ICU. She poured a jumbo cup of coffee and stumbled on a bottle of white chocolate syrup behind the regular creamers. It dressed up her coffee as well as a name-brand coffeehouse would do, and the caffeine perked her up enough to step into Jae's room and reconsider his condition.

The nursing staff now used the central line which Melody and she had inserted. Fluids flowed into one port and a low-dose dopamine infusion was plugged into another. His urine output had picked up and his lungs were still sounding clear.

Annabel remained at the side of his bed as his lungs went up and down with the ventilator. She patted his tattoo and, since no one was around, she spoke softly.

"The time has come to roust yourself awake and recover. I'm leaving the rotation soon, so I won't be helping with your care anymore."

Annabel frowned as she went back to the desk. It made no sense to whisper to Jae, but she had done it anyway. She retrieved her unfinished coffee and went home.

At least home was where she instructed the Uber driver to bring her.

She stumbled into her apartment after the ride, and with all the energy she could muster, she unpacked from call and repacked to go over to Bob's. Desperately, she wanted to wrap herself under her covers, but a promise was a promise. She told herself that he needed her more than she needed her bed.

Although it took longer than she wanted, by mid-afternoon, she was ready to drive over to Bob's. With one more important mission to do, she opened her refrigerator door.

The cool air filtered out while she scoured the shelves. She put the remaining food from her date with Dustin in a brown shopping bag and added more things. Since she planned on being mostly gone for at least a few days, there was no reason to let leftovers go to waste.

Annabel planned on two trips to her car. She needed to bring clothes, toiletries, medical books and instruments, food, power cords, and her laptop. She set out and took extra care walking the bumpy sidewalk with her arms full.

"You moving out?" Travis asked, passing her on the street. A small backpack hung around his shoulders. Coming from his college classes, he carried far less than Annabel.

"No," she said. "I'm too attached to that place. I have a quiet neighbor downstairs and I wouldn't trade that in for the world."

"Flattery will get you everywhere."

"Actually, I'm going to stay at my friend's place for a few days. He's sick, so I'm going to watch over him as well as help him study."

"Sounds platonic, but that's none of my business."

"He's my best friend."

"You need some help?"

"Would you? I'm struggling with no sleep. You'd be a lifesaver."

"It's not every day I rescue a doctor-to-be."

Annabel transferred an armload to him and they walked to her car.

"I'll keep an eye on your place," Travis said after he placed two duffel bags in her trunk.

"Thanks so much." She opened the Nissan's front door and hesitated. "Would you mind? Perhaps we should have each other's number."

"Good idea."

They exchanged numbers and Annabel took off. Since the morning, the gray day had turned cloudless and she soaked in the sun's rays through the windshield as she drove.

After parking, Annabel walked a short distance to Bob's apartment and appreciated that he lived on the ground floor. She rang the bell twice and he opened the door after a delay. His usual stylish haircut looked less perfect and a puffiness had grown under his eyes.

"You look like something a cat dragged over," he said.

"I was going to say the same thing about you."

"Then we're even." He extended his hand and took a duffel bag. "Now I feel bad you came."

"Our night on call stayed crazy with admissions, but don't worry about it. We'll work together on study material and independently catch up on needed sleep. And look ... I brought us leftovers."

Annabel opened the shopping bag on his counter, popped a container in the microwave, and then split up the jambalaya on two plates.

"How are you feeling?" she asked. "Do you think you can eat some Cajun food?"

"I'm not any worse. I might eat Creole." He smiled and handed her utensils.

"There's a difference, you know, between Cajun and Creole."

"Will our internal medicine final exam test us on food?"

"Dr. Raymond's doxycycline prescription must be making you feel better. You're joking."

"I hope so."

"No kidding. This rice dish is technically Cajun, so it's a bit more spicey than it's Creole counterpart, which is milder and sweeter."

"Sometimes I forget you're more southern than I am."

"Do you hold that against me?"

"Never. Where'd you get this anyway?"

"I may have mentioned I went on a date with the police officer. Dustin took me to this Cajun restaurant and, well, we didn't finish our food. In essence, we were sidetracked by a woman needing the Heimlich maneuver."

Bob's expression dimmed. "He took you to a place where the dinners were that bad?"

She swatted his upper arm. "Very funny. We better not dillydally because I'm running on caffeine." On purpose, she didn't mention Dustin stopping the robbery at the cash register.

Bob nodded and ate half of what Annabel served him. They went over to the couch and Annabel laid out notes from the last grand rounds and opened her internal medicine textbook.

"Why don't we approach a case history," she said, "like we did in our first and second year in the unit labs. A team-based approach … and work through a patient with a chronic cough."

"Sounds perfect."

Annabel buckled her legs under her. They scooted the coffee table closer and used it to spread a chart and books. They worked through an entire algorithm for the diagnosis and treatment of a chronic cough and ended up studying all methods of testing, disease entities, and treatments. They even ended up at a dead end workup with a patient who had a psychogenic cough.

They took a break; it was getting late and both of them poured a half glass of wine. Annabel slumped further into the couch. She could not keep her eyes open any longer and fell asleep, but Bob didn't want to disturb her. He was half dozing himself. With an easy pull, he lowered her to a pillow near the armrest and draped an afghan over her.

Bob started for the bedroom, knowing he needed to set an alarm for her for the morning. On the kitchen counter, he heard her phone beep with an incoming text and decided to lower the volume so she wouldn't be disturbed. His finger hit the screen and the text message popped up.

Our night together was awesome. I hope you weren't dead tired being on your call.

I do plan on making us the dinner I promised. This weekend?

Bob's heart skipped a beat and then it palpitated like it was hit with a club. He wished it weren't so, but the text from Dustin was blatant.

Not only did it appear like Annabel and the cop had gotten hot and sweaty together, but she might have lost sleep doing it. And by the sound of it, they made more plans to be together in the near future.

His lethargy from Ehrlichiosis grew worse and he craved sleep that much more.

CHAPTER 24

Patty Caye found out the hard way how much she and Jae kept the William Taft National Historic Site operating efficiently.

Since her colleague's hospitalization, her work had more than doubled. She finally asked the national park system to officially lend her the part-time ranger who was filling in for Jae. They agreed to commit him for the next month. At least now, she thought, she didn't need to scramble every few days to write up the paperwork necessary to request extra help.

She ladled the sautéed venison which she'd just prepared on the stove to a dinner plate. Jae had given her a few single-serving freezer bags of his last processed deer meat. Since presently he was living his life in an ICU, she was glad he had given her some before, but eating venison made her remember him and miss him that much more.

She looked down at the dogs.

"There's not enough to go around. Besides, this is my dinner."

She frowned at Twist. "Plus, you're getting better after your bout with that Leptospirosis disease. There's no way I am going to feed you something exotic."

The dogs understood the gist of her words and stretched lazily on the throw rug. She cut the slices she had prepared into smaller pieces and ate a sample. Pleased with her preparation, she spooned over the accompanying vegetables.

Sometimes Jae worked way too hard, she thought. The last day he hunted, processed, and hung the buck was crazy. And then his big payback from nature was to shower and find ticks. He had told her on more than one occasion how much he loathed them.

She guessed a tick bite might not be important in Jae's medical history, but she wondered.

Had he told the medical team upon his admission that he had recently hunted and was exposed to, and bitten by, one or more ticks? Like the dogs, she and Jae were exposed to the positive and negative secondary gains of the great outdoors, but with Jae, it was much more. His deep woods adventures were as redneck as they came.

Patty was overdue to pay Jae a visit in the ICU, so she decided that tomorrow she would weed out the time needed to see him. She wanted an update on his condition, but it wouldn't hurt to check if the team knew about his endeavors in the woods and his recent intimacy with a tick.

Annabel woke with a start upon hearing an alarm clock. Disoriented, she kicked off the afghan draped on her legs and then realized she was on a couch. Bob's couch.

Bob stumbled out from his bedroom with the portable clock in his hands and clicked off the noise.

Annabel rubbed her eyes. "Thanks for setting the alarm. Now please go back to bed. I'll be fine."

"You were a super teacher last night and we covered a lot. I'm the one who should be thanking you. Feel free to make a single-cup coffee with my machine in the kitchen. I'm taking your advice and going back to bed, especially if you're going to repeat another session tonight like last night's."

"I will dream up a different topic for us and you're welcome."

Annabel scrambled, left shortly, and went to her own car. It was weird waking up in Bob's apartment, but she was glad she did it. They were so "at home" with each other, they were almost like siblings. Or better, she thought, because she wasn't even on speaking terms with her own sister.

She punched in her iPhone password to unlock it and quickly checked for any important overnight messages. When she saw Dustin's message about their date, and that he wanted to keep his cooking promise, she broke out in a smile. She scrolled him back a response.

You'll have stiff competition outdoing our Cajun dinner, but I'll take the chance.

She signed off with an emoji smile and started the car.

At the hospital, Annabel went to the ICU first before seeing any patients on the regular floor. When she passed through the automatic doors, an RN signaled to her from the desk.

"Dr. Tilson," she said, "the park ranger friend of Mr. Nixon is here to talk to anyone from the medical team."

Annabel spotted Patty standing inside Jae's room. She was hard to miss since she wore her uniform. "She sure is an early bird."

"I'll say." The nurse raised her eyebrows. "I'll pour you a cup of coffee since you often put a pot on for us."

"Thanks." Annabel poked her head into Jae's room. "I hear you want to talk to one of us."

Patty nodded and Annabel pointed past the door. They walked out and stood by the entrance.

"Has he made any progress?" Patty asked.

"Overall, he's about the same. We're managing a few more things, however, because his length of stay is getting longer."

"The meningitis is still there affecting his brain?"

"Yes, I'm afraid so. Part of the critical care he's receiving is medication to reduce the swelling in his brain."

Patty gritted her teeth.

"You're here extremely early. Can I get you a cup of coffee from the kitchenette?"

"No thank you. I must leave soon to drive back to work. I don't know if Jae told this to any of you. It may or may not be important. I remembered it last night and, since you doctors are unsure why he's sick, I couldn't bear to not tell you right away."

Anabel's interest piqued, and she tilted her head. "A thorough history is the biggest chunk of the puzzle. What did you remember that may be helpful?"

"Jae uses a crossbow to hunt. Not that that's important, but his hours in the woods and handling of deer is. Before he got sick, before he went to the hospital the first time and they told him he had the flu, he killed a buck. He brought it home, of course, but later he told me he'd been bitten by a tick."

Annabel let out a gasp. Her thoughts raced straight to Bob and his Ehrlichiosis. One very bright family practitioner had hit immediately upon his correct diagnosis. Bob was sick enough, but if someone hadn't figured out what he had, he could be in an ICU right now like Jae.

Maybe Jae had the same disease. Or, the possibility existed that it could be some other lecherous disease brought on by the same bloodsuckers. Maybe Lyme disease? She had a lot more studying or rereading to do about parasitic diseases.

Annabel needed to stop her racing thoughts and address Patty Caye standing in front of her. The poor woman's hands were wrung into a knot.

"I took his history as did several other doctors. Nowhere did I read that in anyone's notes. Mr. Nixon sure didn't tell me and I never asked about bites or his extracurricular activities.

"I'll be sure and tell the others. Especially Dr. Enno, the infectious disease doctor. This piece of information may be important."

Patty gave a sigh of relief; her input was welcomed and appreciated.

"Thank you," Annabel said, "for taking the time and effort to let us know."

Annabel rounded the corner into the office where she found the whole team quiet and distracted with their index cards or pocket manuals. Jordan's head was lowered over a new iPhone. Donn leaned against the desk, his paper folded near the window.

"I have a news flash about Jae Nixon," Annabel said.

"Instead of rounding at this moment," Donn said, "why don't you tell us? It'll give me the opportunity to eat something. I'm starving."

"Why are you starving?" Stuart asked.

"Peanut butter and jelly for breakfast?" Jordan blurted out after glancing up.

Donn pitched cellophane in the waste basket and grasped half of his sandwich. "It's probably better than what you eat, since you can't come up for air from another phone device." He frowned, knowing he shouldn't be talking to the students that way, even if he didn't like one of them.

"Stuart, since your curious mind needs to know, I'm hungry because I didn't eat a thing after leaving yesterday after call. I was back to the office for paperwork, over to the department for a meeting, and then a five o'clock appointment with my attorney about the Helm's family lawsuit. Then I crashed at home because of getting no sleep on call.

"Does that cover it?"

"I'm sorry, Dr. Schott," Stuart said.

"Yeah, well ..." Donn looked at Annabel. "Go ahead and fill us in about Jae Nixon."

Annabel gulped. She sure didn't want to ruffle his feathers. "The other ranger, Patty Caye, was waiting earlier to talk to one of us. She wanted us to know that Jae was bitten by a tick before he got sick. He went hunting; it seemed like he caught it from the woods or the deer he caught."

Donn's eyes grew big. "What the hell?! Do we have a medical student and a patient incapacitated from a little bug?"

"That was my first reaction," Annabel said.

Donn chewed on his sandwich and washed it down with a swig of cold coffee.

"How can people get bit now?" Stuart commented. "It's winter."

"You're chatty today," Donn said. "Did you sleep through the fact that they're not forested down anymore throughout winter? Temperatures are warmer and their range has crept more to the north."

"Dr. Schott," Melody chimed in, "Dr. Enno needs to turn up so we can tell her right away. We're not exactly experts in this area."

"An unskilled family practitioner knew what Bob Palmer had," Jordan said.

Donn scowled. "Unskilled? Don't ridicule other doctors, particularly in that case. Behind my back, people may be ridiculing me right now because I'm being sued, but I practiced the standard of care for my patient."

Annabel looked at the floor. Jordan was an idiot, but Donn was taking the lawsuit too seriously.

"Let's get back to Jae Nixon," Annabel said. "and I'll hunt down Dr. Enno this morning. We're not experts with tick-borne diseases, but everyone's heard about Lyme disease. We should have a group discussion about it."

"Transmission is misunderstood by most people," Stuart said while everyone's eyes locked onto him.

"How do you know?" Jordan asked.

"The topic of Lyme disease came up for me last summer. I must digress too, about how I spent that season of the year. After all, between the first and second year of medical school is the only summer that a future doctor will ever have off again. After that, our 'childhoods' are over forever.

"Anyway, I didn't really take off. I shadowed a hospitalist at least twenty hours a week. He also wanted me to become familiar with writing medical papers. I co-authored a paper with him on Lyme disease."

"Jeez," Chineka said. "Was it published?"

Stuart nodded.

Donn shook his head. "The disease is an important topic and I can see to it that it shows up on a test." He gave them a weak smile.

"Before we go any further, however, Jae Nixon does not have it. He was on antibiotics, which would have made him better. So, let me wrestle with the rest of my pb&j and, Stuart, you can teach these knuckleheads a thing or two about Lyme disease. Why is transmission misunderstood and what's a major symptom that we don't see with Jae Nixon?"

"Working on the subject," Stuart said, "I came to understand that many laypeople believe it is the tick itself which is the direct cause of the disease. That is not true. It's the tick's saliva which is transmitting the infectious agent – a bacteria, a virus, or a parasite.

"With Lyme disease, it's bacteria that's the culprit. She's called Borrelia burgdorferi. I'm sorry, ladies, I call it a 'her' because women are more harmful and entrapping than men."

"How about that?" Donn asked flatly. "You have a personality capable of making a dangerous joke under that nerdy exterior."

"Only when it comes to academics."

"He just annihilated his female colleagues," Jordan said.

"You took that spot a long time ago," Melody countered.

Stuart shrugged his shoulders and continued. "I know what major symptom you are referring to, Dr. Schott. Besides symptoms such as a fever, muscle aches, a headache, or fatigue, the rash called *erythema migrans* is classic. Seventy-five percent of all patients with the disease show the rash within a few days or a month. Usually within the first week. It spreads from the site of the bite, but it really isn't itchy or painful. The skin area looks like a target or a bull's eye."

Stuart looked back at the floor. "One of the reasons Lyme disease is so disruptive to people's lives is that it can be a long-term, debilitating illness. It can cause severe joint pain and swelling. Imagine hiking to get exercise or to take a break from studying, and you get bitten by a tick and contract Lyme disease. You end up with severe arthritis when you're only twenty years old because of your walk in the woods!"

"Bob was bitten by a tick," Annabel said, "and we weren't even in the woods." She shuddered and Donn wiped his mouth, his sandwich finished.

"Stuart, thanks for the synopsis on symptoms," Donn said. "Now let's go round on our patients."

He pulled ahead of all of them and spoke over his shoulder. "Annabel, hunt down Dr. Enno and tell her what you heard."

CHAPTER 25

Annabel wrote updates in her patients' charts after rounds and kept her eyes peeled for Dr. Enno. When she went back to the unit, she found a note from the infectious disease specialist on Jae's chart. She had missed bumping into her, so the next likely places in the hospital were the doctor's lounge or the cafeteria. More attendings and residents filtered in and out of the doctors' lounge during the day than medical students.

Annabel never visited there very long, but she wished she could. Conversations often focused on the care of doctors' current patients. Listening was an educational experience; she yearned to be in their shoes.

Even though Shania Enno sat facing the other way, Annabel knew it was her from the bun in her hair and Alejandro slanted alongside her chair.

"Dr. Enno, do you have a moment?"

"For a medical student? Always."

"I noticed you went by to see Jae Nixon. I have information from his co-worker which, I believe, none of us knew."

Shania's slow hand picked up her cup, but her smile faded when she peeked in the bottom.

"Serve yourself from the counter over there and, if you don't mind, fix me an herbal tea. Come back and we'll discuss our patient."

"Sure thing," Annabel said warmly. The spread of bagels and fruit proved perfect since her stomach was running on empty except for coffee. She dropped a cinnamon spice tea bag and hot water into two different cups, made herself a small plate, and bused them over to Shania's table.

"The young ranger's brain swelling is under control," Dr. Enno said, "and your crackerjack medical team is managing his respiratory support and IV fluids like a champ."

"Dr. Enno, I worry every morning I step into the ICU that he's taken a turn for the worse. I've heard of patients spending months on a ventilator in an ICU. How do medical care providers and families maintain their optimism under such conditions?"

"People in our modern society have lost the ability to be docile and tolerant of situations they cannot control. Under the scenario you speak of, they must unwillingly adapt and practice enormous patience."

Annabel nodded as the older doctor steeped the tea bag and pulled a single packet of honey from her pocket.

"Now, what did you hear about your patient?"

"Before Jae Nixon initially came down with flu-like symptoms, he was bitten by a tick during a deer-hunting expedition."

Shania stirred the honey around in the cup while processing the missing part of Jae's history. "In some cases, ticks are the size of a pinhead or a watermelon seed. It depends on whether it's in the larva, nymph, or adult life cycle.

"Certainly, one of them could have injected Mr. Nixon with an infectious agent. This is an important piece of information.

"And most cases of meningitis are caused by viruses. Which is so critical, because meningitis accounts for one of the more important causes of hospital admissions."

"My dad's a neurosurgeon, so I'm always interested in the brain; from the neurology and medical aspect as well as the surgical standpoint." Annabel opened a pat of butter and began spreading it on a bagel. "You went straight to talking about ticks transmitting viruses. Yet our absent medical student has Ehrlichiosis caused by a tick transmitting a bacteria, not a virus, and this morning, our medical team also talked about Lyme disease, a tick-transmitted bacterial disease."

Shania gave her a half-smile. "Then your group is keeping up with the times. This gives me an idea. Are you aware of who the department asked to give grand rounds in the near future?"

Annabel paused, took a bite, and shook her head.

"I will be the speaker. Although I had a topic in mind, now it will be something entirely different." She wrapped her hand around Alejandro and clicked it once on the floor. "I don't know if ticks are our tiniest threat, but for the purposes of my discussion, they will be."

Annabel raised her eyebrows. She wished she could sit with the woman the rest of the day.

"My talk will be called 'Our Infinitesimal yet Colossal Danger.'"

"I won't miss it, Dr. Enno."

"So, back to Jae Nixon. Fortunately, the CDC does not put me on hold when I call, so I will talk to them soon, as well as our state health department."

"What should I tell Dr. Schott and Dr. Burg?"

"Supportive care is of utmost importance. Dr. Schott understands that. I will get us a diagnosis if it kills me, zone in on any other possible curative treatment, and you fine doctors will keep him alive.

"And the next time Mr. Nixon's co-worker is here, let me know. I'd like to talk to her."

At the end of the day, Annabel veered home to her apartment instead of straight to Bob's. She repacked but, more than that, she wanted to stop at the corner café.

"Hey, Pete," she said at the counter. "I want to surprise my friend Bob with something light yet nutritional."

"What about a 'take two?' Half a sandwich and a cup of soup?"

"How about two grilled cheese sandwiches and tomato-basil soup that we can share?"

"Are you finally dating that young man?" Pete turned and handed the order through the door to the cook.

"Bob? No, but I'm dating the policeman again that I dated a few months ago." She picked up a box of chocolate espresso beans as well as a box of chocolate-covered blueberries from the bin in front of her. "I'll share these with Bob as well."

"Seems like you share a lot with him. Bob, that is."

"Yeah, well, right now, we don't share our medicine rotation. He's hung up with a disease from a tick. Thank God he's been diagnosed and on his way to recovery. The lives of medical students are fragile; one wrong turn and our education blows up in our face."

"College students can suffer the same fate."

"So true. My college boyfriend in our last year suffered a concussion, his schooling was terminated, and it took him a long time to get back on track. We split up too, because our lives went in different directions. At least we're still friends. As a matter of fact, I could count on him in a pinch just like I can with Bob."

Pete stirred a long spoon in a paper cup and handed the drink over the counter.

"What's this?"

"On the house."

"A mocha cappuccino. Thank you."

Pete soon packed up Annabel's order and said, "Tell Bob I said hello."

Annabel held the cup carefully and the bag in her other hand. She wanted to sit on a bench against the wall and sip on the hot drink but, more than that, she wanted to hang out with Bob.

At Bob's apartment, Annabel showed up first with the food. "I'm hoping your appetite has improved today," she said while checking him out. His hair was less messed up than yesterday and a small pile of folded clothes was on a chair behind him.

"I'll take these while you go back to your car."

When Annabel entered again with her bags and books, he was pouring orange juice into a juice glass.

"What a day," she said. "But, first, how are you?"

"I'm still very tired, but it was the first afternoon I didn't feel like I was hit by a train and left for dead. I washed a small load of laundry."

"Wow. You've made progress … like going from an ICU 'critical' condition to 'stable.'"

"I won't be joining you for any marathons, however."

"Don't worry. I'm not up to speed either." She smiled at him and pointed to a chair.

"I did hear from Dr. Raymond's office today," Bob said as he sat. "They were called about the Ehrlichia IFA results earlier than they anticipated. Sure enough, I tested positive. Leave it to me, I passed the disease's gold standard laboratory test."

"Bob Palmer, that's not a surprise. Hallelujah that you are already being treated for the correct diagnosis."

"Then we should celebrate," he said, "with a grilled cheese."

"And our flavored champagne tonight is tomato basil." She pulled the Styrofoam container out, warmed the soup, and then ladled it into two bowls.

"So what happened today?" he asked.

"There's more to tell you today. I didn't want to overload you yesterday."

"I'm listening. Any juicy gossip?"

"Dr. Schott is anxious and Jordan is his usual self. I'm glad he's obsessed with iPhones."

"If he lived in New York City, he'd be like one of those people you see in videos. Walking along and not seeing where they're going. Bumping into taxis and pedestrians rushing along on the sidewalks."

"He'd never make it in that city. He's just a small fry with a big attitude. I wish he was the one who took the run with me. A tick needs to take a bite out of him."

"Feisty today, are we?"

"Maybe so. Anyway, getting back to what's important. My patient, May Carter, came into the clinic the other day. Remember her?"

"Absolutely."

"She followed through with everything modern medicine had to offer to no avail. The metastases from her lung cancer are choking the quality of her remaining days to being intolerable. She refuses admission to the hospital again and I'm sure that was the last time I'm going to see her."

"I'm sorry. For her and for us too."

Annabel took the last sip of the cold cappuccino.

"And the female ranger friend of my ICU patient came by this morning and told me that he was bitten by a tick." Her eyes shot over to him. "Yeah, just like you. But he was hunting deer."

Bob's mouth fell open. "I'm glad I'm not as sick as he is, but I don't have venison to show for it either."

"Spare the hunting, please. Don't get me started on my opinion about killing beautiful animals like them."

"Uh, oh. I won't. What does Dr. Enno think?"

"Your Dr. Raymond said that your case was a reportable tick disease. Dr. Enno is also going to talk to the CDC about Jae Nixon. Since we've narrowed it down to a virus, which one, transmitted by a tick, can put a previously healthy, non-immunocompromised person on death's door?"

A shudder ran through Bob as he held half the sandwich.

"Before I forget," Annabel added, "she's going to present the next grand rounds. Your energy needs to ramp up so that you can attend. Can you imagine a doctor in her seventies teaching young medical students the latest on CDC-reportable vector diseases?"

"I'll probably be dead when I'm seventy."

She squinted her eyes. "We'll make a deal. Neither one of us should die before eighty."

"Will we still know each other?"

"With Facebook and other social media, it's difficult to lose touch. Plus, there will be medical school reunions to attend as well."

"So true. Plus, we may work in the same town."

They both made progress on the food Annabel brought and she rummaged through the bag for the boxes of chocolate-covered treats. "Dessert," she said.

"What about your sister, Nancy? Still no word?"

Annabel shook her head.

"How about if I text her?"

"She liked you when you came home with me ... when Dakota died. I didn't tell you that before. Her interest then became diverted to Jordan and we both know how that ended." She rolled her eyes and popped a chocolate in her mouth.

"She had a crush on me?" he asked mischievously.

"You scamp. You're not supposed to return to your normal behavior this quickly."

He shrugged his shoulders and inched his hand forward for her iPhone. "Do you mind?"

"Go ahead."

Bob found Nancy's number and texted.

Yo, Nancy. It's Bob, Annabel's friend. We're wondering when you're coming up again to visit. There's much more to see and do in Cincinnati!

Bob read Anabel what he wrote. "All right with you?"

"Sure. If you can't elicit a response, then nobody can."

He pressed send and glanced at her questioningly. "So when are you going out again with the cop?"

"Dustin? Soon." Annabel looked at her watch. "No more wasting time. Let's start studying. And, by the way, have you gulped down all your antibiotics today?"

"Yes, Mom. What's the topic for tonight since we only have time for one?"

"Anaphylaxis. It shows up on tests and we've had no exposure to it on the wards."

Bob nodded, enticing her to go on as she opened up a small textbook to a bookmark and began reading.

"Consider anaphylaxis an acute and life-threatening response ... a type I hypersensitivity reaction. IgE mediates the activation of mast cells. When those cells degranulate, they release inflammatory mediators, interleukins, and the biggie ... histamine.

"And here's another definition we must know – angioedema."

"Swelling of the face?"

"Yes, but the body area can be less than that. Technically, it's swelling of the lips, periorbital region, face, feet, or hands. And this is super important. What's the most common cause of drug-related anaphylaxis?"

"Penicillin."

"Good. And overall - beta-lactam antibiotics.

"What about the most common cause of food-related anaphylaxis? I would not have guessed this, although I hear discussions about food that mistakenly carry it as an ingredient."

"I was going to say some kind of shellfish."

"Nope. Peanuts."

"Goes to show. You never know what's in your granola bar that could kill you."

Bob tired before Annabel had read for an hour; she had to coax him to go to bed. She tidied up his apartment and then readied for sleep. There was no answer from her sister regarding Bob's text. She settled on the couch and put her medicine pocket manual on her abdomen.

Before she closed her eyes, she thought about the evening. Even when Bob was sick, she enjoyed his company. When she arrived a few hours ago, her speech had been pressured to catch him up on recent developments.

Was that what married life was like?

In a way, yes. That was what she had seen in her own home with her parents. She sighed. Marriage can't be too bad, she thought. But, of course, when it came to Bob, there was a big difference. There was no sex between them. That would be a whole different thing.

Actually, she wondered ...

CHAPTER 26

Annabel slept restlessly. The alarm clock was about to ring, so she stepped to the nightstand just inside Bob's bedroom and snapped it off. He remained fast asleep on his side and she ducked back out.

This morning, she made one of his single-cup coffees. It was a nifty machine and she could get used to the variety of flavors. She drank it as she dressed, gathered her things as quietly as possible, and slipped out the door to a light rain. By the time she arrived at the hospital, the clouds had opened up more, and she ran from her car to the entrance.

She shrugged off the dreary weather. She was more concerned that the rotation was nearing to an end and there were dozens of diseases and patient problems that she had not seen. But, she figured, seasoned physicians, even Dr. Enno, might not see everything during their short or long careers.

After stopping at the office, she went straight into Jae's room in the ICU where his nurse slipped a sheet up on his chest.

"Dr. Tilson, Patty Caye is here again this morning, but she went to the lounge because Jae was being sponge bathed. She'll be back."

"Perfect. I must grab Dr. Enno so we can both talk to her. How did he do last night?"

"We went down on the dopamine a little." She gave an encouraging smile.

Annabel glanced at his vital signs, listened to his lungs, and then went down to the doctors' lounge where Dr. Enno sat in a plump leather chair. The wise old woman could double for a regal Tolkien character, Annabel thought as she approached her.

"Dr. Enno, you asked me to tell you when Jae Nixon's co-worker shows up again. She's here in the hospital. She probably went for coffee because they were sponge bathing our patient in the ICU."

"Let's go." She wiggled her hand for Annabel to hand her Alejandro and they walked out. When they showed up in the cafeteria, Patty stuck out like Dr. Enno did walking down a hallway. Beyond the window, the rain outside had picked up.

"It reminds me of a summer gully washer," Shania said to the women, "but it should be a late snowstorm."

"May we join you?" Dr. Enno asked.

Patty nodded as they sat, the rain outside growing stronger in the parking lot.

"For a hospital admission," Shania said, "a doctor performs a history and physical on a patient. Notice that a 'history' comes first. I would like to know more about your partner's lifestyle. We've been looking for a white glove in an imaginary snowfall and you told us an important element of Mr. Nixon's recent past."

Patty listened with her hand wrapped around a cup of coffee. "Please go on."

"Recent travel, and exposure to unusual places and things, is particularly consequential to an infectious disease physician like me. To give you an example, I recently consulted on a college professor with flu-like symptoms and a red, spotty rash. Her fatigue and joint pain became so bad, she couldn't go into work. I found out that about three weeks before all of that began, she had travelled to New Mexico where she spent time in the desert soil studying ancestral Pueblo Indian villages and cave dwellings."

Annabel's eyes grew wide and she understood the enthusiasm the woman had for her field. "What did she have?"

"Valley fever. In medical terms ... coccidioidomycosis. It's caused by a fungus with a complex life cycle. Since the spores are so small, they are carried by the wind and inhaled into the lungs where nodules of residual infection can later show up on chest X-rays."

"There are many national parks and monuments in the desert Southwest where rangers are stationed," Patty said. "I'll remember that."

"At least out west, doctors occasionally come across the disease. But here, doctors will most likely never see a case of coccidioidomycosis in their entire career. So what's out of sight is out of mind."

Patty put her hands on her lap. "Do you think Jae is infected with some kind of rare tick disease?"

"I believe so. I heard he is a hunter. Any other recreational or job-related situations where he's in contact with wildlife or other mammals?"

"Well ..." Patty thought. "Are you aware that one of our dogs on the property almost died from Leptospirosis?"

Dr. Enno looked at Annabel.

Barbara Ebel

"We happened to know about the dog," Annabel said.

"And your dog could have gotten the responsible bacteria from a tick," Shania said, "At least in Poland, they have found the bacteria in ticks. Or perhaps something else. Does the dog go on the hunting trips?"

"Never. There are two dogs on the property and neither of them go with Jae."

"Any deer or other common critters living in the area right where you both reside?"

Patty blushed. "We both live in separate cabins next to each other." She narrowed her eyes, put her hand back up, and tapped a finger on the table. "We rarely come across deer in the vicinity. The trails and woods don't encompass that many acres and humans traverse them all the time.

"But the vet thought Twist could have gotten infected by mice and Jae could have gotten infected by Twist."

"What mice?"

"White-footed mice. They are more and more prolific, breeding like prairie dogs. Jae goes out there and tries to cut back their population." She grimaced at the unpleasant job.

"Mice!

"You ladies are unconscionable not telling me all this.

"Or I'm slipping on my questioning, like a private investigator who needs to be given a desk job after years of being out in the field. Maybe it's time to retire." Shania's eyes glazed over. "But what would I do? Count the pills I take all day?"

"We're sorry," Annabel said. "We didn't mean to make you upset. None of this may have a direct bearing on whether or not Mr. Nixon pulls out of this. I understand it's scientific knowledge and intellectual curiosity, but don't be so hard on yourself."

Shania patted Annabel's hand.

"The epidemiology side of me realizes that the white-footed mouse has much to do with the spread of tick-borne diseases. People think that because certain ticks are called 'deer ticks,' the ticks are exclusive to deer. Not so."

Annabel glanced at her watch and frowned. "I must get up to the office and meet my team for rounds. Otherwise, Dr. Schott will cause me grief."

"Yes, dear," the older woman said sweetly. "I will sit another moment for a cup of coffee with Ms. Caye before she, too, runs off."

Reluctantly, Annabel hustled to join her group in the office.

That afternoon, Donn burst into the clinic door, dripping water off of his umbrella.

"We don't have clinic next week," he announced to the team, "so make the most of it today. You all have less than two weeks left on the rotation, so next week we're mostly in the hospital and we'll gather for some extra discussions. Think about any medical areas you're weak in."

"Dr. Enno is giving grand rounds too," Annabel said. "If Bob is up to it, he may come."

"How is he? Will he be able to sit for the final exam?"

"He's still very tired, but he's steadily improving. Dr. Raymond's office called and his test results were positive for Ehrlichia."

"I'm not surprised. I'm glad the diagnosis is proven, but I regret the loss of him from our team."

Donn curled up his mouth, hesitant with what he had to say.

"Annabel and Dr. Burg, I received bad news. Our metastatic lung cancer patient, May Oliver, died at home."

"That'll be one less patient to see today," Jordan mumbled.

"Dr. Maldonado, she wasn't scheduled today anyway," Donn said, "and keep your insensitive thoughts to yourself. Besides, no one in the health care profession should ever think that way."

Annabel stared down at her shoes. May had been a patient, but she turned out to be more than that. She would stick out as a memory from her one and only rotation through medicine as a student.

Dr. Burg patted Annabel's sleeve. "I always accept the death of older patients more readily than the younger ones. At least May died at home like she wanted."

"So true," Annabel said.

"Time to see patients," Donn said, "although I think the rain is causing some cancellations. There are a lot of empty chairs in the waiting room.

"I also have another announcement. Instead of the final exam being given at the end of next week, it's been moved up because of a scheduling conflict. The test is on Monday. At least it will be out of the way, but it doesn't mean any of you can turn into slouchers for the remainder of the week. Also, we'll wrap up with Dr. Enno's infectious disease lecture early in the week as well."

Jordan let out a gasp and Annabel curled her mouth. Stuart looked up momentarily.

"Be sure to tell Bob too."

"I will," Annabel said.

In a few minutes, all the students had a chart to look over before walking into a room. Annabel squeezed in on the counter between Jordan and Stuart. Jordan pulled a book out of his lab coat and looked something up in the index. When he laid it on the counter, Annabel noticed it was an extra small version of an internal medicine handbook, nifty and portable. Perhaps she should buy one of those, she thought, but didn't see the point.

At the end of late-day rounds, the rhythm of Jae Nixon's monitors was steadier than the rain bouncing off the window outside his ICU room. Annabel sat in a chair in his room and carefully went through all of Shania Enno's notes and orders for the last two days. Only because of the infectious disease specialist on his case, a newfound optimism for her patient ran through her thoughts.

Annabel pondered one of Shania's notes:

An IgM viral test I would like to run is not commercially available. I have requested and sent one of Mr. Nixon's samples to the state health department laboratory as well as the CDC.

The secretary from the desk stepped in and handed her a paper. "Hot off the press. For the chart."

"Thanks," Annabel replied. Shania had ordered another EEG and an MRI while they were in clinic. Annabel smiled. It seemed like test results came back a hell of a lot sooner when she was the ordering physician rather than a resident or a cosigned medical student.

She read the first report:

Jae Nixon's electroencephalography shows generalized slow wave activity but, of note, there is a marked improvement since his last EEG.

Annabel glanced at the ranger, his body more angular than when he arrived. Maybe he did hear her when she talked to him. "Time to wake up," she whispered.

She went back to the second report:

The mild ischemic changes seen on the last MRI of Jae Nixon's parietal lobes appear to be fainter.

Holy smoke, she thought. She couldn't wait to tell Bob that Jae Nixon had not only stabilized but, neurologically, seemed to be getting better. She clutched the chart, walked over, and patted Jae on his tattoo. "They are waiting for your return at the National Historic Site."

Jae's RN walked in. "You talking to him?"

"I'm embarrassed to say that you caught me."

"Don't be embarrassed. I do it quite often. Talk to my patients ... whether they're awake or not."

"Do you think it helps?"

"I know it does."

Annabel nodded. "I'll lay his chart on the counter. And good night, Mr. Ranger."

Before she started her car, Annabel sat while the wipers washed her windshield with the rain. She opened up her iPhone to messages and still found no response from her sister. That was that, then. Her sister had nothing to say to her and chose to ignore Bob as well.

Unlike Jordan, she had kept off her phone all afternoon. Dustin had texted:

How about I cook for you tonight or tomorrow?

Too bad she had missed it, she thought, and wrote:

I'm just leaving the hospital. Can't come over now. A friend is expecting me over. Tomorrow would be fine!

Tomorrow it is. Dinner at my place around 6 or 7. Text me. Enjoy time with your friend. I suspect you'll be studying with her?!

Annabel grimaced. His assumption that she was going to study with a female made sense, but that was not the way it worked anymore for students. Gender didn't matter and, besides, Bob was a close friend. She bit her lip and contemplated.

Dustin knew a little about her past dating methods and seemed to be overlooking that history. She wasn't sure how he would react, however, if she told him that she was studying with Bob and sleeping at his place the last few nights.

She contemplated. Trust was a big part of a relationship and she and Dustin had not been dating again that long. This information might give him cold feet, even if she told him that her friend was sick and she was helping take care of him.

With her past history, could Dustin really trust her? How would she feel if she had a new boyfriend who was sleeping at another woman's apartment? She frowned. Would she cut off the relationship because it could signal a sign of things to come?

Her fingers lingered. Finally, she avoided his reference to gender.

Studying for sure. Our final exam is nearing. Looking forward ...

Bob wore a sheepish grin as he opened the door. He wore sweat pants, a Caribbean T-shirt, and no shoes.

Annabel walked in and plopped down her bag. "You doing any better?"

"Hanging on."

"I swear, you've lost a few pounds. Despite my feeding you."

He pranced across the cold hard floor and widened his smile. "I had a fabulous idea a few minutes ago."

"Forget it. You'll get caught. Murdering Jordan isn't worth getting a life sentence for yourself."

He widened his eyes. "Ha ... very funny. No, now that you and I are messed up, out of sync with rotations, maybe we could share a dog together. You lost Dakota and always want a dog and yet you can't do it because you're gone from your apartment too much and on call sometimes. Out timings will be different, at least in the immediate future, so we could flip-flop a dog back and forth."

He locked his hands together. "It's a win-win situation. He or she would live in two homes and we'd benefit with a furry companion and all the joy the dog would bring to our lives." Not to mention, he thought, it would assure him of still seeing Annabel on a regular basis.

Annabel lowered herself onto the coffee table and crossed her legs. "Interesting idea. There are pluses and minuses. Are dogs allowed here?"

Bob nodded.

"I can have pets where I live, but I don't know. It wouldn't be as easy as you think. The dog would still be alone a lot."

"Look at it this way. Later in life, you may want another purebred like your family had. However, we can go to the shelter and rescue a poor dog who may end up euthanized. Wouldn't he or she be better off alive sharing two homes with two ridiculous type-A medical students instead of turning into dust?"

Annabel tapped her foot. "If you were taking an oral exam right now, you'd be passing with whatever health care argument you were presenting."

"Good. I need the practice."

"By the way, our test has been moved up to Monday."

Bob stole a glance at the textbook on the table. "That's cutting it close. But what do you think about my idea?"

"I would love to have a dog. I feel like my life is so confined due to medical school and that most forms of enjoyment are being put off for the future. Which is stupid, because residency is only going to be more restrictive. How about we both think about it?"

"Meanwhile, I'll start thinking about names."

"What if the dog already has a name?"

"If it suits him, then he can keep it."

"Who says it'll be a he?"

CHAPTER 27

After the first beep, Annabel turned off the alarm clock. Bob barely shifted in his bed. She was pleased he didn't awaken. They had studied late the night before and, for the first time, she believed both of them were ready to conquer their final exam on Monday.

She realized one thing after she dressed and made one cup of Bob's single serving brew. Tonight she had a date with Dustin, so she left Bob a note letting him know she wasn't coming over later. She also snickered as she wrote him instructions for the day: *Rest, study, repeat. Rest, study, repeat!*

That should bring a smile to his face, she thought as she closed his door behind her. As she drove to the hospital, she pondered his suggestion about the two of them getting a dog. Thinking over the responsibility that a dog would bring to her life was much better than making an impulsive decision. Yet, by the time she walked into the front entrance of the V.A., she realized that just thinking about a dog ... a wagging tail and wet kisses on her hand ... had stuck a silly grin on her face.

Annabel stopped in the office, dropped her things, and slid on her white coat. Stuart sat on the couch, head bent over a textbook.

"Have you seen your patients yet?" Annabel asked.

"Yup."

"You're super early."

"The heat is on. I'm cramming and strengthening what I already know for our test. But you're pretty early too." He gave her a once over. "Your gypsy life style is showing on your lab jacket."

Annabel brushed over her crinkled collar and pockets. "You're correct about that."

"I'm sure Bob will let you use his washing machine and iron."

"I doubt if he owns an iron." She turned to the door. "By the way, thanks for not making wise cracks about me staying at Bob's. We're strictly friends. You know ... platonic."

"No need to tell me. Individually, it's clear where each of you stand."

"Thanks."

His head bent down again. Annabel gave him a second glance and stepped away. Now she felt self-conscious about her jacket and what did he mean by "it's clear where each of you stand"?

She went to the ICU first, made the bend into Jae Nixon's room, and almost bumped into Alejandro leaning against the counter. Today she must be the slacker, she thought, because both Stuart and Shania Enno were earlier than she was.

The cold, impersonal, beeping room was different as well. Although it played softly, music filtered out from a square black radio sitting by the sink. Dr. Enno stood at the foot of Jae's bed.

"Good morning," Annabel said.

The bottom of Jae's sheet was ruffled up by his mid-calf and Shania focused in front of her. Annabel needed to look twice to discover the movement of Jae's right toes.

"Wow!" Annabel exclaimed. "Is he waking up?"

"This is a start."

Annabel put her hand on his ankle and squeezed. "I wonder what music he prefers?"

"It may be the only time in your career that music accompanies your patient's arousal from a coma. Change the channel if you'd like."

"Country." Annabel switched channels and walked back, this time checking Jae's vital signs on the monitors.

Shania straightened her posture. "Let's step out. I was told our young ranger's diagnosis."

They left the music and the electronic beeps. Annabel could hardly contain her curiosity. After a few rapid breaths, she started fidgeting with her hands. Like the dog whisperer, had Shania really discovered Jae's problem and the correct way to treat it? Could she order him the right drug to purge him of his infectious disease and let him do more than wiggle his toes?

Outside the door, Dr. Enno put her back to Jae's window and tapped Alejandro. With bated breath, Annabel waited.

Twice, Shania shook her head slowly and finally spoke as Annabel swallowed hard.

"Mr. Nixon has Powassan virus."

"Powassan?"

"An RNA virus of the genus *Flavivirus*. Injected into him from the bite of an infected tick."

Annabel gasped. She glanced into Jae's room.

"Of course, you haven't heard of it. The general public, almost everyone, is clueless. Except for the CDC. And the unfortunate few people who have acquired it? Most don't live to tell their tale."

Past the window, Jae's chest cycled up and down from the ventilator. "How horrid. We can rid him of this virus. Right?"

"There is no medicine. There is no cure. There is no treatment for Powassan disease."

Annabel shuddered. "He moved his toes. Isn't that a good sign?"

"Yes. The mannitol to decrease his brain swelling, the respiratory support, the intravenous fluids … the present care your team is providing is all that can be done." Her mouth relaxed into a half-smile. "I am encouraged by what we are seeing this morning."

Shania also glanced through the window, told Annabel much more than she could process, and then ended with a final comment.

"All I can say now is that he is lucky to be alive."

Back and forth, and in and out, Jae Nixon's consciousness drifted as he resided in the confines of the ICU where his life was as artificial as junk jewelry. But sometimes when he was imbedded in deep sleep/unconsciousness, the time spent couldn't be more real.

The nighttime hours were fading away and early morning was approaching as Jae was immersed in a dream. His boots snapped branches out back from his cabin as he foraged the neck of the woods for the damn mice living so close. Twist wagged his tail and his tongue dangled from the side of his mouth.

"Not now," Jae said to the dog. "Can't you see I'm busy? You and Curley do a lousy job at rodent control, so I have to do it myself."

The dog cocked his head. Jae took off his brown leather work gloves and wiped his forehead. He took a stick and threw it several feet.

"All right, already. Go fetch and hang out over there."

Jae slipped the gloves back on and leaned back down into the pile.

But slowly, like a wispy cloud taken away by a breeze, the vision in his head ebbed away.

He again listened to sounds he'd heard before. "Beep, beep. Beep, beep." And a "whoosh, whoosh" correlated with the rising and falling of his chest. That much he had figured out.

Over and above those sounds, however, was something much more familiar and pleasant to the ears. Much more heavenly to his senses.

Music.

A pop song played. Something from real life. Not like the other noises, which enveloped him when he was more lucid. He couldn't make it out, but it had a rhythm and a beat.

The music gave him joy and he tried to make that lost connection. The circuitry between his brain and his body. He dwelled on the movement that comes with a likeable song and he forced his foot to move.

He heard something else. Voices. Low but discernable. The lovely voices of women.

He remembered ... his partner was a woman. Patty Caye. She was all right. They stood by each other. Maybe he underappreciated her. Maybe he had feelings for her. What to do about that?

The voices close by were different but not totally unheard of before. Then the background music changed ... to country music. Yes, that was what was playing. A male singer, crooning about lost love, beer, and a pickup truck.

Ha! He owned one of those. A pickup truck. He remembered his Silverado; he had hauled a buck out of the woods in it.

The song continued to slide into his consciousness. He moved his feet, struggled to open his eyes.

The women's voices faded away.

Annabel rushed around the corner and bumped into her teammates.

"You're running late for rounds," Dr. Schott barked.

"I'm sorry," Annabel said. "I was with Dr. Enno at Jae Nixon's bedside." Her eyes were wide; she was dying to spill the news about her patient.

"I swear," Dr. Burg said, "you might as well be the resident on his case."

"I'm sorry again, Dr. Burg. I don't mean to be stepping on your toes. Dr. Enno shows up early like a medical student and tells me things before I even have a second cup of coffee in the morning."

"Go ahead and tell us," Donn said. "Before you have a canary."

"Mr. Nixon does have a virus ... an RNA virus related to St. Louis encephalitis and West Nile virus. It is really rare and deadly, despite the fact that a patient's bloodstream concentration can remain low after an infected tick bite. The name of it is POW or Powassan virus."

Donn stroked his beard. "We figured we were dealing with a deviant infectious disease, but this sounds freaky."

"It is and there's absolutely no treatment."

"How'd she find out?" Stuart asked.

"From the CDC. They detected antibodies made against the virus in Jae's immune system. Dr. Enno had sent them blood and spinal fluid samples.

"But, can you believe it? Mr. Nixon wiggled his toes. We think … maybe …. there's hope for him."

"Let's go," Donn waved. "I want to see this for myself."

Once inside the room, Donn walked over to the radio and shut it off. Annabel glanced at the bed, where she detected no limb movement from Jae.

"Dr. Schott," Annabel said, "would you mind reconsidering not shutting that off? If he's coming out of his coma, the music might stir his senses."

Donn turned the dial back on. Now the lyrics were about two lovers dodging a no trespassing sign and going skinny dipping in a river. Donn shrugged his shoulders. "I suppose it can't hurt."

The team stood around the bed. Melody turned the ventilator setting down to a lower rate. A ray of optimism made her believe Jae would pick up the slack himself.

Within a few minutes, after they left, Jae moved his toes and then turned his feet towards each other.

Annabel left the V.A. earlier than she anticipated and she had to deliberate where she was headed. Nowadays, she was such a gypsy, she couldn't keep up with herself. She lived between the hospital, her apartment, Bob's place, and even Dustin's. On top of that, she went back and forth using two methods – Uber or her car.

Well, she thought, she had enough time to go back to her place, change, and go for dinner at Dustin's. She dragged her stuff up the staircase and first knocked on her neighbor's door.

The door swung open. Travis grinned in the doorway, his eyes alert as usual.

"Yo. Thanks for monitoring my place. There shouldn't be too many footsteps up there lately."

"Yup. You're not up there or you're 'dead-fully' quiet."

"I'm alive and well and studying all over the place."

"Yeah. Right."

"I owe you. Thanks."

Travis nodded and Annabel went upstairs. Inside, she texted Bob.

You better be studying and taking care of yourself.

Big news today about my ICU patient. Dr. Enno should talk about him in her lecture on Monday.

Annabel swung open her closet door and deliberated what to wear while a ding came back on her phone.

I studied twice today between naps. More to come.

I can't wait to hear. Aren't you going to tell me?

No, she responded. *No way have you heard about his disease!*

Have it your way. (As usual!)

She smiled. There was some truth to that.

She put down the phone and opted for a sexy look – a chest-hugging sweater, pair of black pants, and oval-shaped earrings alongside her natural curls.

Dustin lived north and on the same side of the interstate as Annabel and several miles east of Bob's apartment. The area, with small lots and houses, was more residential and his house wore a fresh coat of dark navy paint.

Annabel pulled in behind the car port. The front door opened quickly after she knocked.

"Welcome," he said.

She stepped in to a warm atmosphere with a narrow staircase to the right and a small room to the left with a cane chair and settee sofa.

"Thank you," she said, slipping off her light jacket.

He draped it over his arm and followed her gaze. "Antique pieces from my mom's chair collection. My dad died and Mom downsized from their house to an apartment. She collected many pieces over the years, but we only kept a few."

"They're pretty. Does your mom live nearby?"

"Forty miles from here, which is perfect for both of us. We visit each other a few times a month."

Annabel nodded and they went down the short hallway. The kitchen was modern yet compact. Two pots were on the stove and a bowl of salad greens sat on the counter.

"It smells wonderful in here," she said.

He took the lids off and let her peek inside. The chicken with broccoli smelled like ginger and soy sauce.

"How about a glass of wine?"

"I'll settle for a half glass."

"I've been here a few years. Redid the kitchen, as you can tell. The place is only two thousand square feet, split between here and upstairs. Plenty big for just me."

He popped the wine cork and poured. "Owning my own real estate gives me something to take care of when my head isn't buried in police work."

She held her glass up to his and, at the same time, a couple of "meows" sounded from somewhere nearby in the house.

"Do I hear a cat?"

Dustin took her hand. "Come meet Solar."

He stepped her over to the corner of the family room as the "meow" changed to a "woof-woof."

It was no cat; nor was it a dog.

On top of a wooden perch, walking back and forth, was a bird.

"What's your problem?" it said.

"Annabel, meet Solar. He's a yellow-naped Amazon parrot."

"What's your problem?" Solar repeated.

"Sorry. That's his favorite thing to say … because I say that to him."

Annabel smiled with amusement and then the joy spread all over her face. And she thought that if Bob and she split ownership of a dog, that would be a big deal. As far as she was concerned, for a single guy, this was one heck of an exotic pet. He must know what he's doing.

"Dustin Lowe," she said, "you are full of surprises."

"Full of surprises," Solar said.

CHAPTER 28

Annabel sat at the dark wood table facing the rec room so that Solar would continue amusing her.

"He sure is handsome," she said. "His green hues, his yellow highlights, and his vigilant, vibrant eyes."

Dustin scooped more rice on his plate. "He's also a conversation piece."

"Hmm. For the ladies you entertain?"

"No 'ladies.' There's only one woman I've been courting. The few people who ever come over are a few cops and we watch football. That's where Solar gets his occasional trashy mouth from."

"He seems to be behaving himself."

Dustin rolled his eyes. "Just wait."

Annabel put down her fork. "You are a better cook than I will ever be. My best creations come from stirring ingredients into a crock pot."

"Help yourself to more."

"No thanks. But if you're finished, I'm washing the dishes."

Dustin carried the plates over and Annabel grabbed both the wine glasses. She rinsed and washed while Dustin dried and put dishes away. As she stood in front of the window, the light from the hanging fixture caused the highlights of her hair to glisten.

Dustin gathered one side of her curls in his fingers and tucked them behind her ear.

"Where'd you get such shiny hair?" He leaned in, letting his fingers inch her head closer.

"Where'd you get that dimple in your chin?"

"I asked my question first," he whispered.

Annabel wrapped her arms around his firm shoulders and went straight for his lips. As he returned her embrace, their tongues met, and Dustin's manhood stirred against her. They both scrambled to peel off their lower clothing, then he tightened his grip and raised her off the floor.

Taking a step while holding her in his arms, Dustin moved a pottery bowl off a short sideboard and lowered her. Their foreheads touched and they looked down as he easily went inside her.

Several thrusts later, Annabel arched her neck with sheer pleasure.

Dustin grappled for her lips once again and soon they slowed their pace, their desire spent.

She glanced up in time to see the bird alight on the top of the cabinetry. The two front toes on both his feet were hooked on the edge and he bobbed his head as if wondering what they were doing.

Annabel tapped Dustin to look up. "Before Solar says anything, tell him you don't have a problem," she said.

Dustin chuckled.

"Do you want to stay the night?"

"I would love to," she said, "but not tonight. A big test is coming up as well as the end of my rotation. I better not mess up my sleep time any more than is needed. Can I take a rain check?"

"I suppose," he grumbled.

"And may I see you the next weekend … when it's all over and I can relax and celebrate?"

"Let's plan on it."

After each of them came back from the bathroom, Dustin pulled a plate out from the refrigerator.

"One more thing. Would you like to share, or would you like your own?"

Her mouth watered just looking at it. "A napoleon. What a way to top off sex."

"Top off sex," Solar mimicked.

Dustin looked up. "Don't go saying that!"

Annabel turned and took two forks out of the drawer. "How about we share?" They went to the table again and she dug her utensil into the layered custard. With each bite, they grinned at each other. By the time they finished, Annabel wanted to take back what she said about not staying over, but she knew she needed to be on her way.

At his front door, they kissed, embraced, and said good-night. She tilted to the side and spoke louder into the back of the house. "Nice to meet you, Solar. Be a good bird for Dustin."

How ironic, she thought, stepping to her car. She wasn't going to sleep over tonight with the guy she was dating, but she'd been staying over at the apartment of the guy she studies with.

And … at least there had been no mention of her study partner while she was at Dustin's.

Annabel was as prepared as possible. Whatever weak areas of internal medicine she possessed, the only way she was going to find out what they were was by missing questions on the test. After the date at Dustin's, she crammed as much as she could when not on the wards.

Bob also assured her that he did a solid overview of their notes and his handbook in the remaining hours. The only thing he wanted, or had left to do after the test, was to finish the remaining time on the wards that he had missed.

She texted him one more time on Sunday night. He promised to sleep a solid ten hours before showing up in the department the next morning.

Which was easy. He still realized that he was in the throes of recuperation and needed more rest because of Ehrlichiosis than under normal circumstances.

Besides being test day, the team was on call. Annabel used an Uber driver and dropped her overnight bag in the front of the test-taking room. She pulled out her iPad. The room was wider than it was deep and she took a seat off a carpeted aisle. Students were peppered throughout the room, with or without their white jackets on.

She waved Bob over as he came into the room and dropped a paper cup in the basket. In a pair of blue jeans, she could tell he had dropped a few pounds. He came around her seat and sat next to her, placing his device forward and plugging it in.

"Are you up to it?" she asked.

"I'll try my best. Because of your help, I think I'll pull through."

They tapped each other's knuckles. Stuart passed across the front of the room and nodded and Annabel glanced around for Jordan, who sat at the end of a row.

"We're going to get started," a man said, standing underneath one of the screens. He was a university doctor ... not in an independent practice. "Does anyone not have their own student-owned device?"

When he received no answer, he closed the remaining open door to the lecture hall. "You may all now open up ExamSoft's secure test site and log in."

Within several minutes, not a peep could be heard. Annabel maintained a steady pace. She reread certain questions and mulled over the answers, but others she answered quickly. She was soon halfway through.

Your patient is a 42-year-old overweight woman you send for ultrasonography. The results confirm gallstones. She comes back in a few months after eating a low-fat diet and presents with a 101 degree F fever, nausea, and right upper quadrant pain. You suspect:

A. *An acute gallbladder perforation*
B. *Acute cholangitis*
C. *Acute cholecystitis*
D. *Acute pancreatitis*

Annabel chose "C" and rubbed her neck to relax for a moment. She glanced toward the side of the room and her eyes fell on Jordan. She caught a flash of the small handbook he used ... off to the side of his lap ... his fingers holding it open. Just as quick, he tugged the side of his lab jacket to rest over it.

She felt anger rise in her throat. There he was again, using his own method to wiggle his way through medical school. She looked back down at her next question. There was no way she would allow his behavior to distract her.

With only twenty-five percent of her test still remaining, Annabel again paused to take a break. A woman to the right, slightly familiar to her, rose from her seat and passed the two rows in front of her. She halted next to Jordan and addressed him in a low voice. His head jolted backwards and after she said something and wouldn't go away, he rose and followed her. Out the front door.

Annabel waited for Bob outside the lecture hall. When he came out, they walked shoulder-to-shoulder to the staircase.

"What was that all about with Jordan?" Bob asked with a hushed tone.

She swung open the door. "I don't know. And that woman from the back of the room? She was not one of us. I think she works in the department."

"He couldn't have finished his test."

"He was cheating again. I'm sure of it. Some compact medicine book hanging out on his lap."

"You serious?"

"I believe so. Anyway, enough about him. How'd you do?"

"Hard to say because my brain still isn't up to speed." He dragged behind her on the steps.

"You go home to your apartment and nestle into bed again before coming back downtown this afternoon for Dr. Enno's lecture. However, I hitched an Uber ride this morning. Can you drop me off at the hospital?"

"Anything. I owe you and I promise to pay you back. Especially if I passed."

"Like two minus two, you owe me nothing."

"I'll think of something."

Bob drove her right under the awning of the front entrance. She pulled her bag from the back seat. "I'll go by the office after call in the morning. I'm sure they'll give me your test results if you want. I can call or text you."

"Okay. I'd appreciate that. In one way, I'm sorry our test is over with."

She gave him a quizzical look.

"You won't be staying over any more nights at my place."

"That sounds like something is going on between us. Other than studying."

I wish, he thought, but refrained from saying so. He only narrowed his eyes at her. "Poring over textbooks has been our agenda together, but now that is over. I'll talk to you soon. Besides later and tomorrow, I mean."

"Absolutely." She shook her head. "Just get better and finish your course of antibiotics. One thing I'll never do again is ask you to go running with me."

"Sitting on the ground and letting a tick crawl into my clothes is my own fault. We'll hit the pavement together in the future. Okay?"

"All right," she said. Immediately, she came up with an idea. To give him a present. "Go home now and take a nap because you don't want to miss Dr. Enno's lecture at three o'clock. I bet she's going to be phenomenal."

Bob pulled away and she went inside. Jeez, she thought, that was like an Irish good-bye and they were going to see each other again in a few hours.

This morning, Dr. Schott and the residents had taken care of all their patients while the students had taken their test, so Annabel figured she had the time to pop into the cafeteria and grab a late cup of coffee. She tilted the black lever and poured from the big dispenser.

"No one will know it was because of you."

Annabel looked over her shoulder. It was Donn, holding a to-go cup like her.

"What?" she said, not understanding the meaning of what he said.

"You shouldn't suffer any repercussions from Jordan. It was because of you saying that he cheated on the mid-term exam that Dr. Mejia and I planted a department spy in the back of the lecture hall this morning to monitor him.

"As far as we're concerned," he hissed, "we consider any student cheating through their training to be guilty of breaking the Hippocratic Oath and to have accumulated the grounds to be kicked back out into the general public. The medical school board will see it that way too."

Annabel remembered her hand was still pressing down on the pour knob and she let go.

"I saw him with an open book again," she said, "and saw him escorted out. Dr. Mejia must be disappointed."

"Between you and me, Dr. Mejia needs to be less enamored by the likes of him. The best doctors can come from the quiet, scholarly ones like Stuart, or the ones carrying a smile and a humorous personality like Bob, or a smart, dedicated one empathetic to her patients like you. Not cheaters."

He sighed while she reached for the powdered cream and stirred some in her coffee.

"Society is full of defrauders and schemers and charlatans," he continued. "There is no way I'm going to look the other way. I have a nest of students and residents who I feed every day. None of them will fledge away from my supervision if they can't soar with the feathers necessary for flight and independently fly with character."

Annabel paid for her coffee. "Too bad it happened. We know how hard college students and others in the workforce prepare to gain admission. His spot could have been filled by another capable, honest med student."

"So true," he said as they made their way to the elevator and the doors snapped open. "Don't talk too much about this or malign him. Not that you would. But you never know if someone like him will hire an attorney and claim some type of discrimination for booting him out and make up some nonsense about his cheating."

"I understand." She sipped the weak brew and the doors opened on the medical floor.

"The lawsuit from the atrial fibrillation case, Mrs. Helm's kids, was enough."

"How do you think it will end?"

He half-smiled. "Our attorney says they are softening and there is less legal activity. Maybe as the family's grief fades, so will their demands for retribution of what happened … which was natural and in God's hands."

"I hope so, Dr. Schott."

It was too strange when they walked into the team's office. Their numbers had fallen yet again.

They were on call and the group was down to two medical students, two residents, one chief resident, and an attending who supervised like he should: not too much and not too little.

After a discussion about the content of the final exam and how they think they fared, Stuart was the first one to ask. "Where's Jordan?"

CHAPTER 29

By the time the group lugged up the hospital stairs, Stuart and the residents heard a shortened version of why Jordan wasn't with the team.

Stuart was the most dumbstruck and perplexed. "His actions don't make any sense. Why risk everything he's worked for by cheating? He couldn't have gotten by solely finagling all this time on exams. The guy isn't dumb. After all the preparatory years it took to get into medical school and then to land in the middle of his junior year, he took a chance to blow it all? Doesn't make sense."

"He's just an arrogant dumbass," Melody said.

"For sure," Annabel said, "but I agree with Stuart. From a psychiatry or psychology point of view, his actions don't make sense. It's like he ramped up his risk of getting caught so that he could fall flat on his face and lose his future career. For some deep psychological reason like he was afraid of success. Or maybe he realized more and more that his future lifestyle in medicine was going to be different than he thought and subconsciously wanted a way out."

"What do you think, Dr. Schott?"

"I did not give any thought to the 'why' he did what he did. You two bring up a prudent subject." He opened the door of the staircase and let the team step in front of him.

"There is something going on with him. Perhaps an excellent psychotherapist can get to the root of the what and why. I'm going to mention mental help therapy to Dr. Mejia because he'll be talking to the medical school board. Even if Jordan is out of medical school for good, offering assistance or concrete suggestions to 'turn him around' is the right thing to do."

Annabel and Stuart glanced at each other and concurred.

"One thing's for sure," Stuart said, "he's not going to be any cardiologist."

Donn took a big sigh as the ICU doors broke open and he herded them forward. "We didn't make it to the unit early this morning. Let's check how Jae Nixon is doing."

They crowded through the doorway of Jae's cubicle and perched themselves at the bottom of the bed.

"Will you look at this?" Dr. Schott said.

Not only were Jae's toes and ankles flexing, but his right arm suddenly slinked over and stopped to rest on his abdomen. Donn reached for Jae Nixon's bedside chart, scanned his overnight vital signs, and nodded.

Jae's day shift nurse bustled in. "Out of the blue, he started moving purposefully around 3 a.m. That's what the night nurse told me, but Dr. Enno hasn't been in yet. Boy, is she going to be taken by surprise." She stood there like she was seeing him move for the first time.

Annabel took a double take at Jae's arm. "Dr. Enno is giving grand rounds later. Maybe she adjusted her schedule."

She inched along Jae's bedside, patted his tattoo, and wrapped her fingers around his hand lying on his abdomen.

Melody scanned the ventilator settings from the day before. "May I see his ABG results from this morning?" The nurse left and reappeared promptly with the lab result.

"He's picked up on his own rate since I decreased his setting yesterday. Let's evaluate his blood work."

Donn peered over her shoulder. "Looking good. Pass this around. Mr. Nixon's pH is normal and his oxygenation and CO_2 is the best it's been. We're getting close to a full turn-around. His brain swelling has subsided enough to not be a major concern anymore and his urine output is perfect."

Annabel gasped as she felt Jae's fingers return a weak squeeze. She studied their hands. For a second, she thought she was out of line. It could be construed like the holding of hands between two best friends or loved ones. But, nonsense, she thought. If this human touch he was feeling was therapeutic for him, then it was as important as the ventilator, the IVs, and the medication they'd been giving him.

He hugged her fingers again with his own and then she darted her eyes to his face. Like a polar bear awakening from hibernation and slowly assessing his surroundings, Jae's eyes both opened. Annabel couldn't contain the squeal of excitement which escaped from her lips.

"Look!" she told her teammates.

"Jae," she said, "you're in the hospital because you've been very sick. Time to wake up!"

Donn and Melody moved further towards the head of the bed on the other side. Tentative smiles came over both of them. Donn grinned. He approved of Annabel talking to him … her words, her soft voice, her reassurance.

Jae struggled to keep his eyes open. He blinked multiple times, which seemed to help. The people around him became clearer. He widened his eyes further, stretching them awake, as if clearing the cobwebs away after being closed for so long.

"You're making excellent progress, Mr. Nixon," Donn said. "We're right here for you … in the intensive care unit. Now that you're awake, the next step will be to get you out of here. You can wish for that, okay? Make it your goal."

Jae squeezed his eyes closed as if he took comfort in everyone's words. His respiratory rate was adequately overriding the respirator. He slipped his hand out from Annabel's and scrambled it up to the tubing from his endotracheal tube to the ventilator. He emphatically signaled. He wanted no more part of these artificial contraptions. They had served him well, but it was time to test the waters and see if he could totally breathe on his own.

His hand now wrapped around the endotracheal tube and he moved his head forward off the pillow slightly.

"Whoa," Annabel said and glanced nervously at Donn for instructions.

"He's ready, Dr. Tilson. You can pull it." He looked at the RN and asked her to send respiratory therapy in.

"Wait, Jae, it will be much safer if I take your tube out." She suctioned out the scarce secretions in the tube and peeled off the tape along his mouth and tube. She deflated the cuff - which helped lodge the tube in his throat – with a syringe, and pulled out while he gagged and sputtered to be rid of it.

"Take a deep breath. Show me what you can do."

The respiratory therapist was next to her in a flash. "Nasal cannula or mask for a while?" he asked.

"Let's give him a moment," Donn said.

Jae coughed a few times and took deep breaths. He wiggled his fingers at them. "I'm fine," he stuttered. "Breathing naturally feels so good. I don't know how long I've been here and I have a million questions." His eyes settled warmly on Annabel like he had known her a long time.

"All in due time, Mr. Nixon. All in due time."

The team lingered at the doorway for some time as new bloodwork was drawn on Jae and they were assured he was fine with receiving oxygen just by a nasal cannula.

Like some script for a "magnificent five" medical team, the residents and students peeled away from the unit. They strolled past the grand windows of the waiting room.

"Dr. Enno is going to birth a canary when she hears about Jae's progress," Annabel said. At that, she laughed out loud because Solar also popped into her thoughts. "Sorry, I was thinking about a bird I know."

"Yes," Donn said. "He opened his eyes *and* you extubated him. And to top it off, he seems, at least so far, like his mental status is intact and no worse for wear."

Donn cocked his head towards her. "What bird?"

Annabel was so bemused thinking about Dustin's parrot, she grinned mischievously and couldn't answer his question.

Dr. Schott regretted the timing of their call day to correlate with Dr. Enno's grand rounds. There was nothing he could do to change things around. He thought about asking Dr. Watt and Dr. Burg to stay at the hospital with him to help out since he'd be taking care of all their patients as well as any new admissions by himself. His seniority dictated that he should be the one to miss Dr. Enno's talk, but he couldn't let that happen to the rest of the team. Especially since her talk was born from the diagnoses brought forward from their own team ... of Bob Palmer and Jae Nixon.

Dr. Watt and Dr. Burg left separately and Annabel and Stuart crossed the parking lot together. The afternoon sky was bright with sunshine. For some reason, it made Annabel think of Easter Sunday when tulips blossomed and marigolds were as yellow as the sun.

Stuart clutched his car keys and since Annabel was hitchhiking a ride with him, she would experience a ride first hand in his 1984 black Jaguar Coupe. Besides studying all the time, he had at least held on to his main hobby of being a car enthusiast. She settled into the tan leather passenger seat, amazed at the pristine condition of the interior, and Stuart pulled away.

"What's the number showing up on your odometer?" Annabel asked.

His eyes never left the road, but she could make out his proud smile, like a father at his kid's winning soccer game.

"Eighty thousand, give or take a few."

"Amazing. Don't you hate to drive it, though? Accumulate more miles and chance making the body rusty and worn?"

"What's the point in having a classic car if I don't use it? I'm not Jay Leno and didn't buy her to store her away. I'm gonna use this baby."

"I would do the same thing, but I thought that would only happen with a minority of people owning old cars."

"Probably so."

She enjoyed riding in the Jaguar as well as his careful driving. There was more personality to Stuart than she previously guessed. Funny how many of the people you work with, she thought, have personal aspects to their lives that you never know about.

Stuart took the exit off the interstate. "I've been looking forward to Dr. Enno's lecture for a week," Annabel finally said. "And it'll be reassuring to see Bob back at a clinical function. He's been gaining his strength back. I'm hoping he won't tire out too much by attending."

"Since he also sat for the test this morning, you're right. This is like a spring break's amount of activity for him in one day. He's having a heck of a first day out."

The only parking outside the building was metered and Annabel shoved quarters into the machine. They both went inside to the second floor lecture hall, different from where they'd taken their test, although there were high tech screens and gadgets in the room as well. The absolute first thing they did was to scan the room for Bob.

Not seeing him in the crowd, they took seats in the middle of the room as a young man from the tech department helped Dr. Enno set up in front. Dr. Mejia was also seated in a forward aisle.

"Do you think we should tell her about Jae Nixon?" Annabel asked.

Stuart grimaced. "We should let her to concentrate on her lecture, in my opinion."

"Okay. You are being more objective than I am. I won't disturb her."

Bob ambled in and gave them a subtle wave as he made his way into their aisle. He handed Annabel an envelope as he lowered himself next to her.

"What's this?"

"I stopped at the department office and, on the way out, the secretary asked me to give this to you. It's addressed to you."

Perplexed, Annabel squinted her eyes. The envelope was sent to her care of the internal medicine department and the return address was from May Oliver, her lung cancer patient who had recently passed away. Her lips quivered with sadness when she realized May must have written it before her death and put the note in the mail herself or maybe her mother had.

She peeled it open and unfolded white stationery with a pale blue border. The handwriting was written in black ink, a feeble attempt at being neat and pretty. But May had nonetheless done her best with the circumstance she found herself in at the end of her cut-short lifespan.

The writing filled the paper like May had measured out her words to fit perfectly. She read from the beginning.

Dear Dr. (student) Tilson,

I am happy with myself to fire this off to you, yet I believe you will be sorry to hear that I am no longer here.

I have no idea if doctors ever receive 'thank you' notes from their patients, but I suspect since you are in training, this will be your first one.

Thank you for your help in taking care of me and especially for your kindness which made it more personal for me ... like we were friends and that you really cared. Going through the lung cancer was more difficult for me than the time I spent serving in Afghanistan and I found it ironic that I made it home from there only to be attacked at home by an adenocarcinoma. Particularly because I never smoked.

I'm writing several letters to people who made it easier for me in the end and perhaps allowed me to face death in a more refined way by thinking there are magnificent people in this world.

I did truly miss my dog in the end after that terrible tragedy at the dog day care center and I know you are missing your family pet as well. Maybe someday soon you will be able to own your own dog despite your training and career. Please give the endearing creature love from me.

Don't lose touch with your kind heart as you continue to train. There will be more patients like me who will appreciate you. And don't worry about me ... I'm probably where I should be.

Sincerely,
May Oliver

A tear fell down on the note before Annabel could swipe it away. Bob's fingers landed on hers for a moment and then he withdrew his hand back to his lap. She set the letter on her knee and wiped her tears. After giving Bob a short frown, she folded the keepsake and inserted it back in the envelope.

"Are you all right?" he asked.

She nodded. "May I make a request? If you and I get a dog like we're thinking about, do you mind if we name her or him 'May' or 'Oliver?'"

"Not at all, but I have a request too."

His tone was pleasant and light and she figured he was trying to make her feel better.

"If we get a dog together, I will be the one absolutely responsible to make sure that he or she gets a monthly tick preventative medication. I have experience with the downfall of what can happen to either one of us otherwise." He tried on a smile to see if it would work on her.

Annabel nodded and swiped her hand across her cheek to remove the last tear.

"Okay. It's a deal."

CHAPTER 30

The lecture hall soon filled up. Few seats remained. Shania Enno followed the activities of the young man setting up the technology for her lecture with keen eyes. When he appeared to be finished, she leaned Alejandro against the podium and fiddled with the electronic pointer. The cover page of her lecture was prominently displayed on three substantial screens:

Our Infinitesimal yet Colossal Danger by Shania Enno, M.D.

Shania tested the microphone to make sure everyone heard her just fine. She nodded at the young man, who gave her a little salute with his right hand and walked to the back of the room where he switched his duty to the recording of her lecture.

Annabel crossed her legs, ready to be comfortable and as attentive as possible. Bob nestled further back into his chair.

"I bet she's going to knock the lecture into orbit," he whispered. "I can't imagine being on stage with a pointer and a microphone at her age."

"Why not? I'm going to try my best to be like her. And did you see? They have set up to tape her lecture. Maybe they'll send her talk into NPT!" She giggled and focused forward.

Shania cleared her throat. "Good afternoon. Today is this week's medicine department Grand Rounds. In case any of you are in the wrong lecture, you are welcome to stay." She pranced the blue light of the pointer up on the title of her talk. "Our Infinitesimal yet Colossal Danger discussion today may take longer than an hour, but the department has cleared the time from clinical duties for all of you. So sit back, listen, and learn.

"As a foreword, this discussion must include my notes on global warming. The medical aspect of my lecture is not complete without the inclusion of that subject matter. We can't talk about one without the other. However, here's my caveat. On purpose, I am not going to call the weather phenomena 'global warming.' In my opinion, that term conjures up politics, political rhetoric, and a right and a left side of a political spectrum that usurps what scientists say after they research and investigate weather phenomena on our planet.

"Instead, I will only use the term 'climate change.' Whatever your political views are, go dump them outside. The necessary foundation of my medical and biological discussion today rests on climate change because, without it, the medical diseases I will speak of would not be rearing their ugly heads as much as they are.

"So you also understand where I'm coming from," Dr. Enno said while she still stayed on the title slide of her lecture, "again, this talk is politically neutral. Although there must be climate change occurring for the infectious diseases I speak of today to propagate, I make no statement as to why the planet is warming. If human beings are responsible for it and whether or not they can do anything to change it, is not part of my discussion."

She looked all around. Satisfied that she made her point, she nodded and moved ahead to the first slide.

"The ice sheets are melting. This here is a big chunk of Antarctica which broke off this year. The seas are warming from below the ice masses, which is causing, and will continue to cause, major collapses of mile-high ice. This is, and will be causing, rising seas.

"And on the opposite end of this pole, passages are being made by Mother Nature in the Arctic ... allowing shipping vessels to travel in previously unnavigable seas; and in Greenland, two men recently spotted open land from a helicopter ... surrounded by snow and ice. They landed and it is believed they stood on that soil for the first time as far back in history as can be imagined. These events are heretofore a thing of one's imagination.

"Of course, man's coastal areas are in ridiculous trouble. In a residential area of Miami, four years ago, residents kayaked during high tide through their neighborhood because of rising seas but, since then, they are not. Because 500 million dollars of taxpayers' money was spent to beef up a barrier against the tidewater which kept creeping higher. Mind you, not due to storms, but due to rising seas. When will that stop? To pump in massive monies like that for the short fix of a few years? And granted, that is only one little area. Beach restoration and the funds needed are going on and being spent year after year along our sandy coastlines."

Shania sighed with despair, which echoed through the microphone.

"I am pleased I am an old lady who will no longer be around to continue to witness the stupidity of government funding and the communities which demand shoring up of land that is inevitably doomed."

She changed the slide to an expansive aerial view of the cold continent of Greenland with the section of earth she alluded to.

"Now bear with me. Although I am an old lady, don't underestimate me. My roundabout way to get to the infectious diseases that came to light for Dr. Mejia and Dr. Schott's team this month is not unwarranted. My wits are with me and I will paint the entire picture which precludes the story of the foxy diseases I will present. Yes, they are clever!

"I say 'foxy,' which means clever, and although I could possibly use fox in my discussion, I am going to instead bring in the white-footed mouse. Because ... my main patient with today's premier infectious disease presented with an unknown history to us of having been knee deep in their environment. So much so, that he was trying to cull their population from the grounds where he lives.

"Our patient is a thirty-five-year-old Ohio National Park Ranger," she explained, "who helps maintain the inner workings and tours of a former presidential home as well as sees to the outside grounds and safety of the nearby woods and trails.

"Anyway, getting back to climate change and the white-footed mouse." She popped up a picture of a horde of scurrying mice. Many medical students were previous biology majors, so she knew she had a captive audience interested in animals, their behavior, and their range.

"What heavily influences a species' life cycle? Climate! Over time, the weather dictates the environmental conditions which affect an organism's reproduction, behavior, phenology, physiological tolerance, and its sensitivity to habitat quality and food supply.

"And above all ... its absolute survival. Because of recent climate change, fluctuations in the weather are faster and of greater amplitude than ever, ever before in the entire past. This affects the distribution patterns and niches of a species.

"Scientists have empirical evidence which is mounting by the day that the earth's species are responding to climate warming and the temperatures have already had a dramatic effect on the flora and fauna of geographical regions in the 20th century.

"What's going on is that the stability of a species' niche is being challenged. Its tolerance and adaptability is being pushed to its outer limits. They shift themselves poleward or upward in their geographic elevation. At the same time, this climate change increases the ability for invasive species to establish themselves in new areas.

"A stark example of a species shifting poleward in its distribution is the successful Eastern North American native rodent, the white-footed mouse. Scientists have calculated his increased and expanded rate of migration on the Upper Peninsula of Michigan for the last forty years. Records also document his northward trek in southern Quebec. The numbers are quite appalling.

"The white-footed mouse usually lives a couple of years, but in northern climates it lives a bit less - one or two years. They eat insects and seeds and, in particular, gather and store seeds and nuts in the fall. They often live in the walls of apartments and homes where they store their food and build their nests and are also the most abundant small rodent in mixed forests in the eastern United States. And, last year the northeast had a record abundance of acorns, which fueled them into a booming population explosion!

"On the other hand, their usefulness is that they eat fungi and spread the spores on the ground in their droppings. This allows local trees to gain nutrients through their roots. They also do eat harmful insect pests and do not engage in harmful activities towards farmers' crops.

"So what's the big deal and why do I bring up these mice? The significance is that their northern migration is a public health concern!

"And everything is interconnected, isn't it?"

She gave them a moment to think about that and began again and said in a louder voice and with more passion:

"The prolific, northern migrating white-footed mouse is known to be the main host for *Ixodes scapularis,* the black-legged tick at the larval stage. And each summer, fall, and spring, the tick population increases because of milder winters and the growing mice and deer populations. Dozens of ticks can attach to a single rodent!"

Dr. Enno skipped ahead to her first photograph of the life cycle of her publicized tick. Of the larva, nymph, and adult male and female tick, the larval stage was the beginning of the cycle and the tiniest specimen on her slide of the entire life cycle.

It gave Annabel the creeps to see the slide with the little vampire, especially the premature size of the larva; she glanced at Bob and shook her head while Bob shuddered.

"The thirty-five-year-old male national park ranger who presented to our medical team first presented to the ER staff with flu-like symptoms. He was sent home with instructions to get rest and to treat his cold symptoms. He came back approximately one week later with worsening symptoms - a fever, headache, vomiting, and central symptoms such as slight memory problems.

"As far as preliminary testing suggestive of an encephalitis, an EEG and an MRI were useful, but a brain CT fell short of being helpful. And to the gloom and frustration of our team, and to the jeopardy of our patient, he soon lapsed into a coma and was in the ICU on life support.

"As most of you can appreciate, the possibilities, the cause of his situation and diagnosis, were prolific. And time was of utmost importance to discover and treat his disease. Would this man succumb to his death, stay unconscious for the foreseeable future, and/or could we start him on an antibiotic and reverse his path of ruination?

"As Mr. X's day by day hospital course unfolded, the internal medicine team worked their magic to keep him alive with respiratory support, intravenous fluids, and drips to decrease intracranial pressure while I chipped away at unearthing and discarding possible diagnoses. But here is where I tell you physicians and students-in-training that the history of your patients is of paramount importance.

"From our patient's coworker - a woman who lived in one of the cabins of the national park like our patient - we later learned two important aspects of Mr. X's lifestyle.

"First, as part of his park responsibilities, he was practicing extermination techniques on the white-footed mouse living in the park and their cabins - the very rodent so incriminated in carrying the dreaded ticks, which cause severe illness in humans.

"And secondarily, our patient is a deer hunter. According to the time frame of a recent bow and arrow expedition he had taken, and the fact that he spent the latter part of an entire day hauling in a buck, and skinning and processing it, his body could have become the habitat for one tick or multiple ticks from his activities with either the mice or the deer. In addition, even from the dogs the rangers take care of on their property.

"We know for a fact from his coworker ranger friend, that on the day of his last deer hunting expedition, he pried ticks off of his body. No one likes to do that and people unaccustomed with these critters sometimes don't even know what they are. However, I am sure our patient knew what he was dealing with, and most likely took certain preventative measures, which were not one-hundred percent effective. We will talk about that and I'll give you my two-cents about alarming your patients to the vastly increased threat to them regarding ticks.

"So, back to the possible diagnosis. Much to our disappointment, and along the course of our patient's workup, bacterial infectious diseases were eliminated as the culprit. He failed courses of antibiotics and continued to lie in his stuporous state.

"At the core of helpfulness in a situation like this is a patient's own immune system. As we are at a loss with discovery, his or her own body is at war with whatever is slinking around in their bloodstream. An immune response is generated against the foreign substance ... cells such as those from the thymus, spleen, lymph nodes, and lymphocytes become warriors against the invasive intruder and, most importantly, antibodies are formed. These high molecular weight proteins, normally produced by B cells, act specifically against the antigen and can be detected by laboratory tests of blood or spinal fluid.

"Thank goodness for the specificity and know-how which emerges from our CDC. They are at the forefront of new, emerging diseases, and have the wherewithal to develop diagnostic tests and deliver diagnostic conclusions where possible. After sending off our patient's laboratory samples, we were told of Mr. X's rare tick-borne disease.

"A positive POW virus IgM test result was confirmed.

"A virus! Powassan virus."

She nodded her head to several residents who had befuddled expressions on their faces.

"That's correct. Powassan virus. You've never heard of it. Our patient is the seventy-sixth patient diagnosed with the disease in the last ten years, but the incidence has heightened in the last two years. The numbers are clustered and are ramping up just like we discussed the ramping up the geographical northward expansion and numbers of the white-footed mouse. Don't forget we had that population boom."

Dr. Enno reached for the plastic cup of water on the podium and took a sip.

"Many states north and northwest of us have recorded cases, but we now have the distinction of being the first reportable case in Ohio.

"So what is the cure for this potentially catastrophic or fatal disease, which causes inflammation of the brain and/or lining of the brain? What is the treatment for this disease, which can cause mental confusion, seizures, memory loss, and long-term neurologic problems?

"There is no known pharmaceutical drug in our armamentarium to cure or treat Powassan virus!"

A hand shot up from a senior medical student in the front of the room. "Penicillin or doxycycline doesn't work?"

"No. No such luck since Powassan is a virus, not a bacterium."

Another arm rose for a question. "The specific tick you mentioned before – *Ixodes* something – has it been conclusively linked to this particular disease?"

"*Ixodes scapularis* maintains a life cycle with the white-footed mouse. The answer to your question is 'yes.' There are also two types of Powassan or POW viruses. Type 2, also termed Deer Tick virus, is the one associated with *Ixodes scapularis*. This tick often bites humans. It's also the primary vector of other human diseases such as Lyme disease."

Dr. Enno took another sip and sat down on the wooden chair on the stage. She spoke clearly into the microphone.

"Speaking of Lyme disease, however, there's a big difference between the possibility of acquiring that disease or Powassan. If you find a tick adhered to your body and remove it within the first day or two, you can escape acquiring the spiral-shaped Lyme bacterium because it takes them forty-eight hours to transmit. And we know how awful Lyme disease is.

"However, Powassan goes through the tick's body into its saliva and into the patient's bloodstream within a few minutes of a bite. So even though the virus is only present in about four percent of *Ixodes scapularis* ticks, lower than the 30 to 40 percent presence of Lyme disease bacterium in *Ixodes scapularis*, if the right tick bores its little head into you, you're sunk."

Shania leaned forward.

"These blacklegged deer ticks have a super taste for human flesh and since there is no treatment for POW virus, half of all patients who contract it will suffer permanent brain damage and ten percent will die."

CHAPTER 31

Dr. Enno stood, gripped Alejandro, and paced across the stage from right to left. Annabel dug into her pocket and pulled out her chocolate-covered blueberries. She sucked on one while she passed a few to Bob.

"Thanks," he said and smiled.

"I'm so glad you came."

"I am too. A test and a lecture in one day. I'm tired already, but she's worth it. She's so thorough and she hasn't even brought up my case yet."

"Did she ask you if she could use your name?" Annabel whispered.

He nodded. "I have no problem with her doing that. Many of the medicine people here are aware that I'm off the wards because of some kind of illness. At least there won't be a doubt as to my credibility."

Shania stopped behind the podium after the bit of activity she had afforded herself. She cleared her throat and chuckled. "Making sure my bones don't freeze up.

"After Powassan virus quickly reached our patient's brain and held his body hostage, the team kept him alive, we received his diagnosis, and I communicated back and forth with the CDC and local health officials. And above all, we maintained our hope and vigilance for his recovery.

"We are thrilled to report that today our patient not only opened his eyes and is lucid, but his very own medical student extubated him and he will be on his way to recovery. Hopefully, he'll be out of the unit soon, transferred to a regular room, and engaged with a small dose of physical therapy to gain his strength back.

"Now, many of you are familiar with the tickborne diseases from the newspapers or television or the occasional case we see in our teaching environment. They are more commonly the illnesses caused by infected ticks carrying wretched bacteria such as Rocky Mountain Spotted fever or Lyme disease. But lo and behold, our own medical student, Bob Palmer, had grander plans than acquiring those. He has been recuperating from what's called Ehrlichiosis."

She looked straight at Bob and several people in the audience also acknowledged him. Annabel tried not to add to the attention he was receiving.

Shania went to a slide of a tick burrowed into someone's thigh. "You see this one here. He's plumper than the one in the picture I showed you before. As they suck blood, they engorge themselves and plump out; they can lose all their physical identity and their forefront can disappear into their host.

"A carpenter can pull a nail out of a wall with the opposite end of a hammer, but a victim of a tick is lucky to root out the vampire from his skin with a tweezer. It's a death grip to the end.

"And the bacteria they carry? Take your pick: Ehrlichial species of bacteria with Ehrlichiosis, the rickettsia group of bacteria with Rocky Mountain Spotted fever, *Borrelia burgdorferi* bacteria with Lyme disease and so forth and so on.

"With Ehrlichiosis, our medical student was bitten by the lone star tick, a different tick than that which latched into our ICU patient. Symptoms for this disease include fever, headache, muscle pains, confusion, and low energy. Laboratory clues as to the diagnosis include a remarkable thrombocytopenia, leukopenia, and elevated LFTs. Diagnosis is also confirmed by the detection of antibodies, but you all must recognize that once a suspicion of this diagnosis is made, treatment should not be delayed. The appropriate dosage of Doxycycline for one to two weeks is the magic first line treatment.

"Unfortunately, the case fatality rate of Ehrlichiosis is up to two percent and, like Powassan disease, a patient may need hospitalization and care in an ICU. In this case, IV antibiotics may be needed."

Shania tapped Alejandro on the wooden floor. "I am happy to report that Dr. Palmer is slowly getting better. Our support goes out to him to get back on track with his rotations."

Dr. Enno glanced at the wall clock in the back of the room and raised the water cup to her lips. She flipped ahead to another slide, which made the audience cringe more than before - an adult bull dog – his poor body bombarded with plump ticks, some of which were too big to hold on any more and had plummeted to the floor.

"Since we also talk about preventative medicine besides treatment, I would be amiss to not include the measures which we should all take to help prevent tick bites. Part of my sneaky presentation right now is to stir the brain cells of you youngsters in training to do me a favor. In the future, you will be giving your patients the normal pitch to stay healthy with a good diet, exercise, routine medical care, etc., etc."

She slid to the next slide, which showed a number of items. "Bring up year-round preventive measures with your patients against ticks. Tell families to avoid wooded, brushy areas if there is no need to be there, and to walk in the middle of hiking trails. Tell them about repellents with DEET, and tell them to cover as much of their skin with clothing as possible when they're outside. There is even pre-treated clothing that repels ticks. Tell them to check for them on their bodies when coming inside and bathe carefully to find them or wash them off.

"Please, treat your family dog with preventive products and don't let them end up like this fella. They are also susceptible to tickborne diseases and if you don't treat them preventatively, ticks will be hitching a ride on your four-legged companions and coming into your home.

"Be cognizant of the area around your home. It is possible to apply pesticides in yard areas. Mow lawns frequently, remove leaf and wood clutter so as to not attract rodents, and think about fences, which discourage other unwelcome animals, such as the white-footed mouse that harbor ticks.

"I attest to adding some of these remarks to your patients when you deem it worthwhile and possible. An idiom from my day is 'An ounce of prevention is worth a pound of cure.' Alert your patients, especially during yearly wellness visits, of the growing problem with these diseases."

Shania moved on to another slide. A long list. "My lecture time is up. You may want to jot some of these down but, if not, be aware of the many, many tickborne diseases in the United States besides the ones we dwelt on: Colorado tick fever, Anaplasmosis, Heartland virus, Tularemia, etc., etc. Don't be afraid to reach out to the CDC in the future and keep up to date with the information that they post.

"Take note of your patient's symptoms on presentation and never forget how important their social endeavors and recent travels are in the big picture. And remember … ticks aren't going anywhere, except just about everywhere."

Annabel, Bob, and Stuart stepped off the curb into the parking lot.

"I bet that will be the first and last time you're a subject in a grand rounds lecture." Stuart raised his eyebrows at Bob.

"I hope that's true," Bob said.

"I, for one, am not going to easily forget her talk," Annabel added.

"Being that our test taking for medicine is over," Stuart said, "it was better yet to sit back and relax and not have a final exam hanging over our heads."

Annabel and Stuart veered off to the right as Bob stayed straight. "I guess I'll talk to you," she mentioned, glancing back over her shoulder. "I hitched a ride with Stuart."

"I can drop you off instead. The way I see it, I owe you some transportation."

Annabel shrugged her shoulders.

"Go ahead," Stuart said. "After all, studying for the test is over for both of you. Might as well enjoy social time." He kept walking without checking on her decision.

Annabel caught up with Bob and they proceeded to his car. The beginning of the drive, Bob stayed shrouded in silence.

"You're awfully quiet," Annabel said. "Are you worried if you passed the written?"

He looked over. "Not only that. What Stuart said struck home. Our studying together for the final is over and I can't impose on you for help anymore. I'm feeling well enough to take better care of myself through the tail end of this tick disease."

"Hmm." Annabel thought it out some more and also realized they wouldn't be on the same rotation after medicine so, in essence, they wouldn't be seeing each other at all. Unless they got a dog together and unless they arranged to do something together. And with conflicting schedules, how often would that be?

She frowned. Bob was too good of a friend to not hang out with on a regular basis.

"I see what you mean. I'm sorry you're not finishing the week with us. But listen, I'll keep you posted about the wards and my Powassan patient that I extubated today. Plus, let's keep the discussion going about sharing a dog."

A smile formed on his lips and she sighed with relief.

"At least you don't have Jordan to contend with anymore."

"Ha! So true."

Bob weaved through the parking lot and to the front entrance of the hospital. Annabel scrambled out and passed in the front of the car. She gestured her hand for him to roll down his window.

"Thanks for the lift. You stay at home tomorrow and I'll find out our test results in the morning after call. I'll let you know. I'm going to miss sharing my chocolates with you for the rest of the week."

She surprised herself and Bob too. She leaned in and gave him a mini gesture like a hug.

"Talk to you later." She stepped back, turned, and disappeared into the hospital.

"I'm impressed!" Annabel exclaimed, her eyes glued on Jae Nixon as she came around his bed in the ICU.

Jae was sitting up against the pillows in his bed and a tray table was in front of him. A food tray with a bowl of broth and a cup of applesauce was on top and Jae had a spoon to his lips. He slipped the contents down his throat and nodded.

"Dr. Burg said if I slide this down, sometime later today, one of you will take this out." He patted the central line on his upper chest. "You're the one who took that nasty tube out of me, so maybe you can whip this out too."

"And I better check on all the lab work that was done on you this morning. We don't want to take things away without knowing the total picture."

"I heard this disease I have can kill people."

"The infectious disease doctor just gave a talk about that."

"I've never been so popular. I wish it were under different circumstances."

Annabel nodded. "You will come to learn that the tick that bit you is called *Ixodes scapularis.* You can blame him."

"There are better living things to be intimate with." He checked her expression to see if she was amused, and they both laughed.

"Do you remember me from before?" she asked.

He narrowed his eyes. "For sure. You drove me to the hospital ... the first time. And now I'm certain."

"Certain about what?"

"These latter days ... I was going in and out of dreaming and, occasionally, I heard things going on around me. It was you who told me."

He gave her a fixed gaze and imitated her. "It's time to roust yourself awake and recover. I'm leaving the rotation soon, so I won't be helping with your care anymore."

Annabel's eyes widened; she opened her mouth, but nothing came out. Jae smiled. "You see ... I took your instructions to heart."

"That really makes my day, Mr. Nixon." She wrapped her hand around his empty applesauce container and pitched it into the garbage can. "Looks like that big bore IV is coming out tonight too."

Annabel and Stuart raced around all night between the ER and the medical wards and never made it to their call rooms. The best they did was sit down a few times on the couch. Dr. Schott postponed rounds for a short while so everyone could go freshen up, maybe even put on a fresh pair of scrubs.

With the pressure of the final exam over, Annabel knew after she made it home, she'd crash into bed as soon as possible. She took the allotted time and jumped into the shower in the call room, dressed, and headed back for rounds. Along with Dr. Burg the night before, they had taken Jae Nixon's central line out. His electrolytes and blood counts were no worse for wear and they had written to have him transferred to a regular room in the morning.

Dr. Mejia joined them. All decked out in a sport's coat and a crisp tie, he strolled up front with Dr. Schott. "Too bad you missed Dr. Enno's lecture yesterday," he said. "You should ask her for some kind of handout."

"Rumor has it that it was a hit," Donn said. "It better have been since I held up the fort here without my residents and students."

Dr. Mejia turned his head toward Annabel and Stuart. "Bet you're both going over to get your grades after this. I'll let the cat out of the bag ... you both passed."

Annabel pumped her fist and Stuart nodded.

"I'm sure you want to know your scores," Dr. Mejia said. "I'm not divulging those."

They turned into the first room in the hallway off of the nurses' station. Jae Nixon's new room.

Jae grinned at the group and pointed at the lightweight checkered pajamas he was wearing. "Patty Caye left these off for me yesterday. I feel like a real person with one foot in the hospital and one foot going home."

"Those legs will be leaving us before too long," Dr. Schott said. "One step at a time." He turned to Annabel. "How's he doing this morning?"

"He was being moved, so I missed seeing him," she said. "May I listen to Mr. Nixon now?"

"Yes, go ahead," Donn said.

Annabel took her stethescope and listened to Jae's lungs and heart. She checked his pulse and evaluated his respiratory rate.

"As good as before," she said and smiled.

"Mr. Nixon," the attending said, "you are fortunate. Not that you contracted the Powassan virus, but that you are recovering and have no neurological damage that we are aware of. Today we're going to have a physical therapist evaluate you. A little therapy to motivate your muscles wouldn't be a bad idea."

"Thanks. On all counts. And I'm indebted to Dr. Tilson."

After rounds ended, Annabel hitched a ride with Stuart over to the office. She scored well on the test. On par with Stuart. She couldn't ask for more than that.

"What about Bob Palmer?" she asked the woman sitting at the desk.

The assistant licked her finger to separate a clump of papers. She was obviously proud of her role in holding the most desirous information of the day.

"Bob Palmer passed." She turned her mouth down and showed Annabel the result. He hadn't passed by much, but she was thrilled nevertheless. He would be too.

"Thanks," Annabel said.

Outside, she called an Uber driver, and when she got home, she dived into bed before texting Bob.

CHAPTER 32

Annabel slept off her call with a long nap and woke to her darkening apartment as the afternoon light faded outside her window. She rubbed her eyes and reached over for her phone. There was no message from Bob. She texted him right away.

I crashed after coming home. You passed your test! We all passed.

She went into the bathroom, threw water on her face, and studied herself in the mirror. Her long hair needed a trim and her face could use some color. Having the entire upcoming weekend off after her medicine rotation, perhaps she could take a hefty outdoor run or walk and pick up some sunshine.

Her phone dinged and she glanced down.

I figured you were sleep deprived! Super! So what did I score?

Annabel twisted a lock of hair. *Passed with a seventy-eight.*

Yikes. That was close. Not like me.

Under the circumstances, she wrote, *you deserve to give yourself some latitude.*

So true. Anyway, all I have to do now is make up my missed ward time. And that'll be easy! Later...

Annabel went into the bedroom and put her phone to bed on the charger. She studied the tree outside her window before closing the blinds. With no breeze outside, it was placid and sleepy, like it waited for the true stirrings of spring. In essence, she felt as tranquil as the view outside her window. Fulfillment from the third year of medical school rotations was beginning to escalate and she realized that she was beginning to think more and more like a doctor.

She closed the blinds and turned back to the kitchen, where she threw together a sandwich and a glass of milk.

Late the next morning, Annabel peeled away from a nurses' station and headed to the cafeteria for lunch. On the ground floor, however, was the physical therapy department. Therapists sometimes worked with patients in the hallways near their rooms, but she'd never stepped into their central work room. She deviated passed the cafeteria entrance and read "P.T." on a sign outside a large double door. Stepping inside, a few chairs made up a waiting area, and a man at a central desk signed in the outpatients.

She glanced around for Jae Nixon. A male therapist stood alongside the ranger as he walked slowly on the treadmill. He wore a gray T-shirt with a national park emblem. His biceps flexed as he held the hand grip, but his arms lacked the sharp tone they had when he first appeared in the hospital. His scissor-sharp haircut had also grown out and appeared less defined and sculptured.

"Well, look at you," Annabel said.

Jae furrowed his brow and nodded at her. "He's killing me. Like making a bear run a marathon after sleeping for a month."

"No, no, no," the therapist said. "We're going to do thirty minutes max. Only ten minutes of walking here, and the rest of the time, we'll work on your muscle memory. Give those arms and legs something to do. But I can see your analogy with a sleeping bear."

Jae tilted his head toward Annabel. "She's a medical student that egged me on to wake up."

"Aren't you the lucky one?! She's pretty enough to wake up to."

Annabel's cheeks reddened. The therapist, as well as Jae, were both appealing on the eyes and flirting with her. She smiled at the compliment and didn't take it as sexist. Harmless flirting, she thought, was good for the soul and a person's ego.

She waved her hand at them. "I couldn't resist popping in. Dr. Schott said if you handle today and tomorrow's P.T., your lab work is normal, and you're eating and feeling acceptable enough to go home, then we're springing you."

"Then I'm almost out of here. I believe work is not out of the question next week … but I would take it slow. They still have enough coverage at the park through this weekend."

The therapist slowed the pace of the treadmill down further and then it stopped. Jae stepped off.

"Since you students are off this weekend, why don't you and your friend visit the Taft National Historic Site? Volunteers or Patty will be giving tours and I could show you around too. I won't overdo it. I promise."

Annabel gave it serious thought and rubbed her hands together. "What a perfect idea. I'll ask Bob Palmer."

Jae gave her a thumbs-up.

"Now … I'll get out of your way." She paraded to the cafeteria, piled a salad on a plate, and went to a table. First things first, she thought. She couldn't wait to text Bob with Jae's recreational idea.

Want to go to that national park with me on Saturday where my patient works? He wants to show us around. I'll drive!

She drizzled a packet of blue cheese dressing over the salad fixings and kept one eye on her phone.

Sounds great, he answered. *Pop into my apartment first. I have something for you.*

? Pick you up at one.

Friday afternoon was both joyous and sad as Annabel and Stuart mingled in the office with Donn, Melody, and Chineka. The two students had chipped in for two boxes of cream-filled donuts that morning and one box still sat half full. All their work for the day was finished.

"I've never had this high an attrition rate on my service." Donn shook his head. "The loss of fifty percent of my students was a big deal. Except for Jordan, however, I'm proud of the work you all did. If I become an attending and stay with the university, I'll most likely run into either of you in your first year of residency. Your stepping stone to whatever specialty you go into."

"Thanks for everything," Annabel said. "It was a long couple of months and we learned a lot from you three and our patients."

Sitting on the couch, Melody crossed her legs and dangled a brown buckled heel off the end of her foot. "Annabel, thanks for being so conscientious. You too, Stuart."

"I second that," Chineka chimed in. "We had the darnedest cases the last few months and you both performed admirably. And Annabel, how is it that you lure in the most difficult, yet provocative cases? You're like the epicenter of the team with your involvement with Jae Nixon, your entanglement with that Parkinson's patient and her daughter in the beginning of the rotation, and even the cops that got involved."

"Well, I knew them from before."

"There you go. See what I mean?"

"Actually," she smiled, "I'm dating one of them."

"Really?" Melody asked. "Hell if I make time to date."

Annabel shrugged. "But it hasn't been that long."

"Yeah. Right." Melody rolled her eyes.

Donn rubbed his beard, contemplating the donuts. They heard a familiar sound in the hallway. The tip of Alejandro appeared in the bottom of the doorway and the rest of it followed. Dr. Enno came in. A small silver clip clung to the front of her hair bun and a clump of wispy hair draped over her forehead.

"I didn't want to miss saying goodbye to the students." Shania acknowledged them with a warm smile.

"Thanks for coming," Donn said. "We appreciate all you did for us."

She stood well-planted next to the table, holding her cane, as Donn relented and picked up a donut.

"It was wonderful that our star infectious disease patient went home yesterday. Couldn't have been a better outcome. And now we know to keep our antennae up for patients presenting with more tickborne diseases."

Everyone nodded and then Donn pointed to the box … for Shania to help herself.

"Well, I'm heading out." Annabel slid off her white jacket and draped it over her forearm and picked up her backpack. Stuart grabbed his things as well and extended his hand to Donn. His handshake was his good-bye.

Annabel searched Shania's expression and beamed at her. "It was a pleasure working with you. Thank you."

"Likewise. As an attending, sharing a patient's course with a student from the beginning to the end is beneficial to both. It reminds me of a Native American saying, 'We have walked together in the shadow of a rainbow.'"

Annabel's heart warmed. Medical education was something else. She narrowed her eyes and nodded. In another moment, she and Stuart peeled away.

Saturday morning, first Annabel called home to tell them her rotation was officially finished, she passed, and she had something fun on her plate for the day. She explained to her father that one of her patients had harbored an unusual disease. When they finished talking, she told him to say hello to her aunt and uncle and young cousins. She didn't ask to speak to Nancy. Her sister needed to figure out herself that siblings were important to each other and that Annabel had done nothing wrong when it came to her problems with Jordan.

She was ecstatic it was a beautiful day. Since her front window with her soulful tree faced east, late mornings in her apartment were the best time of day if the sun was unobstructed by clouds. She caught up with laundry and uncluttered her backpack. She filed away notes and stored medicine books on her shelf.

Soon enough, she thought, she needed to replace study materials. There were still many rotations to go through, but now she had surgery, psychiatry, and internal medicine behind her.

She'd lounged around all morning in pajamas and now she showered and changed into a rose flannel shirt and tucked it into a pair of crisp blue jeans. As she brushed her hair in the mirror, she wondered about Bob's comment. He had something for her.

She mulled that over as she left and passed Travis' quiet apartment downstairs. Why not surprise Bob with something as well? Something not expensive, a little humorous, and maybe even useful. She knew exactly what that would be. After hopping into her SUV, she made a stop on the way to Bob's and armed herself with what she wanted.

Annabel parked at his apartment complex and sprang over to his door. After ringing twice, the door swung open. He wore jeans like hers and greeted her with a smile.

"Every time I see you," she said, "you look more like yourself."

"I'll take that as a compliment." He stepped aside and she entered. He walked to the counter. "It's not wrapped, just camouflaged with a garbage bag over it. A present. For helping me out … a lot."

She put down her own bag and slipped off the white trash bag. Underneath was a bulky box - a single-cup coffee maker.

"This is really thoughtful of you, but you didn't need to."

Bob's expression turned less cheerful. "But I wanted to."

"Yes." She nodded, realizing his gift meant a lot to him. "Thank you. I appreciate this; it will be used often. Every day! Heck, now it'll be easier to drink a different flavor every morning like you do as I run out my door."

His face glowed. She liked the gift as well as the thought.

"Oh, and this is for you." The top of the paper bag she placed on the counter was tightly rolled halfway down. She giggled. "I guess we both don't make the best gift wrappers."

Bob leaned forward, uncurled the bag, and stuck his hand in. He pulled out an orange and green can. After a moment, his head came down into his other hand as he laughed. "Bug spray. A can of DEET. Just what the doctor ordered."

"It may be too late for this Ehrliciosis, but some hefty spraying with this should stop the next tick before he takes a bite out of you. In other words, never let a tick get a head start!"

"Ha!" he said, "especially Powassan!" His eyebrows shot up. "And when we run again, I'm sharing it with you."

"Deal." She picked up the box. "Now let's proceed. We have a date with a ranger."

Annabel pulled her Nissan into the visitors' center lot and sprung out of the car, looking around. The American flag blew gently from the front pole on the prominent hilltop where a sign said the National Park Service, U.S. Department of the Interior, William Howard Taft National Historic Site. Behind it stood a cream-colored building, the birthplace and boyhood home of the twenty-seventh President and tenth Chief Justice of the United States.

Bob glanced over the hood of the car. "Where to?"

"The path on your side leads over to the rangers' housing. We're supposed to meet him there."

Annabel grabbed a jacket vest from the back seat, slid it on, and they headed over. Cabins nestled before the woods, looking like their own picture postcards. A mostly black, medium-sized dog rushed off one of the porches and greeted them. But another dog bounded from the back, passed his companion, and circled around them with a tail that wouldn't stop spinning.

A front door opened and Jae Nixon put his hand on a beam and smiled. "Welcome!"

Annabel and Bob walked closer and Jae waved them up on the porch. He reached out and shook Bob's hand.

"I heard you also had the same unfortunate problem that I did," Jae said. "An encounter with a bloodsucking arachnid that did more than just bite."

"Yes," Bob nodded. "What fun. Although I got away a lot cheaper than you."

"I'll be all right. Each day is another blessing and I'm most grateful to be back here. I'll start work again on Monday with a modified schedule." He glanced at Annabel, who nodded with approval.

"Today Annabel gave me a can of insect repellant," Bob said.

"Consider her a good friend," Jae said and chuckled.

The dogs both sat, poised ready to follow Jae anywhere.

"This is Curley," Jae pointed, "and this is Twist." He leaned over and tousled Twist's hair. "We're not the only ones who have been sick. He was ill from a bacterial infection because of the mouse population around here. He came down with Leptospirosis."

Annabel crouched and picked up his paw to say hello. "You poor boy. You had a rough time."

"Hey, you all." Patty Caye half ran across the grass. She wore her uniform and greeted them both. "I'm about to give a guided tour. During the week, we also do ranger programs with the kids. They're fun to tag along with too.

"Jae and I were also wondering if you'd like to stay for an early dinner. He can easily grill or pan fry some venison and I'll add a salad and a side."

"The deer meat that cost you a tick bite?" Bob asked.

Jae laughed. "Most likely."

"Expensive venison."

"Whaddaya say?" Jae asked. "I won't make a big fuss, I promise."

"I hate to say no," Annabel responded, "but I have a date tonight. With a bird."

Bob leaned against the railing and squinted his eyes. "A bird?"

"Just kidding. I'm seeing Dustin and he has a funny bird."

"We could feed you," Jae said to Bob.

"No. Annabel can drive me home and, in any case, this afternoon will be enough activity. My life is so boring these days that I get into bed early at night and dream of continuing to increase my platelet count." He laughed. "But thanks so much for the invite."

"Well, then," Patty said. "I'll see you all over there." She tipped her hat and left.

"Let's follow her." Jae stepped forward a lot slower than his partner.

"Bye for the time being," Annabel said to Curley and Twist.

She strode next to Bob. "Sweet dogs. You know if we're going to get one, now's as good a time as any. May if she's a girl and Oliver if he's a boy."

"So you mentioned. Let's not rush into anything, but I guess we could start planning the process."

They bumped shoulders together and Annabel rolled her eyes. What were they going to get themselves into?

- End -

FROM THE AUTHOR

Barbara Ebel is a physician and an author. Since she practiced anesthesia, she brings credibility to the medical background of her plots. She lives with her husband and pets in a wildlife corridor in Tennessee but has lived up and down the East Coast.

Visit or contact her at her website: http://barbaraebel.weebly.com

The following books are also written by Dr. Barbara and are available as paperbacks and eBooks:

The Dr. Annabel Tilson Series:

Dead Still (Dr. Annabel Tilson Novels Book 1)
Deadly Delusions (Dr. Annabel Tilson Novels Book 2)
Desperate to Die (Dr. Annabel Tilson Novels Book 3)
Death Grip (Dr. Annabel Tilson Novels Book 4)
Downright Dead (Dr. Annabel Tilson Novels Book 5)
Dangerous Doctor (Dr. Annabel Tilson Novels Book 6)

The Dr. Danny Tilson Series:

Operation Neurosurgeon (A Dr. Danny Tilson Novel: Book 1)
Silent Fear: *a Medical Mystery* (A Dr. Danny Tilson Novel: Book 2). Also an Audiobook.
Collateral Circulation: *a Medical Mystery* (A Dr. Danny Tilson Novel: Book 3). Also an Audiobook.
Secondary Impact (A Dr. Danny Tilson Novel: Book 4)

Other Books:

Outcome, A Novel
Younger Next Decade: *After Fifty, the Transitional Decade, and What You Need to Know* (nonfiction health book)

Also written and illustrated by Barbara Ebel:
A children's book series about her loveable therapy dog; illustrated with real pictures:
Chester the Chesapeake Book One
Chester the Chesapeake Book Two: Summertime
Chester the Chesapeake Book Three: Wintertime
Chester the Chesapeake Book Four: My Brother Buck
Chester the Chesapeake: The Three Dogs of Christmas
Chester's website: http://dogbooksforchildren.weebly.com

Made in the USA
Middletown, DE
20 December 2019